Hugo Claus

WONDER

Translated from the Dutch by Michael Henry Heim

archipelago books

First Archipelago Books Edition © 2009

Library of Congress Cataloging-in-Publication Data
Claus, Hugo, 1929-2008.
[Verwondering. English]
Wonder / by Hugo Claus ; translated from the Dutch by Michael
Henry Heim.
p. cm.
ISBN 978-0-9800330-1-4
I. Heim, Michael Henry. II. Title.
PT6410.C553V413 2009
839.3'1364–dc22   2008045727

Archipelago Books
232 Third St. #A111
Brooklyn, NY 11215
www.archipelagobooks.org

Distributed by Consortium Book Sales and Distribution
www.cbsd.com
Printed in Canada

Cover art: Francisco Goya, *Tu que no puedes, (Caprichos no. 42),* 1796–1797,
Davison Art Center, Wesleyan University (photo: Rob Lancefield)

This publication was made possible with support from Lannan Foundation,
the National Endowment for the Arts, the New York State Council on the Arts,
a state agency, the Flemish Literature Fund, and the Mary Duke Biddle Foundation.

Tú que no puedes, llévame a cuestas.

(Castillian proverb)

Encounter

The teacher walked the twenty feet from his room to the elevator in wonder. Waited at the latticework of the cage. Stuck three fingers through the mesh.

(This is a beginning. In the hallway redolent of belladonna. And just as one has a chance of winning the lottery if one buys all the tickets, there is the chance of an end.)

There was no sound but the rumble of the elevator. No, not the shuffle of floral-patterned, rubber-soled slippers along the wine-red runner leading from the gypsy woman's room to the elevator shaft, expressly, so it seemed, for her tiny, swift, perpetually unwashed feet in those mules with the violets embroidered on them. Not even her breathless laughter. Though she had a visitor, as the teacher heard while passing her door, which despite the owner's repeated admonitions she had decorated with an India-ink drawing of Pisces. What stood out most was her belladonna scent.

Once he had entered the elevator, he forgot about the gypsy woman. Which was all to the good. Downstairs in the hallway he avoided Bogger, the porter, a lickspittle with light hair who was pretending to sweep behind the glass partition separating the restaurant from the hotel entrance.

What did the teacher look like in the midday sun amidst the holiday makers, balloons, and trams? Hard to say. Full of wonder, most likely. Composed, to be sure. As he had been for the most part during his thirty-seven years. What was the sea like? Booming quite loudly amidst the shouts of children and their parents. Yet one could tell that up close it would flow more smoothly than the noise on the esplanade seemed to indicate. That the ripples down by the sand would be milder than the waves the teacher saw from the esplanade. The teacher squinted into the strong light, having slid his sunglasses – his students must have made fun of them, cheap and unfashionably mica-framed as they were – into his thick hair, which he wore long because his ears stuck out so. "Tacks," his father had once said. "Stick a few tacks in your ears before going to bed and in a few months you'll get up one morning to find them looking as they should – small and Greek, smack against your skull."

Amidst the hostile crowd with their naked thighs and peeling shoulders, their sand-covered knees, eyebrows, and hair; through their iodine-turbid gestures and voices, their hula-hoops, the grand-fathers in tennis shoes, the fathers in green visors, the children gleaming with oil; past one of the twelve ice-cream carts (two nuns and one fisherman licking), he made his way along the esplanade, which was yellow and composed of smooth, neatly jointed hexagons for the girls roller-skating along it. Opposite the beach and the channel of the inlet, which had been turned into a harbor by means of a breakwater that was regularly, every five or six years, destroyed by storms, stood a sandstone ship's captain, the back of his head on a level with the houses' second stories. If one viewed him from the esplanade, one would see his buttocks squeezed together; if one viewed him from the water – from a boat of schoolchildren or tourists, from a two-man canoe – one would soon – no, immediately – notice the innocent smile with which the sandstone Mongoloid head (smooth as an acorn, of course) stood watch over town and sea and the sailors and fishermen, commemorated beneath his feet, who had drowned during the wars of 1914–18 and 1940–45.

In his involuntary perturbation the teacher pictured the beach the previous winter: the hotel façades with their shutters lowered, the abandoned embankment, the pits with the rubble's last remains, the hulking remains of the Hotel Titanic with its two thick-lipped caryatids; he recalled walking through it all (not hurrying through, as he was now) and once or twice, in the cavity of cold the wind blew into his mouth, murmuring, daring to murmur: "Magic. Casements opening on the foam of perilous seas . . ." then reciting the lines – and getting them hopelessly wrong – a while later in his fourth-year class so that it was the botched lines the bleary-eyed class wrote into their notebooks. The only thing the professor had any success with – he had been used to it for years now – were descriptions of the drowning Shelley, the coughing Keats, the dead broke Michael Reinhold Lenz. "And now listen very carefully, ladies and gentlemen, to how the poet seeks to convey the song of the nightingale in his words . . ." They recognized the sounds: syllables became chirps, warbles. They imitated birds, puffing out sentences to the beat of the teacher's index finger. This, together with the lectures he gave them on his highly personal technique of English breathing, helped them when they went out dancing in the evening and sang along with American tunes on the jukebox.

The teacher was on his way to school. He did not so much as glance at the dike, now an esplanade for foreigners. Through the park, with families playing miniature golf, to school. Along Franciskus Bree Street, where he had lived during the first year of his marriage – two rooms, no bath, creaking bed, cauliflower stench – to school. Along the inner quay. Past the warship *Antoinette*, where sailors on deck above the rusty plates were doing their exercises, a dull, tame art of war. Past a boat unloading flour or fertilizer. The teacher walked under the crane near the truck where two workers, white with powder, were stacking the sacks. One of them, the younger, said, "Ahoy there, pretty boy!" Bright red, the teacher raced across the street through the traffic, clutching his briefcase to his ribs. This side of the bridge, beyond which two warty cathedral spires soared, the sails of the Belgian Yacht Club fluttered before him. The Reverend Slosse, Religion, raised a fleshy hand to him as he rode past on his bicycle, revealing a blue-and-gray-checked undershirt in the sleeve of his cassock. "Hello there, Mr. de Rijckel! None too early, I see." And the calves in wrinkled black stockings beneath the inflated robe pedaled on. Occasionally, when the slope was especially steep – at the Albert Bridge, for example – some pupils would push the Reverend Slosse up the hill to the bystanders' cheers. Then the Reverend Slosse would take his feet off the pedals and, once on the bridge, give a triumphant wave of farewell. The Reverend Slosse was frequently seen bicycling with his hands behind his back. He was also generous with his marks. And greatly loved. Lucky man. How do we know? The teacher knew. From time to time the Reverend would sit in the teachers' room between classes, read his newspaper, and smoke his three-franc cigar, holding it upright, twirling it between his thumb, index- and middle-finger and staring at the ash with such undisguised pleasure that it made the teacher uncomfortable. He did not dare ask, "Reverend, what makes you tick? What's burning inside you? How can you be so provocatively calm, so offensively serene here in the teachers' room?" The plump, rosy face would, the teacher knew, have replied as gently and compassionately as he would have to an entering pupil: "Trust, friend de Rijckel," or "Faith, *amice.*"

Once in the playground, a large skating rink, the teacher pulled himself up and took on the bearing of someone who has been spied upon, ridiculed, and overburdened, and crossed the courtyard and the bleats of the youngest pupils accordingly. There stood Nouda, Latin and Greek, wringing his hands; there came Kurpers, the Nose, Geography, neck forward, looking for his next class. Kurpers, the Nose, Geography, was usually late and would make a beeline for any line of pupils as yet un-shepherded. The teacher had been late three times in the four years he had been working at the school, and three times the principal had, perhaps because the bell had rung twice, sent his pupils off to the classroom. What is more, the teacher had established that when he had no morning classes, as was the case today, the principal never put in an appearance on the playground. As if the only reason for him to turn up were to catch de Rijckel, English-German. As if, when there was no chance for him to humiliate anyone, he preferred remaining in his office, that glass cage emanating from the façade like a cubic wedge. Up there, invulnerable, he kept an eye on everything. Though he was less invulnerable there than he was when he moved among us, up close, all but a teacher himself, with his placid, wrinkle-free face aimed at us, each one of us, at everything.

The teacher went over to the principal, who was standing next to Nouda, Greek-Latin. The two seemed to be sharing a funny little secret.

"De Rijckel," said the principal.

Nouda, Latin-Greek, who never greeted anyone, asked him whether he had seen the floods in Denmark on television. The principal shook de Rijckel's hand but kept his glove on, as he did not with the other teachers. Without releasing the principal's hand, the teacher thought, "What's come over me? What's happening to me?" The principal disengaged his hand and headed for the main entrance with a springy step.

The teacher went up to his class and the line fell silent. He turned and heard them following him up the stairs, the boys dragging the soles of their shoes, the girls clacking their heels. They did not mimic him, as they often did Malaise, Chemistry, whose waddle they occasionally carried to such extremes that a band of epileptics climbed the stairs behind him, jerking and moaning and swaying. They never teased him either. That sometimes bothered him. And sometimes he caught himself wanting to ask them what nickname they had devised for him, because no one in the teachers' room seemed to know. He had thought up all sorts of nicknames for himself, crude and offensive names, but for some reason none of them seemed appropriate. Besides, it was not always possible to account for a nickname's origin. Why was Camerlynck, Physical Education, called the Föhn, and Miss Maes, Assistant Principal, the Nose when she had a perfectly ordinary nose? The teacher had been ashamed of what he came up with while engaged in the search: there was something humiliating about seeking a nickname for oneself, about reducing, confining oneself to, defining oneself by a single physical attribute or trait. Moreover, of all the names he had thought up for himself that evening (he felt a bit like an author seeking a title for his book), the only one that stuck in his mind was the last and, so it seemed, most appropriate, just before he climbed into bed, dead tired, and gave up. Prick. Prick de Rijckel, English-German.

But for Kurpers, Geography, Nose seemed perfectly natural. The man was a drunkard who had once stood fifteen minutes at a class-room door trying to get the key into the keyhole and then sputtered when it went in too far, "I can do it, you little bastards. I can do it." Later he fell asleep, his head on his elbows, for the duration of the class. One of the pupils reported the incident, but the principal scarcely held it against him.

The teacher walked up and down the aisles giving a dictation. The group – mere names, voices, homework, and marks to him – wrote it down. Why this class and the others thought of him as an exception was a riddle to him. He would never know. He was perspiring. Wondering why, he wiped the sweat away. Weighing his good points against his weaknesses, comparing them with those of the other teachers and with those of people outside the school – his few acquaintances, his ex-wife, for instance – was of no help. Nobody told you a thing about it. And you could hardly ask. He was strict. Yes. But Camerlynck, Physical Education, was strict too, and that didn't stop the pupils from behaving normally with him, stroking his sleeve, flattering him, telling on others, which never happened to him, Prick de Rijckel, English-German. He was an exception. A disagreeable, brutal word. No, he was no exception. He had noticed a similar situation before, a few years, two years earlier, when Tienpondt had come as a substitute teacher. Tienpondt, Mathematics. He played on the municipal soccer team, which in principle should have made him popular, beloved, respected. He had even tried to cash in on his glory by devoting the first fifteen minutes of the class to a technical commentary on the previous Sunday's match, but it hadn't worked, and – perhaps out of sympathy for someone in the same boat – he had told de Rijckel about the inexplicable indifference on the part of the pupils. "I feel no resistance," he had said, adopting a term used in connection with gauging a team's defense capabilities. The teacher had forgotten his response at the time in the reading room. Probably something about independent coexistence . . . perhaps something about marriage as an analogous phenomenon . . . in terms of which . . .

The dictation was over. He went to the board and wrote a text for the class to translate. On the roof of the gymnasium some workmen were dragging a cable through the sky, the melody of a march wafting up from below.

The teacher floated through the day, vowels elongating, classes taking him from fifth-form science to third-form classical, the hordes in front of him docile, stammering out answers, at home in the conventions of their customary enemy camp. He had wiped the board for the umpteenth time with a clammy, ill-smelling rag, then rubbed his hands dry, and tossed the little balls of gray grit into the waste-paper basket when, a few minutes before the bell was due to ring, the principal came into the room with a newly lit cigarette in his mouth. The teacher watched him tweak Verlinde's fat cheek and move to the back of the room, where he waited motionless, without a nod, sign, or word. Would it have been too much trouble for him to go up to the podium? Yes. But because the teacher had frozen, the principal finally nodded: Yes, yes, you fool, you can dismiss the class before the bell. Just get it over with and come over here. Chop-chop! The avid, clean-shaven face bit into a piece of toffee.

At a signal from the teacher the pupils shut their desks with less noise than usual, stood up more calmly, and trooped out, whispering, into the corridor. While the teacher closed a window in the empty classroom, the principal said that there was a meeting this evening and that the speaker (he himself! the principal! the guest speaker!) needed to be introduced. The professor replied that he had to oversee the study period from six to seven. You'll have plenty of time, said the principal, aware that the teacher was divorced and ate quick dinners in cheap restaurants.

The study hall was lower than the playground, a glass-walled base-ment room cut off from the vast, endless field by a brick border. The teacher, motionless on the podium, did the newspaper crossword puzzle and watched the sun go down over the school rooftops. The lights went on, turning the harmless room into a poison-green aquar-ium. Pens scratching, paper rustling, sweaty air, chalk dust, heads bent–

the teacher would have liked nothing more than to stay there until it was totally dark. He felt like going to the kitchen to ask for a cup of coffee, but they were always ready to suspect you of trying to save a penny at the expense of the local or state government, and he asked himself, "What's the matter with me?" After a long interval three unruly rhetoric pupils made it clear to him in the obvious nonchalance with which they stood and began talking that it was now seven. Another teacher would have made a biting, arrogant remark like "You leave your seats, gentlemen, when I say so and not a minute sooner," and the principal would have said nothing but "Gentlemen," but the example of the gangly older boys was followed by the entire class before the teacher knew what was happening, so he simply rolled up his newspaper and dropped it into the wastepaper basket. He thought of tossing a lighted match down the hole in the center, but the metal cylinder had pinched the paper too tightly and there were too many orange peels in it to allow the fire to catch; besides, it was on a cement floor. Pushing his way through the pupils, whom he easily dispersed with an unambiguous growl, he moved towards the cool fresh air.

Rid of the shoulderless horde, he headed for the hotel, listless, bent, like a man ten years his senior. I'm going on forty already. He met no one he could nod to on the way. He gave the women a scruffy eye and bought cigarettes at an Albertdijk tobacconist's. The man behind the counter informed him there would be a crowd at the Pavilion that evening and into the night and, nibbling on something with his front teeth, pointed out it was a good time to have rooms to rent, because there would be men changing their clothes and their women three times before dawn. Then in an unprecedented gesture he made the teacher a present of two boxes of matches.

Just as the perpetrator of a crime of passion may sometimes unwittingly recognize the place where he will later lay hands on his unwilling fiancée, so Victor-Denijs de Rijckel, teacher, walked past the Pavilion that evening. There were posters in all the windows. The French and Belgian flags were flying over the dome. A gigantic white rabbit with two human eyes (bought from an optician? with a practice specializing in one-eyed patients?) was dangling on shiny nylon wires from the neo-gothic arch of the entrance. Their irises reflected the light perfectly; the white was reminiscent of milk, skimmed milk, with blue highlights. The rabbit also had whiskers under its nose – these too of nylon but gilded – and a tail tipped with an electric light. The rabbit was moving even though there was no wind in the city. It had probably just been hung up and given a poke by a playful worker. The rabbit laughed. While the teacher was admiring the animal's fur – in the orange neon light the hair seemed modeled out of clay – he suddenly imagined for some reason that its inside had been made true to nature as well, that it contained a soft, bubbly mass, and that it could easily slip from the wires, or the wires from the arch, fall with a thud, a heavy, wet, warm cushion meeting its skull and the pulp dripping out over its ears and the angel-hair of the nylon wire in its eyes. Then the teacher left the entrance behind.

In *The White Sea* he all but gulped down the special of the day. The waitress, as usual, regaled him with stories about her husband, who belonged in a monastery: What can you do with a man who does nothing but dream of sailing to Iceland, of spending whole months there? Throwing away his marriage for a couple of herrings. At breakneck speed – as if in a silent film: since leaving the school, no, since he had seen the white rabbit swaying over his head, he had felt an overwhelming need to hurry – he skimmed the newspaper; too fast; the words ran into one another.

When he got back to his room – whom might he catch in what act? whom might he punish? – the sea, though visible all those floors down only by its whitecaps, was rustling audibly; tourists were calling to one another; sloops were coming in. He made a cup of Nescafé with the lukewarm water from the tap and sipped it on the bed. There was a rattling coming from the gypsy woman's room. He stared down at his briefcase, a gift from his wife when he was starting out as a substitute teacher. The grainy coffee stuck to his palate and lodged between his teeth. He walked to the door in his socks, then to the gypsy woman's door, where he knocked on the belly of a fish carrying its fins high like a cock its crest. He could hear furniture being moved about inside.

"Oh," she said, and came out with a cry of joy that struck the teacher as perfectly misguided. "I just knew you'd come."

"Today?" he asked.

"Today or tomorrow," she said.

Was this a bad time?

"Well . . ." She was still standing at the door.

Or was he inside by then? I was inside by then. I'm sure of it.

The teacher said he wasn't feeling well. She said no wonder: Jupiter and Saturn were in the way.

"Saturn, my foot!" said a sailor, unasked, sitting on the bed pillow, his back against the wall. He was playing with his long, white feet and wiggling his toes.

"Why not?" said the teacher, still near the door, fearing the gypsy woman would get out her charts and star maps while that sailor was still there energetically scratching his toes.

"Just a second," she said, and did in fact head for the cabinet, but at this heated, difficult, unholy moment he mumbled, "Why don't I come back some other time."

Her belladonna eyes, her delicately painted, wax-like face said, "Yes, some other time. Right . . ."

"Some other time, my foot!" cried the sailor. "Here, take a seat, pal!"

"He's my nephew," said the gypsy woman. She touched her two-hundred-and-eighty-times-colored-and-decolored hair, which had taken its definitive form in the twenties, and said, with lips made up – no, lacquered – into a forty-year-old heart shape, that he was in for a difficult time as a Ram now that Saturn . . . "Watch out for Scorpio," she said, her Prussian blue eyelids with their prickly lashes covering her eyes, "though the Moon today . . ."

"My mother," thought the teacher.

A duly warned man was now walking the streets, though how much did he know? The path to the premises of Our House – where the Association for Flemish Culture was to hear the well known lecturer, pedagogue, and head of the Friends of Music, the principal of our secondary school, Dr. Verbaere, speak on the function of classical music in our society – would have taken the teacher through the park, but that was not the path he took. He forced himself to walk slowly, stopping at every shop window, every café, stopping and gaping. At one point (it was twelve past eight) he found himself walking with one foot in the gutter and the other on the sidewalk. What was the matter with him? Even as he clutched the two matchboxes he had been given by a tobacconist for the first time in his life, he asked a passerby in German for a light, then scurried up the spiral of dusty sandstone steps, rounded at the corners, to the lobby of the Pavilion. A man was standing behind a partition made of fir, holding a roll of tickets in his open hand, ready for the discus throw, and said sleepily that it was much too early, nobody came before ten. "If that early." His serious head, under a paper party hat with "Be sociable. Have a Pepsi!" written on it in English, was cocked at a slight angle. "I've never known anyone to come to the White Rabbit Ball before ten. The idea!"

The teacher moved on past three guards wearing the same party headgear and talking over Almeida's chances in the trotters' Grand Prix, past Coronation Hall, past the Hall of the Spanish Court. The ball was evidently an important affair: servants, workers, maids, and waiters were hard at work. Supplementary lighting was being installed in Renunciation Hall, and a group of angrily muttering technicians was putting up a stand for television cameras. The teacher hesitated, turned back. Then, having sunk into one of the dark green couches in the reading room – the artificial leather made his trousers stick to his skin – he leafed through a local newspaper and fell asleep. He did not wake up until a little girl in a Tyrolean skirt sat down next to him and bit into an apple.

Up. Out. Into the street. There the smell of the sea was much more penetrating than in town. The dance halls were nearly empty. In every room in every street people were trying on party clothes. "It's too late," the teacher said out loud, and thought, "I'm starting to talk to myself out loud." "No one," he said, "can change his outfit, his hairdo, or his face any longer; the ball is about to begin; the die is cast. And the art lovers' meeting is underway; there is no way out; they have long since stopped looking for the man who was supposed to introduce the speaker. And yet . . ." Up. Onward. "Good evening, ladies and gentlemen," said the teacher, hugging the façades of the buildings as he passed. "Before I introduce this evening's honored speaker, I should like to point out several facets of his moral make-up. For morality plays an important role in his make-up. Not only is he stingy, sleazy, difficult, dishonest, and spineless but also and nonetheless, consequently in fact, even manifestly, I dare say . . ."

A woman answered. She was wearing a fur. In this season. Yes. She claimed her dog had run away, a small yellowish bitch, chamois-colored actually, a light tobacco-brown, you might say, wearing a collar with little bells. "Sorry," said the teacher.

He joined the woman, calling "Mitsuko!" When Mitsuko failed to come, he gave up and sat on a stone bench in the park next to two fishermen and a maniac in glasses tapping a rolled up map of the city on his knee. The rays of the lighthouse reached both the last tourists and the first arrivals to the ball, while tangos filled the darkness of the park. Eight identical grass-green vans rode past, swerving gracefully as a virginal, discreet young woman's voice sounding right next to him yet coming from the first of them recited:

> Tonight at the White Rabbit Ball
> Drink the wine that has all in its thrall.
> Saint George Wine from the south
> Plants a kiss on your mouth
> Pure and warm like the sunshine in fall.

The teacher wished more than anything that a few or even just one of his pupils would happen past, saunter along the other side of the street, for instance, running an index finger along the ribbed window sills. Then that day's feud could not help but come out into the open.

And he'd tell him a thing or two! "Is that what you call an analysis of the second chapter of *Das Leben eines Taugenichts,* young man? Well then, we'll just have to return to it tomorrow morning (the blood vengeance would once more be postponed). Wir sprechen uns noch!" But he didn't get the chance to tell him off.

The trams ran less frequently now. Then, ladies and gentlemen of the Friends of Music currently listening to your guide and speaker, then the teacher stepped into a shop that usually sold souvenirs – ashtrays with the cathedral in tin, seashells with the Dover Packet painted on them, embroidered depictions of fishing sloops – and there, from a jumble of giant bumpy heads, Ku Klux Klan hoods, pointed hats, balloons, and Chinese lanterns, he bought a velvet domino. The salesgirl put the thing on him, and he glanced at himself in the mirror, took a step towards the stranger, went even closer, not recognizing the strange red eyes, those cold, aloof mussels between their slits, eyes that belong to nobody, no one. He quickly pushed the mask onto his forehead. His face had changed. He stared at it. In the light from the ceiling neon fixtures and the electric bulbs shining in some of the masks he suddenly discovered never-before-noticed nicks of shadows in his face, thick notches even, as in a print made too dark. A teacher of the dark arts. He bared his teeth, and the notches wrinkled. The salesgirl was used to the solitary game and never disturbed her customers while they were at it. The wonder they felt was her daily bread. He made a rabbit face and nibbled, screwed up his face into a grimace of fear so extreme that the black velvet membrane slipped back down from his forehead and prevented him from seeing. Outside he kept an eye out for the little yellow dog, Mitsuko, but no bells tinkled anywhere. The calm, dolphin-like sloops were still sailing in from time to time, their snouts grazed by the skittish lighthouse lamp. It was now hours since the principal had launched into his talk.

The teacher drank two glasses of beer in the company of some men discussing the Tour de France: Belgium had entered thirteen potential world champions. There was also talk about an Antwerp man who had been washed up on the beach, having disappeared the week before and drowned since then. He fingered the shriveled corpse of the mask in his pocket and stroked the velvet against the grain, then twisted an index finger in his eye. The wife of the café owner asked about her son's conduct in school. Franciskus Doelman, age twelve.

The teacher reassured her that with a bit more energy Franciskus Doelman, age twelve, would go far. Did that mean her only son was lazy? No, no. Though is laziness an illness or a vice, Mrs. Doelman? She said, while putting on nail polish, that Franciskus Doelman was good at gymnastics: they sometimes exercised together, in the morning, following along with the radio.

The teacher, who rarely drank, felt the place where the mask had rubbed against his face growing warm. Drinking his fourth glass of beer, he studied a mermaid on the wall. She was about to slip off her rock in an attempt to grab a bottle of cherry-red liquid that was one and a half times her size; there was a nondescript white bump between her thighs and scales, and a farmer was plowing his lava-rocky land in the mist beyond the hills. The café owner's wife blew on her nails while glancing pensively at the teacher. It was an exciting moment: the teacher was all worked up, burning, all atingle, feverish. What was going on? Just like that, on a Friday in mid-August.

Three seagulls paused in mid-flight and swooped down before the threshold of the café. That must have held a significance begging to be revealed. Three seagulls – fat, white, waddling. I don't even need to draw them on my door, he thought; I can just nail them up, the sign of the Seagull. The hotel owner can't object to that. What he accepts in a gypsy woman he can't deny me, an English-German teacher with an advanced degree in Germanic languages, thirty-seven, divorced, clean police record.

Though a real seagull with entrails and blood hanging on my door would never be as attractive as the two Pisces chasing each other on hers, bound together, gill to gill, and the ribbon decorated with Hebrew letters. The fish ribbon is not unlike the tube used to refuel bombers in mid-air. When will they take off? The alarm can sound at any time over there in Cottesmore, and in the two minutes allotted the three elements – pilot, plane, and nuclear warhead – will come together and they'll make the forty-five-minute flight to a pre-determined destination, eggs ready to drop, and if no command is radioed to them, back they'll go, fat, white, docile gulls, and swoop down near the village with its clay farms and straw roofs and children walking to school in Cottesmore.

The teacher ordered a sixth glass of beer, this time a Brussels geuze.

"De Snip?" asked the café owner.

"De Snip?"

"De Snip. The best brewery for *geuze*."

"Fine," said the teacher. "Give me a Betelgeuze."

"Betelgeuze? What's that?"

"It's Arabic," said the teacher. "For 'shoulders of Orion.'"

"Who are you trying to kid?"

The teacher was ashamed of himself.

At five to eleven, after studying himself with approval in the window of a furrier's, the teacher bought an entrance ticket (elegantly torn from the discus that the cocked-headed ticket-taker was still brandishing) and waded through the bead portière that gave access to the White Rabbit Ball. Chaos reigned, an ordered chaos, according to plan, yet here, there, and everywhere – chaos. Five rooms, five orchestras. Five doors opened onto the round hall, and exotic flowers in the form of a letter surrounding a light flashing scarlet topped each doorframe, the five letters over the five doors making up the word *geluk,* luck. During a feverish Viennese waltz in room L the teacher took in the fact that he was not the only one wearing ordinary street clothes, though most of the people who were pursuing one another in a complex but decipherable ballroom exercise in desire and escape had procured the necessary accoutrements and respected the prescribed ritual. He went back to the main hall, where five different styles of music were crisscrossing and the crowd was the thickest. It was as if man-in-disguise felt more at ease where no clear (loud, demanding, offensive) rhythm could be discerned.

The teacher hopped his way through the mazes of the calypsos and cha-chas of room G, the waltzes of room L, the Dixieland of room E, the highly viscous tangos of the room with the horseshoe, whose lamp had broken, and on through the fox-trots of room K and the shouting, the babbling, the running, the whining, the stomping, the sweat and the leaps, the squealing and howling of the entire province plus assorted visitors from the capital, grazing women's backs and backsides and heading – suddenly free from the constraints of his daily hotel-school-hotel geography – towards the regular dull pounding of a wooden hammer on something. Beyond the last room, near the toilets, he found a small man surrounded by four guards and, standing on a ladder supported by two bellboys, hammering boards together to form, as he put it, a parapet to enable a TV cameraman to shoot the ball from an unusual angle. The guards kept at the man to get on with the work and cut the gabbing. Women in Louis XV, Egyptian, and Mexican costumes crowded together giggling at the door of the ladies' room. Everyone, everything had to be upbeat on a night like this! It occurred to the teacher that Fontainas, History, would have his work cut out for him. He would surely have discharged an endless, indignant stream of nasal commentary on the costumed dancers, pointing out the guesswork, errors, and gaps in the historical get-ups of those shameless amateurs who just like that, all feeling, no research, tried to make their dreams come true. Seven Marie Antoinettes, the teacher counted, three Charles the Fifths, several Neros. Yet Fontainas, History, as overwhelmed as the teacher, would more likely than not have forsaken his professorial pretensions before long and peeled off his official status as he would the wrapper from a sweet and (more sprightly than the teacher could ever be) danced like a schoolboy with the most anachronistically accoutred floosies!

Tarantella, tella, tella. Line dances filled the hall. The waiting, swaying ladies by the ladies' door were snatched up by foreigners and disappeared into the oscillating rows. The mask the teacher bought was too small for him: the cardboard chafed his temples; his eyes teared. But since everyone kept his mask on, so did he, and thought: is the whole lot of them crying or had they carefully tried them on weeks ago? And all at once he was absolutely certain: Fontainas, History, would show up in one of the few historically accurate costumes because he approached his appearance as a competition whose outcome (for pupils and teachers) led from level to level all the way to honors. Fontainas, History, would not give him – Rijckel, English and German – the time of day here. He would abandon, betray him. An unbearable thought.

A dragon ambled past, its six legs wrapped in black wool beneath a copper-colored cardboard belly, its head bobbing. And here and there amidst the mobile image-park, in the heart of the horde's painted rags, the teacher hopped his step, a cross between folk dance and quadrille, bumping into classical waltzers and mud-hipped jitterbuggers alike. He thought, this frantic teacher on this Friday night, that he should do this more often, and downed three whiskeys for three times the price of a private lesson for the little ones, three times the price of a grammar session with fat Hendrik Martens.

He had a conversation with a dwarf in a panther skin about the attendance this year as opposed to last. There were no really beautiful women, the dwarf opined, in contrast to last year, when – remember? – a woman came with forget-me-nots pasted all over her body, and nothing underneath. The Pavilion boomed and seethed. The swirling cloaks of dancers of both sexes made a raging sea. The teacher collapsed onto a couch in a niche transformed into a gazebo, smoked three cigarettes, and rubbed a finger between the mask and his clammy forehead and wet eyebrows. There were streamers among the paper vine leaves and plastic tendrils, and each time an indomitable couple bumped into the gazebo's fence a flurry of motley confetti snow fluttered down on them. Perfectly happy – like a hero who, at the very moment the gods have settled upon his downfall, reaches the apogee of pride and presumption – he lay back and placed his two feet on the wrought-iron garden table in front of him. Two figures in costume came up to him.

One was shouting. The woman. And everything was so clear, seen, heard, experienced from so close (as if the teacher were in an intimate theater designed for a one-man audience with a private speaker aimed specially at his ears that toned down the tumult of the five rooms of *geluk*) that he lay motionless on his couch, in his murky bell-jar, invisible, cut off. The man was a portly, graying Venetian courtier with a silver mask ornamented by a triangle of gems at the bridge of his nose, a mons veneris of quartz. He was wearing a dark-red cloak with a black moiré lining. Knee socks. When he fell down next to her – what was she dressed as? – he was breathing heavily, his Adam's apple bobbing, his ring-bedecked fingers seeking support on the sofa back as he tried to make himself comfortable. Hemorrhoids or a weak heart. A bird for the cat. And the cat howling. About payment. About a price. And to make her demand more forceful, she did something the teacher would never have believed possible, not even here in the darkest, most intimate nook of the House of the White Rabbit, because midnight, the hour of nudity on command, was still a long way off: she removed her mask and held it in her hand. The courtier knew her, because he showed neither surprise nor alarm; he simply listened to her raging. Which went on and on. Granted, a price had been set, she said, but she was under no obligation to abide by it, she screamed.

The teacher in his cloud of invisibility dust watched the woman's one-man-show, her one-man gazebo theater. What was she dressed as? What part was she playing? What character? It was a nineteenth-century costume, authentic, accurately copied from documents, perfect and with such an abundance of detail that it was too precise, too lifelike, of a different order from a masquerade costume, with the result that it made a far more masked, more disguised impression than the dancers' wildest inventions.

She sat with her back to him and underscored each reproach with a flick of the mask. She wore a corset pulled tight over her ribs, a thick leather belt not unlike the straps motocross racers use to support their backs, a starched pink dress that reached just below the knee, and black boots made of weather-beaten leather and iron heels like the pens children write with in village schools. Her back was bare and decorated with six painted beauty spots. She had pearl-tipped hairpins in her chestnut-brown hair. A dark, austere, subdued figure. An overwhelming, coarse, common voice. George Sand? The Countess Potocka? She had someone in mind, that was clear, and now she was letting go of the performance like an actress when the curtain falls, vacillating between the role and the dressing room. The courtier was talking to her. He was barely human in the eyes of this actress, but he stood his ground. What did he say in the direction of the teacher, of the far-off, dancing-distant public? That he didn't understand her. That he'd done everything for her, spoiled his whole evening for her, ditched his friends – and they were having a ball now (the way he said "ball" it sounded like a sometime contagious disease), that she had no right, a deal was a deal and couldn't be changed.

The woman's scent was: vanilla. The courtier got ready to pounce, got all excited, mouthed angry words, brushed away smoke clouds. And only then did the teacher notice there had been a mirror opposite him the whole time and he was sitting in it, a young philistine wearing a suit off the rack (black flannel, bought with Elizabeth the first year we were married, she was proud of it, I looked English, she said, the dimwit!) and a stupid black mask. He said out loud he hoped they would excuse him, he hadn't meant to eavesdrop, he was just catching his breath, it was his heart, he had a dilated aorta. They did not hear him. Next to him, the merrymaker, he saw her, with her broad shoulders, her long neck and clearly outlined jugular vein, her painted face, white as chalk but with coal-black eyes, the lasciviously puckered lips that said to the courtier that she was sorry, that he should go back to his friends now to have that "ball." Whereupon she turned away from her attacker. She put her right boot with its cracked instep up on the garden table, and the skirt parted willingly, falling open near the chalk-white thigh, the shiny knee-cap, and the calf, which ended in the moleskin border around the boot. Her black leather glove stroked the knee; three fingers of her hand touched the inner thigh.

The courtier yawned.

"Jew-boy!" said the woman, jumping up and running out of the gazebo. The courtier wiped the sweat from above his mask and dried his hand on his poorly fitting wig, revealing gray hair along the ears and neck. He nodded to the teacher, who stood and followed him.

They wended their way through Tyrolean circle dancers, creatures blowing into cardboard trumpets, and hundreds of Ku Klux Klansmen and Nefertitis.

Then, taking a side entrance the courtier seemed familiar with, they went out into the evening air. There they stood, like brothers, awaiting inspiration. Apaches, Napoleons, and monks bumped along on the platform of an otherwise deserted tram. The courtier pointed: the woman in the 1870s get-up was on her way to the esplanade, inviting pursuit. Her bare back, a wedge in her dress, was whiter than the white façades of the houses.

"She forgot her fur jacket," said the courtier in a hoarse voice. "Wait a second. Too bad!"

Under the hotel balconies, under the dimly lit sky she went her way until like a game animal awaiting a hunter's steps in a thicket she stopped in front of a tobacconist's. She turned. Stood legs apart. A man's voice called out to her from a window one flight up. She started off again. Slowed down. "Come on up!"

The courtier had a Persian lamb coat over his arm. They headed towards a Buick together. The motor started up as soon as the teacher had slipped clumsily into the front seat. The radio was on, the side windows rolled down. The courtier prattled a bit until they drew up to the woman, who quickened her step the moment she became aware of their proximity, the metal of her heels clicking against the stone sidewalk. The car's dance music accompanied her steps down the street and along the hexagonal-tiled esplanade and calm sea. A breeze from the water ruffled her hair, parted her skirt. And when she suddenly crossed the embankment and took hold of the railing with one black hand the car braked. The courtier pulled his mask down to below his chin, where it sat like a jewel-studded collar. He cursed. The woman looked straight at them, then walked down the steps from the esplanade to the beach. The two men in their streamlined coffin on springs watched the woman hurry under a thin moon over the wet sand to the breakwater, awkwardly, legs wide. She held down her hair with one hand; the other, though invisible, seemed from the way she hunched her shoulders to be resting on her stomach. The breakwater, a flash of lightning topped by wave crests, was now under her feet. She jumped up and down and waved her arms as if chasing away mosquitoes. The courtier shook and shuddered behind the wheel, his knees rubbing against the bumpy, curly folds of the shiny fur.

This Is My Notebook

This notebook was given to me by Fredine. No one will ever know, she promised me. And today marks the fifth day since Korneel gave me a stack of paper and a loose-leaf binder together with a penholder made of heavily fibrous wood that had been dipped in red ink. Chew on it hard and you can taste the ink.

At first the attendants thought I was an artist, Fredine said. But Korneel set them straight. He also forbade them to disturb me while I write.

And I write the whole day through. It's colder now, and they refuse to turn on the central heating. If you just sit here, the way I've been doing these past five days, you don't notice the cold for a while, but when you do it's too late and you go to bed with frozen feet.

I've pushed the table over to the window because it gets dark early here. The window lets the wind and rain through. Even now a rain is freshening up the earth and the house. It's running down the window and beating against an awning. I'll never see it because the window doesn't open. Unless somebody forces it. But then there's a chance the pane will break. "If you don't watch out, you'll land back in the cellar," Fredine said. This is a God-forsaken hole, I realize, and nobody ever lands here. I'm the nobody now.

Voices. Especially the drawn-out whine of a woman dealing with her child. Plus someone blowing his nose over and over. Through the window I can see the wash hanging out to dry: endless undershirts and towels. It's getting drenched. But that's not my business. As long as they can't see me from outside, I'm okay. I like it here.

The courtyard is full of boards, and they're all painted a cream color, a color my father thought most suitable for the kitchen, for inside. Furniture painted cream was proper, "bourgeois," by which he meant distinguished. Besides the boards there are broken picture frames, a ladder with a floor cloth draped over it, the bright-red inner tube of a tire too small for a car. Pails. Sodden boxes of food. Crates of discarded wiring. I'm happy. The window, my window, offers material for an inventory that could go on for three days at the least.

Let's start with the walls – peeling, moldy, faded, yet overrun by color; fingerprints; the plaster pattern. I'll jot it all down, organize it. But not now. Now I've got too much to do because Korneel wants me to use up the paper. I've written the beginning. How it all began. But that's not how it began. It's totally different. Still I've got to try. I've got to, as Korneel says, look at it from the outside. And what's left? A dreary story, the dregs, an unparalleled void, while in fact it was totally different . . .

This hole of mine – which is six meters by three and a half and two meters high, judging by my height, one meter seventy-six (the ceiling is approximately a head higher) – this hole will soon be wet with rain, because there's a frayed oval opening in the ceiling about a quarter of the way to the corner on my left and some gray lathwork sinking under the weight of whatever is on top of it and black rings of mold all over the ceiling. The ends of the lead pipe holding the wiring have come apart. Seven electric wires wound round with insulating tape are hanging down like the fingers of a Punch puppet.

Six meters long is enough for me: I never walk the room from one wall to the other; what I like best is to sit on this kitchen chair, at this wobbly little table, which totters if I lean too hard on my notebook. There are three other chairs, but they have no seats. The mahogany bedside table has no top. In the corner, carefully covered with potato sacks (so they're well aware that it rains in), some sticks of half-burnt wood, once a bed, are leaning against the wall. Or does the water come from the thick, black exhaust pipe whose elbow sticks in and out of the wall, leaking now and then over the potato sacks? I'll have to keep my eye on it. In any case, I haven't noticed any leaks in the last five days. I've been too busy. Then again, everything happens when you're asleep.

A woman threatens someone in a high, thin voice. That someone being another inmate, most likely. People threaten me too. "You'd better do this! Why don't you do that? Why didn't you do it this way?"

The bang of a lid against a railing is the response.

The other bedside table – it too of mahogany – has a plywood top. It has bottles of Schweppes tonic water on it. I can tell without reading the letters. I can tell by the yellow label. Gin and tonic for the ladies. The wallpaper is yellow-and-white checks, and even the ceiling was once papered: you can see traces of it here and there. I see everything. And yet several people have said, "Don't you see that this or that . . ."

Spider webs, dust webs, chinks, cracks, new coats of plaster, drippings – I see it all. Keep that in mind, Korneel. Each pipe for water, gas, and electricity crosses another. The strips of linoleum on the floor are of different sizes. They'd probably found them in small lots and glued them together. Cheap and good enough for us. At a sale. Or won them in a lottery. The filth in the linoleum cracks.

Then there were stacks of paper full of stone grit and cement and dust. A refuse bin recommended by the local authorities two years before. There is a matte glass ball in the right-hand sink together with a poster rolled up in such a way as to reveal the letters IL ST KR IDTD and a piece of broken glass you can tell comes from a frame because you can see the remains of the glue along one edge. This sink has no drain.

I didn't realize it the first night they brought me here. I got a bawling out from Fredine in the morning, of course.

Fredine was on night duty yesterday. She asked me which I preferred: writing in the notebook or writing on Korneel's paper. She was glad I preferred the notebook: she had smuggled it in.

The door is important too. Girl's-bedroom light blue. Though it's ages since we've had a young girl here. Through the glass in the door they can see me – though I can't see them, it's a one-way thing, to one side's advantage – the glass has a word engraved in it. They can read it; I can't. Not even backwards. But I think it's my name. I must ask Fredine.

One day I'm going to count up the bottles in the room. Magnums, flutes for Rhine wine, flasks, cognac bottles with stars on their necks. I'll going to line them up in rows too, according to type: by size, shape, or label. Their necks are coated with dust. I'll have to wash my hands again. That means requesting more water.

How can I ever hope to make my description of Almout accurate if my description of this place is so pathetic? I forget everything. A pan, several rusty biscuit boxes, paint brushes, a jar of brown mucilage that was probably used to glue the linoleum down, the screw from a fan, a tap with the word "cold" on it, a box: Product of Turkey. Jam jars in a basin. Shiny blue packing paper. And the position of all these objects. And my pen. My hand. My shirt, the one that used to belong to Korneel. The air. Dust, gas. The odor of urine from under the door.

And the smell of the others, on the other side of the door: tobacco, soap, and the aroma of hair, women's hair.

No . . .

(18 October, two hours later)
I'm drenched. They don't dry me well afterwards.

I shouted, and they beat me of course.

Fortunately I know – I know without fail – when I'm going to shout. So I have time to get the notebook out of the way. I hid it in the . . . No, not even in the notebook will I say where.

(19 October)
Voices. Children crying. And most of all, outside, not far from the window though far enough to keep me from seeing it, the noise of a scaffolding going up. They want to mount a camera on it to film me, get me down on film, so they can study it. I often hear a cracking sound, like a piece of plywood splitting. There are duller sounds too. A rubber truncheon on a shoulder. Or neck. Yesterday a young mother was singing "Sonny Boy." Water gurgles. A telephone. "Come on, come on," a shrill voice says. A child answers, a girl, I think: "No."

"I won't do anything to you," the old man says.

"You can't!" the child shouts.

"Why not?"

"Because I've got to go to school."

I get the papers late. Fredine always brings me yesterday's. What do they want to accomplish by that? One of these days I'm going to make a formal protest, on Korneel's paper. I swear.

A child's steps: featherweight. And the old man panting after her. The child keeps shouting her short shouts. They keep running. The child will fall.

My shoe scrapes against the linoleum, and I'm the only one who can hear it, and now I've heard it, it's over, and no one but me knows it. There's somebody standing behind the door near the enameled trough, which gives off a strong smell. I hear him. Sometimes there are three or four of them standing there close together, chatting next to the rectangular enameled trough. We used to stand like that too, we teachers, between classes, shoulder to shoulder almost, next to the school's enameled trough, stand there and chat. Long, long ago. In an aquarium. In a hall. There are times when you stop hearing and seeing. A fog descends. Just as night is sometimes steeped in a darker night.

(Later)
Stock still. Only my hand moves. And sometimes my stomach against the table edge.

This is the coal shed. Though I know for a fact they have oil heating. Why do they use oil? Why, I wonder, do they use oil? No, no. Why do I think they use oil? I won't give up until I get to the bottom of it.

Besides, I've nothing else to do but sink into the maddening play of images racing through my head, and I refuse, refuse – do you hear me, Korneel? – because if I don't I'll spin my life kaput, always a few images behind, trying to get to the bottom of them. And then there's Fredine and her "If you don't watch out, you'll land in the cellar!" "If you don't watch out, you'll land in the shower!" This hole is worse than a leper colony. Though good enough for me. Until recently I lived in rooms that were spic and span, where, prudent and self-assured, I had free range and thought no other landscape possible. And now look.

Fredine is beginning her night rounds. She'll be here in five minutes. I've got three minutes left. There's nothing more to tell.

I scraped a bit of whitewash from the wall yesterday just before they hauled me off to beat me and hold me under the shower. The clammy powder from the wall is still under my fingernails. Fredine.

(21 October)
What? Self-assured? Free range? Don't make me laugh! Those prison-like premises where I lived and worked: hotel, school, meeting hall, cinema, restaurant? Other people moved back and forth between home and work freely and easily. Not me. Wonder and disgust were as alive in me back then as they are now; it's just that I didn't make much of it. I accepted feeling ill at ease with my life as normal, ditto my adolescent hobnobbing with grown-ups in grown-up streets and premises. Did other people feel fulfilled by their lives, fully fledged?

That was their business. I didn't. Or maybe they were just pretending to. Perhaps. Then I'd do the same. But with a cool eye, a heavy tread.

Korneel must never see this notebook.

But it's less important to know how I was back then than to know who I was. My pupils would greet me with a Good morning, sir, and I would finger my chin or the small of my back, which was a bit flabbier than it was when I was fourteen, but that was all: I remained an outsider I didn't like. Liked less and less. And, wonder of wonders, nobody seemed to find me transparent anymore and neither teachers nor pupils came up to me in the schoolyard and gave me a kick in the pants with an "Out of my way, snotnose!" I would have got out of their way. Then.

Crabbe changed all that. It was Crabbe who pulled me loose from what I was, my way of talking, walking, existing. Crabbe made the snotnosed kid look outside himself. Before: cloying clichés, timid, watered-down diction, chalk-like ideas, a "stands to reason" look; after: none of the above. And maybe nothing at all. Other than this notebook.

Without Crabbe I'd have grown older, happy-unhappy, and perhaps in a way the armor would have become more "natural" with the years and I'd no longer have found the difference between myself, outsider, and the others, outsiders, of any significance. Or even noticed it.

Now there is air, bad air, between me and my armor. The two layers of bark, of hide – the one copper, the other flesh – will die but never merge. They remain separate, Dr. Korneel van den Broecke, as separate as the paper on which I shall deliver the fair copy of the story I'll eventually write for you and this outburst, this notebook.

Calmer now.

The rain is coming to an end, the hole growing lighter. There must be a rainbow. A twice-reflected sunlight is spreading over the wall opposite me: it is first picked up and reflected by the oval glass-in-lead window embedded in the wall, then reflected again by the zinc slats of the awning next to it. It has no meaning; it's just a concatenation of circumstances, and yet it thrills me.

I've written nothing more about the other concatenation of circumstances: my story. I mean to put it down on paper, but not the way Korneel wants me to. When I tried to tell him about Crabbe, he said, "Chance, chance happenings," as if chance were at all possible in my story, which has always depended upon and continues to depend upon a strictly delineated structure that deludes, betrays, and stymies anything that doesn't fit.

Not that I can put my finger on that structure. Instead I circle round the facts, though maybe if I . . . No, I have no choice. Now the story is underway, I'll follow it through to the end. I'm positive nothing will come of it, but what else can I do? How else can I get through all this? I'm trapped.

On my feet. Two steps to the left. Nothing moving behind the door. Fredine will be here any minute. She's as regular as they come. Like everything in this place: the young mother with her baby, the little girl with the old man on her heels.

> *Raindrops are beating*
> *On window and tree.*
> *This is my greeting:*
> *Believe me free, please.*

How did I used to greet people? I would greet the Revered Father, who gave religious instruction, with only the slightest nod or, rather, look at the cleft between his eyebrows and greet the cleft – the way you aim at the bump between a crocodile's eyes before pulling the trigger – but the shot, the greeting, would misfire.

A person can be as locked up as a house. The cold is climbing up my trouser legs. Insomnia awaits whenever I lie down on the camp bed under the American army blankets (which the newly liberated Belgians turned into overcoats). Had I been at home, I'd have taken a few pills. Strange that now I use the word "home" for that sixth-floor, twelve-hundred-francs-a-month room with its morning vacuum cleaning routine (because the chambermaids had to start their work somewhere, and if they didn't start early they'd never be through, and they couldn't start their racket at the three-thousand-francs-a-month rooms now, could they?), the English tourists, the porter's sullen dog, the owner who went sniffing about the rooms, a folding ruler in hand, claiming to be taking measurements for a new radiator. Compared with this hole I call that home.

Somebody in stocking feet is standing on the other side of the door reading the word engraved in the glass that I can't read. A bit farther off, the young mother (young, proud, happy) is talking to her child.

I'll start up again tomorrow morning. Fan the cinders. A cockchafer has just walked onto the paper. After making a full circle, it sits there as immobile as me sitting there looking at it. Calm now. I'm calm.

In my *soledad sonora,* he quoted, pleased with himself.

People et al.

THE PRINCIPAL (he is smooth. I hear a lot about his predecessor. He was from Normandy and had a bit of trouble after the liberation and was oh such a fine person, so fair, the teachers said. But I like the new man. Maybe *because* he's too smooth for me.

His graying hair slicked back in the style of the movie stars of the twenties. His slightly prominent chin, his Adam's apple. The calfskin gloves he keeps on when obliged to shake my outstretched hand. Shoes that make a cracking noise, a starched shirt. Oh, the noble hunter!

Occasionally he deigns to teach a lesson. History and solfège. He rises ever so slightly on his toes when he beats time. Do re do. Re do. Mi fa mi do. So la so ti do. And history is his hobby, his stamp collection, his dovecote. No wonder he's active in the Party's youth movement. It makes sense. He's also started a school chorus. Warbling.

Bliss. The Little Gallows Singers. But when the tenors' throats start swelling, their upper lips sprout down, out they go. Order is order. The principal is the smoothest man I know. That's why he's the principal. The self-control, the knowledge of human nature, the wheeling and dealing within the realm of possibilities, the formal diplomacy – they had to be rewarded. And now he's tapping his finger right under my collarbone. Even though nobody can see him – the boys are out in the corridor and we're alone in the classroom – he can't help posturing, taking a deep breath before the first sentence, like a TV commentator, winking, bending the upper part of his body).

"De Rijckel!"

"Present."

The Principal (encapsulated in his pose like a larva in its cocoon. Never will courtesy be as cruel as his! With what cold perfection and tetchy distance he tilted his head forward as if listening to the flow of life in the corridor, where the boys were growing noisy. And the way he lifted it, sniffing, smelling something, the proximity of humans, a rancid smell. We humans belonged to his race but as imperfect specimens. Oh, the round, nicotine-free ball of his finger with its arched nail, filed and polished by one of his three daughters, the cuticles carefully pushed back to display the half-moon, now gliding along the shaven cheek on the lookout for a pimple, a wrinkle, then hesitating, gliding back, a limb armed with a horn seeking its path as the voice finds a familiar path and says): "De Rijckel."

The hand on the cheek – I notice just now – is holding a gray, flayed hand, a small cluster of used-up fingers, a gnawed-down thumb, a leather hand out of service (its service: humiliating me in public) there on the face of the Man.

He gives his thigh a slap with his glove – thus arousing the horse in him, though he does not go so far as to rear – and fixes my left ear with his eye; the lobe resists his attention. He smells of almond trees, burnt coffee beans, and something metal. The pinnate leaf of his forehead refuses to unfold. Nothing is easy in a principal's beleaguered realm because We, principal of a mirror-smooth playground, a domain suited to absent-minded roller-skating, We were not present, We, ruler and tamer, encourager of talent and discipline among the underage teachers. We experience daily afflictions, and one of them, one of the deluge awaiting Us every day – aches in the stomach, questionnaires in the office – but as I was saying, the first affliction of today – notwithstanding the fact that we stand in the breach the whole day through, tormented and frozen in the icebox of Our iron will – the first veritable affliction We must contend with today, on the spot, before it spreads like a tubercular plague, is this de Rijckel standing here before us, and the Principal says: "My dear de Rijckel, forgive me for interrupting your class, but it is a matter of great importance, don't you see, don't you see, it occurred to me, if you know what I mean, that you might overlook tonight's meeting, don't you see. And that would be, at the very least, shall we say, a pity, because I have big things in mind for you, and as I am certain you know, do you not, my dear de Rijckel, I am very fond of you and would very much like to render you a service that would be highly beneficial to you, but professional discretion prevents me from going into detail here. I shall be speaking tonight, as you may be aware, after the business meeting and the committee report on the annual trip, which will be to Salzburg this year, on the topic "What Does Mozart Actually Mean to Our Youth?" and I thought your introduction might highlight my deep commitment to the education of our young people. You are free, of course, to speak about whatever you . . ."

Whereupon? I refuse. Whereupon. His teeth, which have trouble letting s's through. The a's dating back to the "Fair Flemish" days. The coldness in his eyes, eyes brighter than the streams medieval heroines drowned in and, yes, froze. The sullen mouth releasing doves from an evil dovecote, words like "if you know what I mean, right? don't you think?" that yearned for give-and-take, if you know what I mean. Right? Don't you think? Always the injured party. And clearly: the cancer spread by the don't-you-think? if-you-know-what-I-mean, and right? presume a secret sympathy. As if his pus were melodious! And his fin-de-siècle airs and graces. Along the lines of: this gentleman has seen better days and holds on to their allure! Beset by doubts and pitiful despair this bon vivant, don't you know? right? Yes, truly, a mystery trickles over these immobile, perfectly mature features like a sauce. And is not the sauce the soul of the dish?

How strong he is! He is the key vertebra in the school skeleton, the kingpin in the mechanics of the universe; without him the meridians would rattle; and the axis of the world is: the hand, hesitant, picking over his face in its lifeless glove, wandering over his face in slow-motion.

"Have you got a moment, de Rijckel?" he asks. "Listen. We'll be expecting you a bit earlier than usual this evening. Because I'm scheduled to go on just after the chairman. And make your introduction short. So we'll see you at eight, right? We're counting on you."

The Principal (is for emancipation, re-resurrection, regroupment, for healing the wounds among all sectors of the population and for rallying round what we all hold so dear, for solidarity with, in the framework of, in today's world, in the area of human relations as such, if you know what I mean.

I am a child when he looks at me, a snotnose. Waiting for my punishment. I would never dare hide a firecracker in his office because once it exploded he would turn to me – unscathed, unspotted, unperturbed – and give me a slap with his dry, perfumed palm by way of a harsh blessing.): De Rijckel. Just a minute. A moment of your time, dear friend. Our city is in need of men who can lead. I have become one by dint of energy and perseverance. Follow my example and you won't regret it. You will deliver your introduction, just after eight, with your usual brio. I am certain you won't let us down, the Party and me.

Much remains to be done, my boy, and this evening is a test of the strength of our cultural program. All eyes will be upon us. See you then, right?

THE TOBACCONIST (eyebrows arched in wonder, worried eyeballs bulging a bit too far, and, sure enough, the white-velvet mound of a goiter is lodged in the wide opening of the collar; energetic little teeth chewing away on gum whose sugar and mint have been long since ground into a memory softened and rekindled by the mucus and spittle and gargle in his gullet; the odor of Wervik tobacco and coronas and chocolate; phlegm being hawked up; he lives with the delicate membranes in his throat as other men live with their wives, that is, he is drained, debilitated, provoked by them, totally trapped; hot and distorted, his voice strolls into the street, as hoarse as a child's; he scratches his head and wipes his nails clean on the faded apron that had once, long ago, during the seven years of plenty, belonged to his mother; arranges the piles of various cigarette brands because nowadays you have to stock them all, the customers need to have a choice; behind him – it's been there so long he doesn't see it – an Egyptian princess mounted Amazon fashion on a lion in the shadow of a sphinx, sucking on a gold cigarette holder and blowing the smoke to me, a foreigner, who has been buying his filter tips for two years now, two packs, twenty-six francs. Today I get two boxes of matches as a bonus): Oh, hello, sir. It ain't cooling down at night, but that don't bother me. I can't sleep anyhow. My legs, it's like they're on fire. You know how it goes. Going to the Dead Rat tonight? No? Well, there'll be a big crowd. Ten thousand or more, or so they say in the papers. People are rolling in dough, let me tell you. It's the Congo, they say, but I seen guests change their costumes two-three times a night. First a clown. Then Julius Caesar. You know how it goes. I ain't never been and I been living here since twenty-four, but the likes of me we can't get away. You know how it goes. This is our best time: nobody pinches pennies when they're out on the town.

The things that go on at that ball! It's them youngsters, mostly. The young people today, let me tell you, we don't understand them, they don't understand us. From what I hear they do it right there on the couches. I mean, really. Okay, you're out for a good time, but if you're serious about it you do it in private. Now don't go thinking I'm trying to drum up business, but if you do happen to go, not to worry: you can always depend on us. See what I'm getting at? Pleasure is pleasure, after all. A room, nothing fancy, but clean, see what I mean? Lots of gentlemen will be using our rooms tonight, and we ain't never had a complaint. Well, enough said. I'm at your service. All you got to do is come in and say "Arthur," and I'll know what's up and take you to your room. And don't trouble your head about the next guy. Nobody'll come knocking at your door, ha ha ha. Enough said, sir. Right. Thank you, sir. Bye now. Thank you. Bye, sir. Thanks.

THE HALL (how long? how wide? how high? I'll have to fill it in later. It's urgent. There are so few concrete things left.

The niche where I sat on the couch with my feet up on a wrought-iron garden table was a reception room, an office that had been dismantled for the sake of the ball, though the shelter provided by its walls and screens let me hear the two nearby dancers so clearly that the panels of Burmese rosewood might have contained sound-dampening glass fiber . . .

Under the chandelier of polished bronze and cut glass: the vertebrae and six beauty spots on her back.

And in the beginning, beneath the emerald granite dome and between the walls of white Pentelic marble, I had passed through the silvery bronze doors, propelled by the curtain of warm air at the main entrance.)

THE COURTIER (his Venetian disguise serving only to heighten his Flemish demeanor. The wig of silver-powdered nylon is loose at the ears and neck. And I never see a wig on a head without thinking of my father in an amateur performance of the comedy *At Uncle's*. My mother said, "Look! Your father!" and pointed to the stage, where a thin, surly man in a black dress was delivering a monologue. His head was a mass of flaxen curls powered white. "Don't you see him? There! Look, silly! The pastor! That's him. Don't you recognize him?" Chalk-white make-up on the face, red streaks on the cheeks, three vertical strokes on each side of the nose, its wings brought out by dabs of gray matching the gray beneath and above the eyes, all of which was meant to give the impression of age, poverty, and disease. The man standing bent and coughing in front of the footlights was not my father, impossible, and I lost all interest in the pastor. I also thought that, as usual, my mother was trying to lead me up the garden path the better to mock my gullibility, and I turned my attention to the other characters and tried to recognize my father in the village notary or the farmers going on interminably about age-old memories, though they were too small, too fat, too lively. Then at a tearful point in the play Uncle turned his back to the audience and whispered to his niece that he was not long for this world, and I suddenly saw a familiar, make-up-free, blood-red neck under the wig and between the powdered ears sticking out on either side, and I cried out "Papa!" and my mother hushed me and I started laughing and wailing in terror . . .

The lace collar the courtier is wearing is lopsided and makes it plain for all to see that he has no wife or solicitous mistress, that he pulled on the expensive, ill-fitting costume by himself. He tries to emulate the courtly gestures the costume calls for – the cigarette held at a rakish, provocative angle, the jaunty crossing of the legs and swinging of the feet shod in silver-buckled clergyman's shoes, the eyebrows rising red and wild over the mask – but can't quite bring it off. Anyone looking closer could tell the costume was rented: you could just see it hanging next to the Greek togas and Rubens cloaks and midnight blue dinner jackets in the costume shop, and there is no more a person in that costume now than there was in the shop. He tries to prop himself up behind the tails of his Venetian get-up. Later he buries one of his spade-like fingers in his nose under the mask's pliant scales. He says to her): Are you unhappy here? Tell me. If so, we can leave. I'll take you home. I promise. I swear. No, I won't stop anywhere on the way. Why won't you tell me your name? My name is Albert. I won't tell you my family name: that's what masquerades are for, damn it. Pascale? Dominique? Cathérine? No? All right. Don't tell me. I know it anyway. I know you quite well, actually. You can't fool me. Of course I'll buy you a drink. Champagne.

What? No, I won't go any higher. No. A deal is a deal. A thousand francs is a thousand francs and not one franc more. Here. Take it. A thousand francs. You refuse? All right. That's your affair.

Come on. Stop acting so crazy. It's over and you've got your thousand francs. It's a masquerade, after all. I'll bring you right back, I swear, and no one will be the wiser. A quarter of an hour. All right. I'm on my way, this very minute. You can find yourself another sucker. First you give your word, then, boom, it's off. *What?* Three thousand francs? Are you out of your mind? Nobody's ever paid that much in Belgium. Not the shah of Persia!

And don't think I don't know who you are. I know you perfectly well, my girl. But that's the way they do things nowadays, damn it. So I'll be a sport and throw in an extra five hundred. Not good enough?

God damn it! I know you. You've got the most beautiful eyes I've ever seen. And your costume . . .

Jew boy? Me? That's a hot one. What a thing to say.

The Courtier (more brutal now, his everyday mode. The spade-like fingers grip the steeling wheel. The road ahead stretches out far into the distance, all the way to the ocean, where a brightly lit boat is sailing. The radio is playing; the car is making a muted rumble. Flags are fluttering.): What do you think I am? Fifteen hundred francs – nobody pays that much. Good God, is this why I came to the Dead Mouse Ball?

Well, at least I've got her jacket. And she won't get it back. That'll teach her. You heard her call me a Jew, didn't you, pal? Well, if I'm a Jew, I'll keep her jacket. Good God, if it'd been a man who called me a Jew, he'd have regretted it to the end of his days. Because before you know it, word gets around, and in my line you can't afford that kind of thing. Being a Jew may be okay in some places but not in the car business. Teddy Maertens a Jew – you never know what you're going to hear next. Look, there she goes. A hot bitch that one!

Just my luck to run into her here. I'd heard she stopped showing her face in these parts and went to Brussels for a good time. But I kept up the game, played dumb, while the whole time I was itching to tell her, nearly told her, "Hey, don't you remember Teddy Maertens, who fought with Crabbe during the war? The guy he shot dice with till the wee hours?" But no, you don't say that if you're a sport and it's a masquerade to boot. You're either a gentleman or you're not.

Let me introduce myself. Teddy Maertens is the name. I'm in cars. This is your latest Buick. It's got the wheelbase of the four-cylinder Tempest. The cylinder heads are aluminum, but the linings are cast iron of course. One hundred and fifty horsepower. So the mileage . . .

Look, she's lost. She doesn't seem to know where she's going. If mademoiselle thinks I'm going to get out of my car, she's got another thing coming. She damn well should have figured that out by now. But will you look at that ass!

She'd better watch out or she'll catch pneumonia. Seen her eyes, pal? Purple. And pure iron, let me tell you, pure cast iron. Go right through you. Man, she hasn't changed a bit in all these years. Still crazy as a nut cake. Hey, where's she headed anyway?

I can't take any more of this. Look at the ass on her, pal. Hey, is she walking into the ocean? Don't tell me. I know. Don't say a word. Not a word. What an animal . . .

Her

No constellation is present in its entirety. Or visible. Or restored to an earlier state. Just as the stars never reconvene in the configurations they form on the gypsy woman's maps, never again.

Near the railing the esplanade is set off by the sky, by the green pickets with their rings, by the poles on the playing field, and the two telescopes that, or so people said, the Führer once looked over to England. For fun (a contagious word and out-of-date). The Führer inserted a five-franc coin in the magic slot that activated the long-sighted retina, and saw England.

No moon. A tatter of a moon breaks over the wave crests. Framed by the sky and the intersection of four or five scaly-backed breakwaters, her shape slips past and cuts a hole in the frame. As her shoulders pitch and her feet seek firm ground in the wet sand, one breakwater lurches back into sight, an incisive route into the black water. The shredded, glimmering paper of the light from the sky reaches the woman's hair and back and illuminates her silhouette. (The "hot bitch.")

We're now at the railing, which is cool to the touch. Below, amid traces of horse hooves and bicycle tires, amid fresh footprints, the cabins on wheels rest against the esplanade.

Her knees are no longer buckling; she is taking longer surer steps towards the breakwater. Yet she still has something of the stilt-plover scampering along mossy stumps on the backs of wavy scale-bugs. The breakwater grows smoother and she slows down. Wades into the ocean. So far she nearly disappears. There are three men giggling below us; they are hidden behind the cabins, where the soil begins. So we have in fact followed her, notwithstanding Teddy Maertens' declaration that he wouldn't leave his car for that "hot bitch," and notwithstanding his request for silence he is mumbling incantatory supplications. She is still standing there when a late fishing sloop sails back into the harbor and scans for waves with its beacon. When I put on my glasses, she has retreated several meters, but she is still facing the boat. Is it coming to pick her up? Her skirts are swirling around her spread legs. Far from the port brawls and dancing, she is absorbed by the more immediate violence of the water. And because the insistent, gruesomely placid element is forcing its way into her, we too are drawn into the grayish play of the water, and her offensive stupidity when telling off the courtier, her show of lewdness when stroking the silken insides of her thighs, her awkward, bovine advance through the breakwater's slippery stones – we forget it all, fools that we are, at that moment.

We are standing side by side, Teddy Maertens and I, our organs tingling, our blood surging, our throats going dry in the din rending us asunder. Then, nestling against the porcupine-like beast swirling in the whirlpools, she laughs, audibly, she laughs loudly, and the water rushing towards us rolls her laughter along. My glasses cloud over with sweat. The car salesman at my side says he should never have left his car. "She's going to fling herself into the sea. Just you wait. Then we're really up the creek."

I think of the underwear I've had on for a week and my filthy feet: when I stumble out of the sea with her on my shoulders and the esplanade residents come running (Teddy Maertens is sniveling and yelping) to help the rescuer and rescuee get their clothes off, that will in-dis-putably be the first thing they see. The woman laughs. The tide is making her – and us – dizzy. No stone is firm underfoot. The droning pavement of the esplanade, hexagonal tiles for the roller-skaters, is making to rise up like another, broader-backed beast. The three men are cooing behind the wooden palisades near the cabins. The woman lifts a hand, reaches out for birds, chases away mosquitoes. She is keeping beasts at bay.

Because Teddy Maertens wants to go and I don't want him to disappear thinking of me as the sozzled eavesdropper in the sound-proof niche or the accomplice eavesdropper in the Buick, because – I have other reasons, though what are they?

Korneel wants me to be as accurate as possible: the facts, he says, nothing but the facts. Well, the fact was that I gave him a kick in the ankle just above his shoe with the silver buckle. Through the gray layers of my glasses I see Teddy Maertens vacillating between cry and curse, revealing his teeth all the way to the gums. He shuts his mouth. He has been caught red-handed. Guilty. He has been punished. Folds of fat form where the mask digs into his neck. He seeks out my eyes.

"Is this any way to celebrate?" he says. "Is this why I took you to the masquerade? Is this the way you thank me for plying you with champagne all night?" He is hopping up and down on one foot.

One by one the three men down below straighten up. They walk to the steps leading to the esplanade without a word.

"You shouldn't have done that, pal," says Teddy Maertens.

I go back to my hotel. I have nothing else to do. Behind me the breakwater, overwhelmed by cresting waves, is empty.

I spend the rest of the night – exhausted, dry thanks to the ministrations of the local residents, admired, treated to a hot toddy, smiling at the reporters, honored by the local officialdom – in my room. In my room I fold up my trousers – spotless, unwrinkled – and place them under the mattress. My eyes are still tearing from the friction of the mask. The window is open, and I am lapped by the rays of the lighthouse. Later fog invades the room with a smell of metal and women.

The Smell of Metal and Women

"You can't smoke here," said Elizabeth, tickling my palm. A summer with doves and the hum of heavy cars on the far-off road. The damp wood smell, her young girl smell, and the stench of the sludge in the river oozing along behind the depots of Haakebeen Lumber, taking all the city's filth with it. The pungent air rising out of the enormous beams and disks attacking my eyes.

"I don't want to," said Elizabeth while pulling at my sweater and digging her claws into me instead of pushing me away.

I thought of Haakebeen Lumber's four watchmen, armed watchmen. "But you followed me without thinking," I felt like saying. "I didn't need to ask twice."

"No, I do," she said hesitantly, then stammered something else, and to check the capricious shiver that overcame her she clambered onto a

pile of boards and crouched there, knees apart, letting me hoist myself
up into the dark between them. "I bet you think I came because we're
having an exam and I don't know a blessed thing. You do, don't you.
Well, it's not true, sir. Really it isn't."

"Then why did you come?" I asked calmly.

She bit her thick, young lips. Scratched her knee.

"Why do you think, sir?"

I stalled and waited.

"If the girls ever heard," she said. "Emmy Verdonck. And Cecile
Meert."

"They'll hear soon enough."

"Oh no, sir. I swear. I won't breathe a word."

"It will be the first thing you talk about tomorrow on the playground."

"No. I swear, sir. I'll never breathe a word of it to anybody. It could
really get you into trouble, couldn't it."

"Yes, Elizabeth."

A dove cooed. A wooden dove? They sat in bunches. The boards
swell and crack. I'll never be able to get this odor of turpentine and
tar out of my clothes. I can just see the principal sniffing them. Four
night watchmen with machine-guns could turn up at any moment in
the performance of their duty and run me in, a teacher caught with a
minor in Haakebeen's lumberyard.

I could scarcely bring myself to pronounce her name in class, which the acne-ridden snoops surrounding her on all sides must have noticed: I often skipped over her as I went from pupil to pupil, and whenever I wrote a capital E on the board it came out thicker than other letters. I was twenty-eight at the time.

Pressing against me now, she said with a triumphant look in her eye, "I thought you'd never talk to me. When you came up to me on the bridge this evening, I knew you'd start in about the class. It was the only thing you could do, right?"

Already she spoke the language of the victor, wallowing in her victory.

"You had no choice, right?" she whispered. "I'm your pupil."

Submissive. Innocent. Then she decided she didn't need to bother with all that: licked her upper lip, placed her fingers just above my watch on my pulse, took my hand. Time passed. "Listen," she said. "Listen carefully." And then she said in English, "What if I say I shall not wait." In the weak neon light that erased the childlike contours of her face she smiled no more. I gasped for breath – and ingested a mouthful of the wood-fouled air – so abrupt and unexpected was the shift to the Emily Dickinson poem I had just taught to the class and is addressed to a dead woman and had burst out of her girlish mouth so monstrously and with ravishing lubricity.

"Does she know the second line?" I thought. "Does she want me to recite it to her, even in this dirty, all-invasive light?"

I said the second line – "What if I burst the fleshly gate" – but could not go on: I was chewing on nettles; the roof of my mouth was ablaze. I mumbled a few hoarse words, chewing away, and as if by chance she let her closed hand down on my crotch. I mumbled a few more hoarse words, and she fell against me – as she had seen women do on the screen, arms open wide – and licked my cheek like a cat, thrusting her breasts into me. I shook her by the shoulders. She muttered something and, eyes shut, searched in the folds of her dress until she came up with her handkerchief. She dabbed her eyes; a clump of mud dissolved in me. She tried to get a grip on herself but failed and stammered, "No, no, sir. I don't want to, sir," and took my hand again and pressed it against the nipple under her black sweater. I heard watchdogs barking, watchmen approaching: we were kneeling behind piles of green lumber in the shadow of the licorice plant, Elizabeth and I, she sitting with her knees open over my face, forcing the darkness down my throat, I retching from the smell of metal and woman, my woman Elizabeth.

Haakebeen's Lumber and Furniture Center

We consider Haakebeen Lumber to be one of the town jewels. Edmond Haakebeen, the Founder of the Establishment, and his two sons Jan and Herman, a ne'er-do-well and a lawyer, are known to one and all. Not only for their energy, obstinacy, and business sense but also for their less popular familial characteristics, such as their penchant for parties with artists and naked women, their passion for sailing, their trips abroad, and the way they played up to the landed aristocracy. This and very much more – and in myriad detail – we learned from our elders and friends when as children we heard them tell envy- and veneration-packed stories about the Haakebeens. While attending the municipal secondary school during the war years, from 1940 to 1944, we were fully apprised of their position: we were aware that the Haakebeens not only supplied lumber and furniture to fortify the Atlantic Wall and sang, arms raised, the requisite German songs during the meetings of our homegrown fascists, the Blacks, but that they also supplied the Resistance, the Whites, with money and provisions. No wonder there were grim free-for-alls even during the Occupation. I remember the ones that started up when Herman Haakebeen, the leader of the German-Flemish Workers Association (The Flag), had to stand by helpless while his only brother Jan was arrested for sabotage and held by the Teutons for three weeks in the city jail, which we call The Stroll.

We do not find this schism in the heart of one of our Great Families disconcerting; indeed, in antiquity discord of the sort was actually thought to fortify virtue. Be that as it may, Jan Haakebeen escaped after the third week of his incarceration, when the RAF strafed the city and hit the prison. Quite a few of us expected that in the ensuing months Jan, in hiding at the time, would suddenly turn up at the parental Abode and make a scandal by, for instance, beating Father, murdering Brother, cracking the safe. But nothing of the sort leaked out, and after the Liberation Jan Haakebeen came forth with testimony in favor of his brother and father during the Trial. The Haakebeens were remarkable people. Twice their lumberyard had burned to the ground, once during an RAF bomb attack and once after the Liberation, when the entire enterprise had been impounded. The second fire was naturally enough instigated by old man Edmond Haakebeen and, though nobody doubted it in the slightest, the most hardnosed insurance inspectors practically went blind trying to come up with something. We had no trouble appreciating such efficiency in evil, and so we greet Edmond Haakebeen politely and sincerely when, decorated with several national orders, he makes his way every afternoon at about five to the Bridge Club in Market Square.

We, mere children at the time, were unwilling witnesses to the first lumberyard fire. People usually ran up the hill when they heard the sirens, the hill being just outside the center of town and the site the Haakebeens had chosen for their lumber business. The fleeing crowd looked upon it as a refuge which, though not necessarily safer than their air-raid shelters, did have its advantages: 1) one could follow the bombing in all its phases because the town lay in a kind of valley below; 2) one could derive a sense of strength from the solidarity that came from praying together, weeping together, drinking beer, telling jokes, and so on; 3) one could assume that the (then) enemy aircraft had received clear-cut directives from Headquarters to spare Haakebeen Lumber because once the Battles were over they would make use of Haakebeen's materials, machines, and organization, plus the know-how of its management. (For is it not so that the Mighty of this world look out for one another? Precisely.)

We could give many more reasons as to why the denizens of the city gathered out in the open on Haakebeen's hill, but those were the main ones we heard as children, when the buzz of thousands of hornets flew over our heads just before the bombs fell. One night, contrary to all expectations, they fell on Haakebeen Lumber. We were by then part of the Civil Defense Youth Brigade, and at the signal – the lacerating sirens – we biked to the center of town, where we were generally given an assignment. But that night the center of town was hit by a bomb and all we found at the smoking, blazing hole in the row of houses was a panic-stricken group of three Civil Defense representatives whose shouts failed to coalesce into comprehensible commands. The only thing that came across was that Haakebeen Lumber was in flames.

Then Jules Metzemaekers, the leader of the Civil Defense, said, "Come with me" and drove us to the Hill. Panic reigned there too. There was untold material damage, and the number of human victims was impossible to calculate because people were running all over the place and any attempt at commands or explanations or order was out of the question. Everyone screaming as if injured or dying. One of those moments when people lose all rationality.

We, the Youth Brigade, four of us, and Jules Metzemaekers, were helpless. But not for long. Because we soon realized that the focal point of the fire was not our main goal (help! help! how can we help!): it was nothing more than a pile of boards sending flames into the air with a person here and there; no, our help was needed by a quiet, dull, inert mass. There was a kind of shed built against one of the lumberyard's gigantic walls to serve as a canteen for the workers, and that bench- and table-filled space, which incidentally also served as a banquet hall when the Friends of Haakebeen's Brass Band held their annual banquet, was where the older members of the population would congregate and wait out the bombardments. But this time a heavy bomb had hit the side of the wall the shed leaned against, just where the enormous supply of coal necessary for the operations was stored, and the air pressure resulting from the bomb, to put it simply, had brought down the gigantic wall, crushing the shed and burying it beneath the coal.

The bystanders who had brought this to the attention of the Youth Brigade were in such a state of shock and anxiety that they simply stood there and sobbed. "Attention!" Jules Metzemaekers shouted, and ordered us to start digging. We did as we were told. With spades and shovels. The crowd around us lifted their fists in the direction of the English planes, which were still buzzing overhead. They screamed bitter oaths up at the planes, and we searched the coal for the old people buried in it. We found few that night because they had probably thought the gigantic wall the safest place to be and had gone and stood there, and the place where the wall caved in was right in the middle of the coal. While Jules Metzemaekers brandished his revolver to keep the bystanders from making off with the coal, we dug till morning.

If we have always considered Haakebeen's Lumber and Furniture Center one of the town jewels, it is not only because so many people, cowardly and brave, lost their lives within its walls during this disaster; no, when we say "jewel," we mean it in the fullest sense of the word.

In short, Haakebeen Lumber is memory, chastisement, and sin for us, so that when we happen to go there now – with women, some of us – we can never breathe in the sharp odor of resin and tar without thinking of life and death, and this despite the fact that we live in a time more concerned with bread and circuses.

Reconnaissance

The teacher slowed his pace through the Municipal Park when he realized he didn't need to be anywhere at a particular time, it being his day off. He had not fallen asleep until late the night before and had awoken with a start several times during what was left of the night, and now – there wasn't a soul in the park or street – it was ten past six. There was a powdery mist hovering over the asphalt path that emerged from the bushes and crossed the park, and the teacher made his way through it towards the abandoned tennis court and hillocks with their gaudy exotic plants, each bearing its own name plaque. Once in the not so distant, unclouded past, whose harmony now seemed inexplicable to him, the teacher had read all the little yellow signs with the Latin, French, and Dutch names of the plants. Without putting his glasses on he could no longer decipher a single character, which were made with a Schoolchild's Printing Kit. He gave up.

The mist parted wherever he went. He stood on one of the steps of the bandstand where brass bands from all over the country would come on Sunday mornings to earn their rating in a national competition, and he was about to address the crowd (asleep and longing in sleep for the first tinkle of the alarm clock) when a little girl dressed as a woman walked past. She was wearing silk stockings, high heels, and an open Persian lamb jacket so long that she was all but dragging it along the ground. She stopped and saw a dog turd at the edge of the lawn, picked it up, and put it to her lips. The teacher watched her full vapid face framed in dirty-blond curls. Her lips were smeared carelessly with purple lipstick, her eyebrows covered with soot. Although he had not moved, something – his attention? his disgust? – had betrayed his presence, and the child looked up at him and squeezed the turd in her hand. Then she hurried off over the lawn, awkward in her high heels, disappearing behind the pond's high reeds. The teacher, trying to follow her, went all the way to the water's edge, where the motorboats were moored, but the child (or the female midget returning home from a party for circus artists) was nowhere to be seen. She had probably hidden in the bushes surrounding the tennis court. He kept looking until he came to the bronze tiger on his light-green porous pedestal. The mossy tiger was facing west, guarding a list of citizens fallen in action. A pale sun broke through the clouds. The teacher picked a sprig of the fuchsia clinging to the gossamer-like wire mesh surrounding the tiger. Farther, beyond a hill, a prism whose front surface was covered with multicolored flowers forming the dial of a clock whose numbers were lilies, he came again in view of the city with its slate roofs, posters, and now active traffic lights.

Reluctant to venture into the cool, concrete depot of the houses and public buildings, he turned back into the park and took the path leading to the miniature golf course. He came to a bench with a white-haired man on it and a man dressed in dark green standing behind him, his hands resting on the back of the bench. The old man was rocking back and forth, which meant that his back regularly came in contact with the hands of the man behind him. It was a game. Or the old man had a rocking sickness. It was the longest bench in the park, and large numbers of women with children would sit there in the afternoon sun. When the teacher passed, the old man greeted him with his entire body. Or happened to rock very far forward. His white beard folded against the snow-white shirt front. The teacher did not see the watery, bloodshot eyes and their pea-green pupils. The old man was leaning on an ebony cane whose silver point was half buried in the sand, and was singing a march with many tarantaras in it. The man behind him – guard, male nurse, jailer – stared into his master's neck. Or victim. "Good morning," said the teacher with more vitality than he felt. The male nurse gave him a servile look and hunched forward in self-defense like a green, dark-green bird, when the teacher, Victor-Denijs de Rijckel, an interloper, took a seat at the far end of the bench. The old man – noble, run-down, lonely – was enjoying the sun and singing "Malbrough s'en va-t-en guerre," his lipless mouth occasionally opening extremely wide between the two white growths. The three sat there on the bench for a long time. No one said a word. The light – ever clearer, sharper – cast a shadow under the bench through the branches and back-lit the bandstand's crisscross latticework, lending color to the flowers garlanding the marble bust opposite the old man. It was an image of himself – the same strong nose, the same puritan mouth – a gift from the grateful town fathers. One night the Art Academy students had honored his memory – because he had become a vegetable wheeled around by that awful servant – by spattering it with green, red, and black paint, but now nothing could happen to it because the two of them kept watch. The old man raised a knotty hand. The bones cracked. The back of the hand was flaky, and the knuckles and thumb were deformed. The old man pointed a finger in the direction of a beetle and sang his march a bit more slowly as if to time it with the scrapings of the coleopteron. The male nurse was still leaning forward in his ready-to-pounce position. The old man's jaws started moving, and his blotchy red eyelids trembled like a delicate leaf in a breeze. The teacher left the bench.

Tram bells were ringing, more and more people appearing and scurrying here and there. It was a fine August morning. The teacher crossed the playground, which was used for skating, shooting matches, and children's games. The classroom buildings with their fire-escape ribs and roof gutters were grouped around the principal's lookout tower, where his office lay in a fleece of ivy.

No one. What bestial, memorable, irrevocable damage can I do, now, here, in the middle of this dance floor for giants? the teacher thought. But nothing could happen or come about without the complicitous presence of the others – pupils, teachers, and de Beul with his periscope high up in the ivy-ivory tower. By the same token it was their presence that meant nothing memorable could happen, because no sooner did they make their presence known than the carcass the teacher knew to be encasing him tightened its joints and paralyzed him more than ever, and he was forced to keep rank at the head of the cattle he was charged to instruct. He did so willingly, meekly. Or had done until then. Was he, in turn, looked upon by them as an executioner? No. Well, he wasn't sure. Insignificant? No, not that either. A judge charged with carrying out orders but who for want of orders could come up with dictates and verdicts of his own. He had no name, no pseudonym, no nickname. The teacher followed a precisely traced line to the door of the classroom where the day after tomorrow he would have his first class with the fifth-form classical pupils: High German for ruminants.

In the windows, whose lower panes disappear inexplicably under the level of the playground – what space did the military architect think he was saving by turning the basement into classrooms? – he spied himself approaching, decapitated, then reduced to knees and shoes.

In the reflection of his trousers he could make out the blackboard, the rubber plant, the science charts, and the map of Western Flanders, where, if you got close enough, you could see the varicolored tacks the teachers had used to follow the campaign of 1940. Under the freestone coat of arms with the eagle commemorating the gift of the building by the town council. In the glass door that miaowed. In the hallway of the basement smelling of chalk and rotting boards and stagnant water. The teacher was descending into the depths. The door to fifth-year classics was locked – he should have known. He sat down on a stair, lit a match, turned it round and round, tossed it into a corner, and, leaning back on an elbow, stretched out over the stairs and fell asleep.

In his sleep he heard the rasp of footsteps and, awakening with the languid thought that somebody had *the right* to come and go in the corridors at this hour, he noticed that the sound was coming from behind fifth-year classics, where it was darkest because the four beams supporting the low ceiling blocked the light passing through the window in the door. He saw then that the rasping sound came not from shoe soles but from a sharp-edged brick being scraped along the walls by a slender youth. All the way from the air-raid shelters, the coal cubicles, on the other side of the school most likely. Near the door to fifth-form classics, at a place where the plaster was thick and smooth, the boy

started writing a series of pointy letters. The brick scratched away –
the teacher felt a nervous tic in his eye sockets – scratched through to
the wall's elastic, unplastered innards. "What are you doing here?"
he said, standing. "You shouldn't be doing that. It's much too early.
What's your name? What class are you in?" and the obstinate digging
in the weak flesh came to a halt.

The kids with the rusty daggers, he thought, are the ones who do
the most harm. Aloud he said, "Will you stop that, damn it!" thereby
giving up his status as educator, teacher, adult. Suddenly, wonder of
wonders, he was no longer Judge; he was just a sullen equal holding
back his fury. He read the letters ALESA and asked the boy again what
he was doing there.

The boy's name was Verzele, he said. He had lank, wet hair. Had he
been here so long that the dank cellar air had given his tangled locks
the sheen of purified water, or had he taken a shower in the gymnasium? The boy – shiny-cheeked, open-mouthed, pointy-chinned –
stood in the doorway of fifth-form classics and said he would rather
be early than late. He was smiling a cocky smile and turning the brick
in his red-powdered fingers. His basketball shoes told the teacher he
was in the sixth form: their first period today was gym. Eyes far apart;
deeply set. He did not expect to be punished, the boy; he was beyond
threats: he smiled as if he had caught the teacher, ill at ease, cowering
in the shadow of the beams. He inserted his pinky into one ear and
shook it.

"The poetry classroom is open," he said. "Did you know?"

I'm perfectly happy where I am, thought the teacher. Why should I go to the poetry classroom? What's the poetry classroom to you, snotnose?

The boy, who could not have been more than fourteen, spun around on one leg, then, unable to stand the silence in the hallway (the teacher's silence), said, "I saw you last night."

"Me?"

"At the Rat Ball."

"Me?"

"You weren't in costume, but I was."

"You? Why? When?"

"I called out to you by name."

"You did? I didn't hear you."

"You didn't? Really? I tugged at your sleeve too."

"Why?"

"I shouted like a fishwife. Don't you remember? I was dressed as a Franciscan friar."

A dwarf? A friar? There were so many of them.

The teacher sat back down on the step and lit a cigarette.

"And you didn't dance. Not once."

"No."

"It was really crowded, wasn't it. But not a good crowd."

He had a West Flemish accent, from around Tielt. He spoke very fast, trying to catch something in his speed that had been just as fleeting the night before: No, yesterday was nothing special. It had been much more chichi the year before – as if he went every year – and there weren't enough people from Brussels and not enough people had worn theme-related costumes and the theme for the coming year had been decided upon: The World of James Ensor.

"What was this year's theme?"

"You couldn't tell? The East India Company. The women with brown make-up? The men in white wigs?"

"Okay, okay," said the teacher. Early as it was, the principal could put in an appearance at any moment. He stood up.

"You don't have a key," the boy said.

"No." Then he read "A-les-i-a" out loud.

"Pardon, sir?"

"Alesia. The Latin name for Paris."

The boy smiled again, a sullen yet inviting smile that made him older, and added an "n" to the last "a" with his brick.

I'll have to stop this, thought the teacher. The word stood there, irritating, bright British red, meaningless, right next to the classroom door, in neat capital letters, with the little clerk waiting provocatively for the teacher to guess, to identify his intention. He was thirteen at most.

"There's a mistake in the word," the teacher said.

"It's not complete," said the boy, but the teacher cut him off by saying the it should be Ale-zzzz-an and he hoped that the scorn with which he buzzed the "z" conveyed the following: If a snotnose like you can go to balls with a 150-franc entrance fee and hang around all night there, then you must also go to the races, and the least you can do, you clodhopper, is read the posters and get the spelling right. And he thought, Alezan. What a wonderful word for a chestnut horse: how well it evokes the coat, the mane, the speedy hoofbeat on a bright afternoon at the track at the Palais des Thermes.

"I haven't finished yet," said the boy, and the other – who had now given up his office as adult and teacher, thinking, What's happening to me? – turned to the scornful thirteen-year-old man and said, "What? What?"

"It's her name all right, but the word isn't complete. I haven't finished." ("*I* haven't finished" is how the teacher heard it.)

"Alesandra," said the boy, correcting not so much the word as the role the teacher had now allotted to himself. "I saw you last night, remember? I saw you sitting near her the whole time. And not once did you dance with her."

"What?" (How tiresome. A teacher standing at the blackboard with a wet rag, nobody listening.)

The boy made to finish off the word on the wall, then forgot what he was doing and said, "Her name is Alesandra."

Without a second "s"? Or was it Ale-x-andra?

Buckets, rubbish bins, and milk pails were rattling outside. The playground was being invaded by the army of old women who came to clean the classrooms.

"I don't know any Alesandra," said the teacher impatiently. "Besides, it's none of your business, none whatsoever, understand? And there's nothing between her and me." His voice sounded empty, a monotone.

"Well, then . . ." The boy passed a red finger over his brow: he had stretched a string in front of the teacher to trip him and was concentrating on the attack – that was clear – and the teacher said apologetically, "I didn't know her name was Alesandra. I've seen her only once. Yesterday was the first time."

The boy was wearing black jeans despite the fact that the principal had forbidden pupils to dress like "American dockworkers." His lank hair hid the tops of his ears; his face was light and formless. While the old crones outside shouted to one another, lumbering over the fish market of a playground with their buckets, the boy said that Alesandra lived in a castle called Almout at Hekegem, near Veldonck, which you got to via St. Laurentius-ten-Distel.

"What's that to me?" said the teacher.

"I thought you'd want to know."

"Well . . ." The teacher hesitated. "Do you think she's there now?"

Later the teacher was unable to remember who made the decision, who first learned from the other that he would follow him through thick and thin, who suggested that they might go there, not meaning in a few days or right after school, but now, on the spur of the moment, before the cleaning women came in, before classes began. But it was definitely the boy who threw his brick on the floor and cried, "You bet!" and the pedant of a teacher who dressed him down with a "You mean 'Of course.'"

"Of course," said the boy and, as soon as they were outside, thrust his hands into his pockets. Already independent.

We crossed the playground in the sunlight's glaring white monochrome. The old crones stopped what they were doing, leaned on their brooms and exchanged glances, but made no comments. The teacher, ambling in the lead without haste but not without direction, proceeded under the arches of the entrance, where the porter, at once excessively familiar and excessively obsequious, touched his cap. He was about to stop the boy but then saw that he was with the teacher and reported the fact to someone (the principal?) in the room.

Like a trusted servant who may spend an occasional evening of debauchery with his master, the boy pranced along beside the teacher as they left the quay for the esplanade. They were in a new relationship now: he was a deserter and had to behave. Or was it the teacher who had done the deserting? He found it hard to listen to the babble coming from the boy next to him: that the young woman in Hekegem lived with her parents and the bus went there six times a day, that it was a half-hour ride through the villages of Smitsvoorde, Rijsegem, and Robberzeke. Children were on their way to school by now and nodded to the teacher but did not dare to say anything to the boy, who they assumed had been commandeered to pump a bicycle tire or load tools or was on his way to the teacher's house for a private lesson.

The teacher bought two bus tickets at the Hazegras ticket booth. The boy stood to one side. Then they sat down. The Hazegras was deserted: the shutters of the groceries and sailors cafés were shut. The boy bought three packets of chewing gum from a vending machine, hobbled around in the gutter, and kicked a margarine container along the street. The teacher – teacher no longer, though neither father nor friend – did not try to stop him. The boy kept giving the container side-foot kicks as if trying to make a pass to a member of his team. He was tired by the time he had reduced it to tatters, and he sat down quietly next to the teacher, giving him time to himself, time for reflection.

When one or another pupil escaped from his cage, from the gigantic dragnet that the principal and the teacher had stretched over the school buildings and playground, from the line in front of the classroom, from the row of desks, from the ranks of the march formation on national holidays before the Monument to the Unknown Soldier looking up at the principal and his wreath, that pupil became another child. Often when the teacher met one of his pupils in the city, he caught himself feeling touched by the awkward greeting, the averted glance. You're out of bounds now, he would think whenever it happened: we, the principal and I, have no hold over you here; here you are prey to other, greater powers.

But, he thought now, not this Verzele character. He had lost none of his suspicions, his wiles, his strategies, none of his vigilance. The girlish smile is a weapon, the willingness to help potentially harmful. The widely spaced oblong eyes with their childlike blue-white whites and gray pupils take everything in, forget nothing.

The boy sat there stiffly, waiting for the teacher to say something after the time he had granted him for reflection. Slowly the square was becoming populated with cars, people, policemen, bicycles. The day had begun. The teacher was afraid – though only for a moment – that people he knew, people from the hotel, the brutish porter Bogger or the gypsy woman would happen by and recognize him and ask him to explain what he was doing sunning himself so nonchalantly on a bench on a day when he (or so they thought) was supposed to be teaching Grammar or Pronunciation. But it was too early for the hotel denizens; at most, a chambermaid might ride past on her bike.

Then, without seeing the man approach and before his smell of sweat and muck had filled the booth, he noticed there was someone sitting near him, below him: crouching against the wall under the ticket window and against the edge of the bench was a blind fisherman, a folded bundle of stinking clothes with a capped head sticking out. The fisherman took off his cap and set it down by his shoes. The leather band, shiny from wear and tear and sweat, was bent inward, forming a kind of slot. He did not move; he seemed to have been carried there, folded as he was, from one of the neighboring cafés and tossed down on the ground. Feeling the boy's attentive eyes on him, he said, "A very good day to one and all." He had cataracts. The boy carefully threw a one-franc coin twenty centimeters from the cap. The blind man felt around. His chapped fingers, the color of the red rims of his eyes, were unable to find the coin. He bent forward in such a way that the top of his head with its bumps and scars was turned towards the teacher, and, rummaging, groaned, "Anybody see that pretty little thing?" The boy looked at the teacher and put a red-powdered finger to his lips. "Come on, boys! Stop the nonsense. It's money, I know it is." The rummaging grew desperate. "Come on, boys! Find me that pretty money."

The bus pulled in and honked. The humiliation that beast is putting me through, thought the teacher. Here I am, taking it all in and not moving a finger, letting him do as he likes, with that crooked smile of his.

The boy threw a second coin near the cap, this one a fiver.

"There's another, pal. Twenty francs this time."

"Come on, boys! Come on!" the fisherman cried.

"We've got to go now," said the boy. "Our bus is here."

"Just toss it in the cap, will you?"

"Let's go," said the boy, and the teacher followed him.

"Go ahead," the fisherman cried, "and have a good trip. I'll find the money somehow."

Even though there were empty seats in the bus, the boy remained standing and grabbed a strap. Once the bus left the city proper and passed the coast guard barracks, the teacher told him he was in for a serious punishment. The boy nodded. Nothing defiant in his acceptance of the situation. He understood justice and had expected nothing less.

Past the harbor with the Belgian fleet, the docks, the outskirts where the fishermen lived, through open fields, villas, garages, woods with pylons, cranes, and clouds behind them. Car cemeteries, supply depots for the American Army, cows, farms, restaurants with French names in Gothic letters.

When the boy said they were there, the teacher couldn't distinguish the village from all other villages in West Flanders: a church, a community center, eight shops, eighteen taverns, and one monument, which represented a slate-colored, heavily laden soldier sinking to his knees, imperfectly supported by a woman carrying a palm branch. Advertisements for car tires, margarine, public auctions; two cedars; a few people out walking.

The teacher followed the boy, who babbled animatedly as they crossed the marketplace, saying that Alesandra and, even more, her mother were responsible for the death of a man named Crabbe, a local celebrity, and that the time would come when they would put up a statue to Crabbe, here in the main square, with fresh flowers daily, as was only fitting. The side street they turned into was so narrow that a tractor coming in their direction could hardly get through. The driver, a young man in overalls, gave the boy a cheerful wave.

"So you live here too?" asked the teacher when they were back in the middle of the paved road.

"No."

"Have you got family here?"

"No," said the boy restively.

"But clearly you're at home here!"

It turned out he had lived in Hekegem five years before, when his father decided you could earn a living breeding chickens. The boy did not like being interrogated – it reminded him of school – so he cut the teacher off and asked, "You wouldn't be hungry, would you?"

"No," said the teacher, who was hot in his thick flannel suit and was wondering why he had taken his briefcase with him.

The street split into an asphalt road and a country road. The boy hesitated. Because he didn't know where to go from there? Later the teacher thought that the brief delay the boy was indulging in represented a deep breath before the leap, before the inevitable, indispensable meeting. He stopped at the fork in the narrow, quiet street.

"Don't you know where to go?" It sounded nasty.

"It's a fifteen-minute walk from here," said the boy, and moved over to the edge of the asphalt road, the instep of his basketball shoe grazing the grass as he started down it. Sudden long bursts of the sour, irritating odor of rot, hay, and animals wafted over the stubble. It could have nothing of the flax field about it: the river, the Leie, was kilometers away; nor could it have come from the nearby, all but tangible black smoke rising out of a pile of burning rags. The odor-laden air the sun was now burning seemed aggressive in a manner different from sea air, which at times the teacher found unbearable: it made him simultaneously restless and lethargic. For no apparent reason – the landscape had not changed, there was no break in the asphalt road, no sign, no gate – the boy leaped over the ditch next to the road, crawled under some barbed wire, and took off over a meadow. The teacher followed, and when he caught up to him the boy put on speed while explaining to him they had nearly committed a faux pas: arriving at Alesandra's house in broad daylight was not the thing to do. But since he was walking too fast and leaning forward, as if looking for a ping-pong ball or some lost coins in the grass and cow dung, the teacher could not follow his line of reasoning very well. On the other side of the meadow they crawled under electrically charged barbed wire and proceeded along a willow-lined country road.

"I'm hungry," said the boy. "What about you?"

The area ahead of them was called the Rode Hoek, and the boy headed straight for a tavern. "Because," he said, looking at his watch, which he wore with the dial on the underside of his wrist like a parachute jumper, "it's nearly two. Did you realize that? Or don't you eat lunch."

The teacher searched the boy's face for a sign of derision and, finding none, thought, "Even so, everything he says has an ulterior motive. I let him lead me around by the nose. He seems about to storm a fortress, but instead of orders he gives hints – and of what nature? Were I to protest or refuse to follow him, he would accept it without hesitation, and yet . . ."

Once they were inside, in the cool semi-darkness, he ordered two cheese sandwiches and two pilsners. The peasant woman who served them was pregnant and kept wiping her hands on her apron. Then he ordered a Coke for the boy and a coffee for himself. The pupil read the local paper; the teacher passed the time observing the Rode Hoek's humdrum existence: a coal merchant, a pastor, a notary public or a retired school principal out for a walk, a few children, four strapping women. Then the teacher played three, four, eight rounds of darts with three farmers and a construction worker, defending himself vigorously to the boy's shouts of encouragement. Since they had left the school, the boy had looked or at least acted distinctly younger than fourteen or thirteen. After each round the darts players drank a beer, and as the afternoon wore on, the teacher grew flushed. Not since his military service and the brief period after his wife Elizabeth had left him had he drunk so much. And after each round the boy was treated to a chocolate bar by the loser (not once the teacher) together with exhortations to do well and behave in school.

By then the teacher had forgotten what had brought him to that hole-in-the-wall (or if he had not forgotten, he had pushed it to the back of his mind the way you leave a homework paper that needs correcting on a bed in a hotel room) when the construction worker asked him what he was doing in there. All he could think of was the sloshy, wobbly disturbance in his stomach and said nothing, but the boy gave the pock-marked worker a surprise, intimate little poke in the ribs and said his uncle was taking him on a walk through the countryside. Nature was so beautiful here, the pregnant barmaid said. And so good for city folk, the farmers said by way of confirmation. The construction worker, not wishing to remain in the background, opined that the air in the city was contaminated by factory emissions, the water poisoned by sewer pipes, which he claimed were porous. Though the air here too was being polluted by factories, the farmers pointed out. The teacher kept nodding agreeably, almost enthusiastically, and thought, I'm not drunk though I've never drunk so much; before I know it I'll be taking my clothes off and dancing around the tavern with the pregnant barmaid. Then dusk came through the door, and the house across the road turned bright orange, the stand of trees behind it deep green, while the teacher stared at it all, transfixed. The beer in his glass sloshed when a rowdy farmer pushed the boy against him.

"Let me through," said the boy, slipping out. "I'll be right back." He had been sent to buy sausages.

Through the cloud of tobacco smoke the teacher counted up the number of patrons. It had risen to fourteen. With the fall of evening they spoke differently: more leisurely, solemnly; they spoke about the bombing, the war, exchanged memories, made allusions, as if rehearsing for an eventual definitive performance or keeping a past performance alive by repeating it over the years.

The boy was greeted with a cry of joy, and he passed out smoked ham, headcheese, and sausages, and calling out to the barmaid how much it had cost and giving the patrons nasty nicknames. He was elated. Yet his arrival failed to re-establish the friendly, informal darts atmosphere: the episodes, the plots, the introductions and incomprehensible epilogues of the farmers' stories droned on, saying the same things over and over, slowing down, getting stuck. Certain voices sounded particularly unsure of themselves, and the construction worker began challenging them and proposing they join him outside.

Darkness, like a parachute unfurling and descending in uneven, cloud-like patches, fell on the house across the road and dampened the few remaining street noises. The neon letters of the sign and the lamps, their lampshades adorned with beer advertisements, came on at the same time, and everyone looked at everyone and all the familiar faces of the regulars were distorted, their hollows and bones newly configured by the electric light. The teacher, now an uncle with a childish, loud-mouthed nephew, paid and pushed nephew through the door by the shoulder. They had not let each other out of their sight the whole afternoon, though they had exchanged no more than a word or two. Now they were walking side by side, each with his right hand in his pocket. The teacher made a vague remark about the different route they seemed to be taking and added, "Where's the barbed wire? Watch out. It's electrified."

"It's much shorter this way," said the boy. "You'll see."

Which made no sense, because not knowing the village the teacher had no basis for comparison, and he was going to point this out to the boy but then let it pass. "We'll see," he said.

As they walked, he kept wiping his face and thinking how similar the chatter in the tavern had been to the parties his wife Elizabeth had given in their Franciskus Breestraat apartment, cocktail parties for her female friends among whom she was queen, the affable magnet, and the stuffed yet oddly empty feeling in his stomach grew worse. He walked faster; the road turned into a dried-up ditch: mosquitoes in the hedges, dogs on chains all across the landscape, a swaying bicycle with no light. Passing them, the man pedaled harder. Did he have a message to deliver? Trudging along in the shadow of the hawthorn hedges, the boy pointed to the cyclist, who had blended into the wet-paper sky, and said, "Know who that was? Ange."

"Ange?"

"No, Sprange. Sprange from the castle," said the boy. "A bastard, as you'll see."

"Sprange," the teacher thought. "Sprange with a hard g."

They followed a low, white-washed wall to a small, wrought-iron grill, and the boy, with a flick of the wrist that made it clear he had done it more than once, lifted the latch and pulled up the grill, holding it in the air while swinging it open, which meant that the lower part was above ground. The grill squeaked – a field mouse. An avenue with chestnut trees and beeches. The boy and the MA in Germanic languages, who at this hour was usually at the cinema or in his hotel room reading a book or correcting homework, were now squeezing through an opening in the shrubs running parallel to the avenue, whereupon they saw the house where Alesandra lived with her parents. The daughter of the house. As they approached it from the back – Indians, commandos, marauders – the boy, totally absorbed in the reconnaissance mission, broke branches and flattened bushes, while the teacher fixed the house in his brain – a nineteenth-century French mansion – placing an Alesandra, not the dancing shade by the sea but the pure outline of a hot, dark face, out in front, just below it, in a clearly delineated rectangle as on a cinemascope screen, and the house, which on the contrary came closer and grew larger, flickered vaguely in the background out of the range of the lens, which focused on a face still bearing traces of the mask in the inhumanly smooth, shiny skin. Between them and the white house with a dull lamp on the terrace stretched rows of fir trees, a flat English lawn showing through where they were planted more widely apart, and regularly spaced pedestals (like trees in an orchard) supporting statues, columns with busts, and bare pillars. The capital of the closest pillar sported a number of curved bars with fragments of stone and cement hanging from them.

"Crabbe," said the boy, poking the teacher in the ribs as if he were a fellow pupil or one of the farmers in the tavern. Just a while ago it was Sprange, thought the teacher, confused.

A tall man with jet-black hair and eyebrows running above his nose in an unbroken line and keeping his eyes in the dark stood near one of the statues attired in what looked like battle dress and short black boots. There were swallows skimming over the pillars. How long did the two stand in the bushes and the man by the statue, motionless? Later it seemed a long time. Suddenly – a bird called, a lapwing, thought the teacher, who had noticed an inlet or two in the neighborhood – the boy made a few angular, nervous gestures, and the teacher, not understanding what they meant, crept up closer to him. The boy said something to him, and when the teacher looked back over the lawn the man was no longer there.

"It's Crabbe himself," whispered the boy. "There's a hundred thousand francs on his head. Dead or alive." But the teacher had no desire to play games and said – too loudly, because the boy gave a start and hissed a "Sh!" – "Shut up!"

They climbed out of the safety of the bushes onto the statue-strewn lawn that lay before them, a space easily within machine-gun range from the house. The teacher, who always and everywhere felt insufficiently protected, even here, where his bent back and head were swallowed up by the darkness between the statues, thought it would be better to beat a retreat. The boy, who was bravely standing erect, called out, "Hey! You coming or aren't you?" Didn't he see that the teacher was following him? "Hey! De Rijckel!" the boy cried.

The teacher, shocked, now stood up straight as well, lunged at the boy's clothes, seized his collar with a trembling hand, and spun him a quarter of the way around. "*Mr.* de Rijckel!" he snarled. "And don't you forget it, you hear?"

"Sure, okay," said the boy. "I won't say it anymore." And to calm him down and take his mind off what had happened, he added, "She's at home. The light is on in her room."

"Which room?"

The boy pointed, but the teacher, who was not wearing his glasses, could see no light except for the terrace lamp. They crossed the lawn and the closer they got to the house the less they sought out cover. Anyone looking on would have assumed they were on their way home after a day's work. At the edge of the grass was a stretch of gravel that wound its way around the house in four identical lines. The house was closed, the only light coming from a lamp that hung from the ceiling of a rectangular terrace furnished with wrought-iron chairs, a folded chaise lounge, and a few fishing rods. The fence, which consisted of round spikes, was unpainted, new. Before the two could reach the man-high terrace wall – they had made for the side wall with its Gothic arches and wide lead-latticed window, slowing down and finally stopping altogether – they saw something moving in the windows. They ran towards the side wall, potshots for machine-gun snipers, spurting to reduce the firing angle and ending up in the shadow of the house. Unseen. A man came out of the French window, its unlit glass like ebony panels, speaking to someone inside. Given the band of increasingly white light emerging from the window, the assailants withdrew further into a corner, into the dark, and the boy – out of fear? – broke wind. The man, in a diagonal line to the right of their heads, cut off his sentence. There was a fragment of silence. A space. A slit. That could not be undone or filled in.

Then, a rustling in the beeches, swallows or bats skimming past, a lamp sputtering, the buzz of the telephone wire transformers, and a stifled female moan coming from inside. The man above them – whose shadow, cut off at the hips, fell onto the terrace – said in a high, malicious voice: Sprange didn't need to worry; it would be a fine meeting; everyone would be there.

The teacher had so much trouble stifling a laugh that he felt a pain in his midriff and was tempted for a moment to burst out of the rhododendrons shouting "Woe unto you!" but at that point, as if the boy had anticipated just such an ejaculation, a small, thin hand clutched arm. Like the four or five times this had happened to him before 'iceman, a sergeant, friends – so this time the teacher automati- ˙d his biceps to demonstrate his brute strength and imbue the clutcher with a friendly respect for his sheer physical supremacy. The hand let go.

They could hear the two men on the terrace: breathing, tongues clicking, swallowing, clothes rubbing. They would never leave. Then the thick, stifled, gargle-like blubbering from upstairs started in again. It came from an old woman in pain but forbidden to cry out: something was holding her back – a gag, a hood of penitence, a constricting hand. The statues on the lawn, a few of which were made of aluminum, shone in the surrounding gray. Somewhere above the two intruders a glass scraped against the stone. The teacher, who was in an uncomfortable position, felt a sudden cramp in his calf and had nowhere to lean but against the boy; however, as that was out of the question, he put some weight on the crooked foot and, whether as a result of his having moved or not, the boy clutched him again, this time with both arms, which perhaps prevented them from crying out, because heading straight for them from behind along the gravel path, huffing and puffing, came a colossus complete with branches and horns, its hooves crushing the stones and sending them flying in all directions, its grass-green maw open wide and spurting smoke. There was no escape: the mad cow did not brake; hoof-and-mouth disease was upon them. The boy let out a scream, jumped into the light, then ducked back into the shadows and ran off in the direction of the beech row with the teacher in his wake, ludicrously slow and limping. All the time he ran the boy screamed, "Bella, Bella, Heui, Hier, Horrrrra, Gurr!" and the teacher, at his side, thought admiringly, "We are two angry peasants chasing escaped cattle. How clever of him! What a quick mind!" Panting in rhythm, at a swift clip, they reached the porter's lodge, dark and lifeless, and the main gate of the house, two columns topped by stone lions. They were weak by then and slowed to a jog, then shuffled on side by side along the all-engulfing, all-concealing wall.

"It's getting dark," said the teacher, who could scarcely see where his own feet were going on the uneven strip of land next to the tram tracks.

"Don't worry. I know an inn where city people sometimes stay the night. It's right near the Rode Hoek. It's where the tourists go."

"Tourists? In this godforsaken hole?"

"They come to fish," said the boy.

"So it's their hobby."

"Right. Campers too sometimes."

"And a traveling salesman now and then," said the innkeeper. "But we don't get many nowadays. Their kind have cars of their own nowadays."

He had an attic room for them, a room with two beds. He brayed over to an unsavory-looking flaxen-haired little man to bring a bar of soap. It was a choice room he showed them, windowless with a bed and a couch side by side. The teacher, dead tired, nodded his approval, and they went back to the common room, where the innkeeper pronounced in a loud voice, as if to demonstrate his obliging nature to the six guests present, that he would do his very best to satisfy the gentleman and his young son.

"That's not his son, Pier," said someone in a nasty, shrill voice. It was the construction worker. He was leaning against the wall, holding a glass of beer at ear level.

"It's not?"

"No, they're uncle and nephew," said the construction worker, slurring his words.

"Is that true?" asked the innkeeper.

"Sure it is!" said the construction worker, leaving the wall and staggering up to the boy. "Hey, kid, it's true, ain't it?"

"Sure," said the boy.

"What's sure?" asked the innkeeper.

"That he's my uncle," said the boy.

The teacher blushed bright red at the inquisitive, no, downright accusatory look the innkeeper gave him. He scratched his neck, asked for cigarettes.

"Aren't you hungry?" the boy asked softly, but the innkeeper heard him and hastened to point out there was some stew left, pork stew, first rate. They had the stew. The other guests played cards. After dinner the teacher read the radio and television listings while the boy listlessly spun billiard balls. The teacher, who was downing one beer after the other, tried as hard as he could to evade the tumescent images thrusting themselves upon him and making him relive – ludicrous, helpless, humiliated, emasculated – the way the trip had begun, and he had difficulty predicting the field of obstacles and torments that lay before him now that the trip was underway. "Was it Alesandra I heard just now, that muzzled old woman's voice upstairs in the old French mansion?"

He attempted a conversation about the evening's radio programs with the innkeeper, but the man answered that he was in the market for a TV set, and gave a suspicious snort. The teacher noticed that from then on he cast an occasional see-what-I-mean glance at the construction worker who, though in an advanced stage of inebriation, upheld his part of the complicity with the requisite wink. When the teacher played a song on the jukebox ("What do the peasants want to hear? 'The Dance of the Peasant Women' of course!"), it disturbed the card players; when the teacher stood behind one of the players, the man brought his cards to his chest; when the teacher went outside to relieve himself, he could hear them grumbling and could tell it was about him; when he came back into the hot, smoky room, the boy was kibitzing.

"What?" he cried out. "Are you crazy?" He pointed to a card.

"You think so?" the player asked and hesitated, but put it on the table. It was the king of hearts. He took the trick.

"Let's go," said the teacher in a hoarse voice, and much as he tried he could not come up with the boy's name: he had never heard it. The construction worker pressed his index finger against his nose, and the innkeeper recognized the sign.

No one responded to the teacher's goodnight.

It took a long time for the teacher to fall asleep, not least because the boy, released from the onerous duty of the day, shed his day-long taciturnity, his pent-up fever as it were, and began to babble on monotonously, and even though the teacher interrupted him regularly, thus prompting a new stream of words (and even though he did not call for peace and quiet, which is what he wanted in fact, or ask about what he thought of school or of himself in relation to his classmates, a ludicrous pride holding him back), certain phrases grew long and drawn out, coming up over and over as night and sleep grew thicker, frailer, darker, until in the end – the boy got up several times and when he came back he fell into bed with a great thump, wrestling with the sheets until pressing only the pillowcase to his body – both of them were lying in the same direction, both with knees bent and an elbow under the head. The cardplayers' chatter below had died away though there was an occasional coming and going in the hallway and the sound of commands, and then, after one last phrase ending with a hinny of a snicker, the boy too fell silent.

Just before the teacher fell asleep, the room (like all rooms, like a bedroom in a Franciskus Breestraat apartment house with a woman in the bed, like a room in a hotel near the gypsy woman's with her Pisces) extended its walls on all four sides and the bed began to float in still water and arms and legs swelled and sought after recognizable objects like an elephant's trunk. The teacher, wading through a glassy bog, came to a field crossed by tram tracks where no one was present when he cried out, on his head a steel helmet, on his chest a shield and chains that made everyone give way though there was no one to be seen, nothing but a landscape full of ditches and rivers and bogs. Someone called him by name, but he did not turn; he slipped hunched, furious, between the beeches and school desks to an opening in the woods.

Who Will Read My Notebook Now?

(22 OCTOBER)

What noise? This is torture. Because I can't make anything of it (the noise). There is too much. I have no way of placing it (*place* is a dry word and yet too full of meaning, too full of the past for me to apply it to this place, this room, where a peeling of paint or plaster is likely to fall from the ceiling; besides, I can't place it, put it anywhere: sounds jump out at you, bite, take hold), of knowing what sort of flotsam is flying around in it. If I were Kurpers-the-Nose Geography and took notes . . . but I had to give that up because if I could catch the flotsam and write it down, pin it down in notes, then I *would* be Kurpers-the-Nose Geography. And, between you and me, thanks but no thanks.

The rattle of a van. The clatter of an empty trailer. The exhaust of a racing car. A motorbike or a light Vespa. Child. Distant school.

My heel on the linoleum. If this keeps up, I'll scream. The boards of a bridge, an emergency bridge, a car driving across. A great din. Knots in the wood too. A beetle behind the loose wallpaper. Everywhere, even if I don't hear them. I don't hear anything. Hear that, Korneel? The miserable, rapacious, voracious, throat-rending, crystal-clear, close-at-hand barking of dogs.

If I were Kurpers-the-Nose Geography, nothing would keep me from counting the dogs, classifying them according to breed, age, rage. I (once a teacher) know nothing – nor do I wish to know anything – other than that they had been chained up and were released, released with such haste and rage that some still dragged their chains along the ground and human voices, women's screams, stirred them up even more.

The torture is: what is hanging there, what past is there between the death rattle, the yelp, the ear-splitting bark of the dogs and the screams of the women in hot pursuit, and the scratch-scratch-scratch of the beetle behind the wallpaper? Between the hot summer air and the powder moving about my hole here. Between yesterday – no, much earlier – and now, the accursed, paralyzed *now*.

Like an old woman wont to groan when twilight falls . . .

Someone is standing next to me. Someone who could be an old man: he has trouble breathing. He takes root in my shoulders. I keep writing. The tentacles full of seed are sliced off as soon as I write. As soon as they become manifest, visible, palpable, someone starts breathing in fits and starts. I breathe. And I swear, Doctor, it's not me. I

The hand not writing is poking about in my jacket pocket. The jacket belongs to the man who saved me. An angry man who had a hard time being friendly and couldn't stop himself. He handed me the jacket. I waited. He put the jacket on me. I waited. A disgruntled, doubting look in his eyes. He forced me to accept what he had put in those eyes: gallantry, fellowship, solidarity in need – what a joke! I waited while he went off in his shirtsleeves – his wide, gray suspenders bunching the loose trousers – walking with a sway of the arms like a comic in an American movie who is set after by his wife at the unfortunate moment when she finds another woman (whom, all atremble as he was, he had not been able to enter!) in their marriage bed. That is how he walked.

Thanks, my boy.

Your Uncle-Krüger-minus-the-beard face expected no thanks. Removing one's jacket to give it to the naked was perfectly normal, a good deed, something one did in such circumstances.

It is a serge jacket. Much too large. The sleeves too long. Every time I tried on a jacket, Elizabeth said I had short arms. At the cinema too: "Will you look at the long arms that Gary Cooper has!" To which I replied, "Yes, he's back there with the ape-man." Which made her snort and laugh: she wasn't having any of it. The stranger's shoulders are hanging far – about ten centimeters – over the farthest corners, the declivities of mine. The collar is of pre-war vintage, the waist untapered, straight. What I find when I rummage in the left pocket is: dust, crumbs, grit, fluff, wires. And now I inspect my index finger: there are some strands of tobacco between my fingernails and finger-flesh. Remains of German or Russian tobacco from '43, bits of dry dirt he'd taken with him to the front. Squatting between torn-up trees near a bunker, he rolls a cigarette of German or Russian tobacco and the machine-guns start rattling and he curses, and his trousers, suspenders and all, sink to his heels and he trips over them, crawling all soiled on his hands and knees to the bunker and stuffing the wet cigarette into his left jacket pocket. And (not he, of course, because he got away and gave me his jacket) eight, twelve, twenty-eight of the men squatting next to him, who had opened their fur and leather garments, expose, so to speak, the unnamable aperture – with which the Hathayoga Pradipika tells us to wink so as to become one with Brahma – to the element they are fighting, the lethal ice that the Seer-with-the-Blaze thought he could force into submission by storming it with his Bearers of the Fire, and now the world-ice is attacking the unblinking aperture and it freezes on the spot because, if I may remind you, in December '42 the temperature fell abruptly to forty below and millions of men teetered and bit the dust.

But he couldn't have been wearing a suit jacket there, at the front. This civilian jacket. Wasn't that forbidden? Perhaps.

What I find in the other pocket is: a scrap of flambé horn that had been the bridge of a pair of glasses and was now worn down to a knuckle, a blue-and-white checkered handkerchief, an advertisement ("A check in any amount delivered to your domicile tomorrow. Only Flemings need apply. Guido Gezelle Loans"), and two five-franc coins. In the breast pocket: grit and part of a stamp. The SS-man must have emptied his inner pockets before he threw me (handed me, helped me on with) his jacket. The edges of the left-hand pocket stick together in the corner where a crust has formed. He walks, he dances around the field of snow that refuses to melt, anything to get warm. He carries a little cat in his left pocket, feeding it every day so as to eat it later, and when a machine-gun rattles and he takes cover against the ice, the cat's skull is crushed between the butt of his rifle and the cement-like earth. The blood coagulates, no, freezes and then coagulates.

23 OCTOBER (TWO O'CLOCK)
I can't sleep. Nobody will see the light because everyone – Korneel, Fredine – is asleep. There's nobody on duty. Not a breath to be heard.

I'm wearing his clothes. That's what's keeping me awake. I feel his jacket on my skin and can't cry out. Though it would do me a world of good. Now.

Thank you. For the jacket. For everything, man without name. I who have had so many names I didn't want. The local Rode Hoek farmers, the curate, the masters in the Almout castle, the women in white up and down the corridors, Korneel, Fredine – they've all given me names and they're not always the same.

My pupils had no nickname for me. De Rijckel was enough to make them tremble. At least that's what Albert Verzele, the boy, said. My mother used to say: Victor with the stress on the *tor*. That made it sound like the French for wrong, *tort*, so I was accused of being wrong before I knew what it meant. Elizabeth, who was my wife after being my pupil, would coo "Torrie, Torrie" while on her way, coo it lower and louder the closer she got, and when she came it turned into groans and a rippling murmur. I renounce all my names: they have no more role to play. Except in the story that Korneel is making me write and that I keep on with conscientiously and ply with choice adjectives and metaphors. I want no new name: I am still accustomed to the other one.

It used to be that each name-giver gave me a confident look as he pronounced a (my) name, a placid look, all but indifferent, as if he were convinced the name suited me like the lid on a pot and would never (as it always did, every time) slide down me like water off a beetle's back.

The only name that (though I never recognized it) made me burn and tremble was the most impersonal; it wasn't even a name the way she, Elizabeth, pronounced it that tepid day in the sweet-and-sour-smelling woodpile and under the neon lighting overexposing the lumberyard: "No, no, sir. I don't want to, sir."

(25 October)

A vacuum cleaner. Or an electric pump. If it was closer and fainter: a refrigerator. Someone is beating a piece of tin with a wooden mallet. I press a little cleft into my chin with my left hand. It never stays there. Elizabeth thought it looked good on movie stars. A rush of water in the pipes. A sneeze. The back of my hand. Dried out.

Why do they give me a day-old newspaper every day? It can't be so hard to slip the paper under the door after *everybody* has read it, when nobody's on duty and the coast is clear, like now, when the hallways are empty. But no. They do it on purpose: they want to be ahead of me, to know what is going on in the world for a whole day and what can't go on for me until a day later; they want to make it obvious I depend on them.

Don't worry, Doctor Korneel. It's nothing new to me. I was dependent on my parents, on the teachers-training college, on the army, on the principal, on the university and its exams, and most recently on the ladies and gentlemen of Almout. Now I depend on you. Nothing has changed.

I'm comfortable here. Nice and warm. I see everything there is to see. You, all of you. Nero with his glass eye during the circuses.

Without knocking. She's there. I don't look up. She looks dead drunk. She shuffles around. As always: in her white uniform spotted with grease and soot. She puts the food on the table. I don't smell a thing: it must be cold. A glass of beer with no foam. She looks down: my hand scratching away. Fredine.

"What are you writing?"

"That the beer is flat."

"That's not true."

"Yes, it is."

"Sure the beer is flat. I know that. But that's not what you're writing."

"Yes, it is."

"Let me read it then."

"No.

"What are you writing? Come on, out with it."

"That you're saying I'm not writing this."

"You think I'm crazy enough to believe that?"

"You're the one who thinks I'm crazy."

"Not another word about that. We can't talk about that."

Quiet. She won't leave. She wears white, but it doesn't become her the way it does the others, the women in the starched white caps or the men in the surgeon's aprons.

"I'm not supposed to disturb you, the doctor says."

"So?"

"Especially when you're writing. But you don't mind, do you?"

"No."

"Tell me. You're not writing anything bad about me, are you?"

"Uh-uh."

"You don't want them to kick me out. You wouldn't do that, would you?"

"No."

"Is it a report?"

"No. Yes. Something of the sort."

Her right leg is bandaged; the leg is swinging at the level of my head; she is sitting on the windowsill. She has trouble with her legs, circulation trouble. She told me three or four days ago. As if we were fellow martyrs, colleagues in affliction.

"Little Willy's starting to talk real good, you know? A kid of his age. Unbelievable. Why, he can say bomb."

"Bomb?"

"Right. And he can say mama and papa, and last night – they don't give him a minute's peace, they're forever fussing over him, talking to him, and in that High Flemish of theirs – last night he comes out with: 'Bomb.' Were they thrilled!"

"Couldn't they teach the child something else?"

"What for? That's all he knows: his mama and his papa and his bomb."

"His bomb?"

"No, no. Not bomb like in bomb! Oh, I see now. I should have told you first off. You're going to laugh yourself silly when you hear. You thought little Willy was saying bomb like a bomb that goes boom? No, no. You must be crazy! It's his way of saying *bonne maman*. Though maybe you don't use that expression over there in Holland. What do you say, then, to your grandmother? What do you call her?"

"Granny."

"What?"

"Granny."

"They're crazy, those Dutch."

Her strong, broad hands brush away the cigarette ashes she has spattered over her strong, broad, vaultless breast.

"What are you writing now?"

"That I'm well cared for here. By you."

"Oh, good."

She dallies. She should be going back into the hallway, with the others, but she doesn't feel like it. She lacks womanly hips; her back is straight and flat. I know her. That is why I ask her, "How old is little Willy anyway?"

She suspects nothing, supposes little.

"Going on two. Seeing him toddling along with his curls and that laugh of his, you'd think he was an angel on earth. My sister lets me change him all the time except when her husband's there: he'd grab him out of my hands, the brute. But that kid does go on. Never stops.

'Mama,' 'Papa,' 'Bomb.' And he was walking at ten months. Bet you don't believe me. You don't, do you. I can see it on your face. You don't believe me. Well, in the lingerie shop on my sister's street they wouldn't believe her either. My sister, she just said, by-the-by-like, 'Little Willy's started walking.' 'Good,' said the lady who owns the shop. 'Good for him.' But when my sister went outside and stood looking at the display in the window she heard the lady saying to another customer, 'She's crazy. Her baby's only ten months old.' 'What's that!' my sister says to herself, and she runs home, mad as a hornet, and takes Willy by the hand – poor thing, he could hardly keep up with her, but he had no choice – and throws open the door of the lingerie shop just like that and shouts, 'See him? Is he walking or isn't he?' And Willy walked. No, my sister, she's really crazy; she comes up with the craziest things. Specially when it comes to Willy. Which is perfectly understandable. She's right. You can go too far making fun of people.

"Hey, you're writing faster than I can talk. What a fine thing education is. There's no harm in telling you, I guess: I never went to school. The war got in the way. World War One, I mean of course. Hahahahahahohohohohoaaaaahehehehe. Ooooee. I thought I couldn't stop myself. Thought I'd get stuck. Ooooee. Whew! Thanks. It's over now . . . It happens sometimes. You start laughing and you can't turn it off."

Quiet. No sign of meekness in her avid if decrepit face. A body completely lacking in curves. Hips narrower than shoulders.

"Why aren't you eating?"

I eat something. She takes the tray to the door.

"You were hungry, weren't you."

"Yes."

"You're used to better food in Holland, right?"

She too thinks I'm Dutch. Why all these lies and deceits? Why does Korneel keep the most important things about me secret and spread false rumors about me and let them think I'm Dutch the way they did at Almout?

"Tomorrow we'll be having stew, Wetteren style. Bet you never had it before. It's got lots of vegetables – leeks and turnips and all – mixed together."

"Tomorrow?"

"Yes, well, not every day is a holiday. Know what I mean?"

"Fredine, what's that noise I hear all the time?"

"All the time?"

"Well, a lot of the time."

"You hear it now?"

"No, but this morning I did. Hann hann hann."

"Han han," she says, imitating him, though it sounds different. When she does it, it's like a boxer worn out in the fourth round. That's what she's like too.

"Oh, that's Max from next door. When he does his exercises. But don't let on I told you. I really like talking to you, but keep what I say to yourself. Anyways, you know how you write and do your homework to keep your mind going? Well, he keeps *his* going by doing exercises, get it? Outside, in the fresh air, all the time. Just what you can't take. 'Cause Max has worked out of doors all his life. He was a farmer. It was the war, World War Two this time, that did him in. You're not to breathe a word of this to anybody, understand? Anyways, he made a lot of money in the war and put it all in his wardrobe in banknotes of a hundred francs and a thousand, piles and piles of them, and one morning his wife asked him for four of them, four thousand-franc banknotes, so she could go to town and buy a hat, and she put them on her bedside table because she had an errand to run in the neighborhood first, and while she's gone Max comes home from the fields, and what does he see? His four-year-old has ripped the banknotes into hundreds of pieces and eaten half of them and thrown the other half into the air to make believe it was snowing, and when Max saw that, something flared up in his head, a flame, he said, and he picked the poker up from the fireplace and busted the kid's head in. He's a real animal, that Max, but you can't say so to anybody and you got to look after him just like any other. And now he needs all those exercises."

"Thanks, Fredine." She knows that's my good-bye. Still, she doesn't move. No, she does: she rubs her chin with her fingers as if she had a beard.

"I'll be back."

"Good."

"To make your bed."

A heavy man, Max, bends his knees, and Korneel, who watches over murderers, slanderers, suspects, and the accused, gives him a poke in the neck. Max sinks to the ground, his arms bending at the elbows like two well-oiled hinges. Korneel puts his tennis-shoed foot on Max's neck and counts out loud. A death rattle emerges from Max's hairy, flabby chest, his pajamas steam, the calories burn up, and death approaches. Hann hann hann. He exhales his penultimate steam, and suddenly he sees the snow falling in paper flakes, and after a final woodcutter's hann he just lies there, and Korneel straightens up, regards the long anticipated wreckage at his feet, and says, "Time to move on to eighty-four."

I am number eighty-four. So for the first time I shall see his true hangman's face. A man who, even now correct, long-distance cruel, pursues his prey from a watch-tower. Oh, he is nothing if not correct.

I don't complain. I am fed on a regular basis, I read yesterday's paper, chat up Fredine, and apart from that, I do my homework for Korneel – the details I'm supposed to recall in the notebook he gave me for the purpose, my bile, my diary, on the paper Fredine smuggled in for me. It is enough for a man all alone. I'm comfortable here. The paper is lined and I follow the lines. (I've always been a line-follower, Doctor: in school, in the swimming pool, in the town hall waiting to be married.)

The only thing is, my handwriting has become that of a stranger.

Not that of a teacher correcting homework in his hotel room but of a former teacher who now has his own homework to do. And redo. Even though he knows better.

25 OCTOBER (11:30 P.M.)

A monk. That's what I am. More than a clerk. I've woken up. I believe once more I . . . I can't do without it. Have I the time to hide this notebook? Yes. And something else. Above my head in the wavy, scaly skin of ceiling paint: all those cracks, grooves, crevices, fissures, lips, hairs. I am assaulted from within. Crabbe is present, breathing.

The Village and Crabbe

A construction worker he is not; he is a plain and simple one-day disguise; he looks like a foreman playing the white-collar worker by the good graces of his boss, doing office jobs dressed in overalls to show he is still one of the boys, whereas in fact he should be wearing an office smock. The picture of complicity, servility, and blackmail. And the innkeeper he keeps exchanging knowing winks with is either a member of his family or his boss, while he, the willing underling, pretends to be drunk, reeling from one cardplayer to the next, patting their heads and kibitzing. It must be his connection with the innkeeper that makes everyone in the inn accept his intrusive peals of laughter and the way he slips here and there among them, ending up by the jukebox, distracted, hand on groin, looking not at the twirling disk skewered by the needle but at everyone in the room, one by one, his stool-pigeon eyes taking it all in, whereas the objects to be examined and catalogued (the cardplayers) scarcely pay him heed, less fearing him than recognizing him as a necessary evil in their midst and consequently speaking about far-removed, dead-and-buried events over which the police dog no longer had jurisdiction and at which they could not be caught red-handed. And he just sat there moon-faced.

"But," they say. Though there is no preceding sentence that calls for contrast or restriction: no one has claimed anything provoking a "but." No, all the old bits of their old anecdotes emerge in isolation and open with a "but" that raises no objection unless it be to an immense collection of remote facts that took place centuries before and are taking place again in the café. All the cardplayers know the ineffable (unutterable in its entirety) past and the only possible resistance is the particle "but," a springboard to another anecdote.

"But Bogger, was he the porter there or wasn't he? In that hotel."

"He was. Definitely."

"Just the job for him."

"He carries the suitcases as if they belonged to him, and checks them at the station as if he hated parting with them. At least that's what people say."

"Right."

"It's a good profession."

"There are no bad professions. Look at Pier and his rope. Makes me laugh just to think of it." (They all laugh, including the informer, who has changed chairs, as if he wanted to get closer to the anecdote that he had no jurisdiction over and that had no importance for him.)

"'Cause it all began with a joke. And now look at him."

"And he wasn't worth a penny, Pier wasn't."

"They wouldn't even let him into the army."

"Right. One day they were ragging him after High Mass and Tsjeef, one of them Smenske boys, says to him, right in the middle of a laugh, he says, 'Hey, Pier, how come' – we were talking about pigs – 'how come you never go to the farmers with a bear?' And they laughed again and Whistle Daneels says, 'Yeah, with a rope around its neck.' And Pier, he thinks for a while and says, 'Not a bad idea' and tucks it away in his head, and before you know it he's going around with this bear. You see him on the street and in the fields and along the back roads walking his bear, leading him on a rope. From farm to farm. Well, a year goes by – this is in '48 or thereabouts – and 'Monsieur' is riding around in a jeep with the beast in the seat next to him. You can imagine what that jeep smelled like."

"To say nothing of Pier. Man, even from down the street . . ."

"And then he bought a little van of his own. And the two bears would climb in and make their rounds in this diesel deluxe that must've set him back 350,000 at the very least. Then he bought his brother's house and built a pig sty as big as Town Hall."

"We laughed all right, and now we're green with envy!"

"Speaking of bears . . ."

"Who took the eight of clubs? Well, take this! And this! Here. The ten of spades and a trump and another."

"Now that bears have come up . . ."

"We're in big trouble. Count up the points. We're ten short."

"Hey, are we playing or aren't we?"

"He was custodian at the municipal theater during the war and had loads of friends. A real charmer he was: Lucifer – you remember him, the Prince from the Land of Smiles – would give him a box of chocolates every New Year, and not them tiny ones neither. Well, when the attack began, the one people say ruined Haakebeen, they dropped the bombs in a wide circle like chocolates, and bam, one scored a direct hit on the theater, a bomb the size of the Sarma department store, and my Uncle Henri, who was down in the basement, all by himself because his wife was staying with her mother in Lauwe, flew up with the rest of the basement into the courtyard and landed without a scratch except his left leg got wedged between two beams . . ."

"Who trumped?"

"And then the cesspool right next to him cracks in two and starts flooding the courtyard with night soil – it was your talk about the bear's stink that reminded me of it – anyways, it was just a small courtyard, three-by-four meters, and Uncle Henri couldn't budge, and the muck keeps rising, up to his chest, up to his face, and just when he's about to fall over in a faint from the gasses and the stench and he thinks, 'A strange way to say au revoir and merci, may I be struck dead if that ain't the truth,' another round of bombers flies overhead and lets fall another Sarma-size egg, and this one hits the building right next to the theater and the walls come down and make a hole in the courtyard and the night soil flows out. Yes, sir, so Uncle Henri finally worked himself free and ran out into the street like a madman and began to laugh and laugh, and he ran into a German soldier and put his arms right around him, like he was, stinking to high heaven and laughing all the while, he couldn't stop, and three days later he was laughing still, and they had to put him away for two weeks."

"Did his medical insurance pay? I mean, for the asylum?"

"Half."

"Oh."

"Better than nothing."

"But Jante, if I bid a hundred and forty, that means you've got to bid a hundred and fifty, with my sixty in trump."

(The café has had a jukebox for four years: it is no alien monster in the landscape, no miracle to the farmers, only to me. First an avalanche, then saccharine strings. A human voice – high, noble – articulating the notes, elongating the syllables, the strings supporting it, letting it fall, the voice climbing back to the heights, alone. Quiet. A flute. "Sei tu, come stai pallida," the man laments, and the music moves on, the voice in pursuit. Oboes. Desdemona, the man sings and collapses, sobbing "mo-moo-moortaa." Dignified, the heavy, tense, turbid wind section, a storm, slumping trills in the violins, a lone horn in the wood, a high-pitched human voice almost.)

"Time for diamonds, Amedée!"

(And the throaty sounds that no one understands but that reveal the misery of the dying woman, the sobs, the bass tubas underscored by a low drum roll.)

"Who put that record on? Who paid five francs for that?"

"A lover of classical music."

"That gentleman over there. The city gent. He's the one."

"Oh. The gentleman."

"Are you a tourist, sir?"

"True, you never hear classical music these days. Just jazz."

"Right. But the city's still the city, isn't it, sir."

"I hope you don't mind me saying so, sir, but the air in the city is pretty bad. It's all you can do to breathe. All that gas and oil. You can't get away from it, like it or not."

"And the things the city has done to us!"

"We were a place to be reckoned with during the war, sir, and then the city lit into us."

"Pissed in our soup in '45 is what they did!"

"Right, Remi. In '45 it was."

"Lit into each other too, the cities. Take Knokke, for instance. If the good people of Knokke hadn't talked the Germans into blowing up the Ostende Pavilion, where would Knokke have been after the war? Nowhere. Think of all the money they made while the Ostende Pavilion was kaput."

"Our burgomaster and his men in jail, six civilians executed by the White Brigade – it adds up."

"Look, are we playing cards or chewing the fat?"

"But it's nothing to you, sir, all the grief we've got coming to us, the things Our Lady of Fatima has predicted. The fourteenth of October there's going to be a worldwide catastrophe. Those are her very words. True, she hasn't said where or what, and she's been wrong before . . ."

"Well, I've laid in twenty crates of beer just in case!"

(They all laugh, including the informer.)

"Go ahead and laugh. But you'd do better to stock up on things. Soap, coffee, rice, anything that keeps well."

"Detergent."

"Bacon too."

"She's never been wrong, Our Lady of Fatima. Remember she said a new pope would appear. And what else did she say? 'Those you presumed lost shall return and great violence shall be done unto them.'"

(This is the second beginning, the second skin of the onion I must peel, because at this point – then – they began speaking of The One Due To Return so naturally, with such easy familiarity, that the change in tone made me sit up and take notice. I knew nothing of them, of these men who do a given number of things over a given number of days with no expectations or hopes or uncertainties other than those of the weather or the price of potatoes, and who spend the rest of their time in the simple passions of sniffing their soil, their gin, and their women, while a bit of politics encourages them to keep their family feuds going or honor their notary public, but otherwise I knew nothing about them, which is why the sudden flare-up in their conversation struck me so.)

"And return he will. Mark my words."

"I got this bet on with Miel, Miel Necker. I said he'd be back before '65. Bet him a thousand francs."

"He's in France, Crabbe is. Waiting it out."

"Or with Degrelle in Spain. The two of them showing up together. Wouldn't that be something!"

"No, no. In France. Crabbe always liked talking French."

"More than Flemish. Go ahead, say it."

"Only to prove he knew it better than the Frenchified Flemings, damn it!"

"Have it your way."

"You're wrong. Talking French was part of his game. Because the Leader, de Keukeleire, said that the Kingdom of Belgium must survive and we must fight for Leopold. And the Leader, de Keukeleire, let me tell you, was a turncoat. First it was down with Belgium and Flanders,

Flanders, and only Flanders, then poof! the Belgian cause never had a greater champion!"

"But that's because Belgium, all of Belgium, was going to be annexed by the Reich, damn it. Can't you see that even now?"

"And Crabbe went along with de Keukeleire in everything, naturally."

"But not in May of '40, not until the bullet got him."

"No, not then."

That was how Crabbe made his entry. Into me. Foretold by Our Lady of Fatima and evoked by the cardplayers. Or had the boy brought up his name before? The smell is of flax; it suffuses furniture, clothing, hair, makes the coast dwellers gasp for breath; it is the smell of noisome air rising out of the nearby rettories. The villagers – it is hard for me now to get them right, to come up with a collective picture of them – were a gray, dingy lot, always grumbling, and I thought them the ugliest people in Europe – including the working classes in English cities and the French in Tourcoing – and I am one of them from head to toe. They spoke of Crabbe with devotion, of his universally admired feats of arms; they never ceased evoking and invoking him, and his deeds – though recent developments like Katanga and the king's marriage had diminished, even tarnished his fame – remained milestones in their history.

And they said, "One man lives on in our history and geography, and he is not the Leader, de Keukeleire; he is de Keukeleire's shadow.

Because the Leader was assassinated by French scum in the year 1940 and Crabbe, like the squire whose knight falls in the heat of the battle, took over his weapons and virtues. We witnessed it, and much as we deplore what leaked out subsequently from the camps of Death and so on in the land of the occupier, we find little, even now, to alter our position in the Crabbe camp. Our village contains the highest number of men executed in West Flanders, Blacks and Whites both, though the number of the former predominates with the seven Flemish guards who stood watch over the German arsenal and were court-martialed and sentenced to death in the space of one afternoon. And it is in the name of this death that we speak when we say that Crabbe lives on in our midst and binds us together, as if we carried him within, collectively, like a tapeworm. Just as we believe there is no point in spending a whole evening trying to win at whist when the cards are bad, just as we believe that the Virgin who appeared in Portugal and whom we worship with prayers and money and love will announce at the appointed hour that Crabbe will return to us, so we believe that we did nothing wrong when we followed him on his dark paths, even when the Germans had us by the short hairs. We would rather provide the TV news with our own skeptical commentary, we would rather close our eyes to the public sales announced on the pages of the *Brugs Handelsblad* than to imagine that in the boundless space over which Our Lady of Fatima holds sway there should be no room for Crabbe. We do not need to do anything; we simply wait. And if now, in this café, *Honesty Fears No Man,* a lieutenant should arrive from Crabbe and speak to us (even with the zeal that Crabbe, lieutenant of the Leader, de Keukeleire, displayed when he recruited our young men to demonstrate against an ailing parliamentary system), we would reject him, stare him down disdainfully, so tied are we to the miracle that will resurrect him and him alone. He will not bestow his grace upon those who refused to recognize him during all those wasted years when he was present by his absence: strong, simple, insightful."

"How can you pick up cards like that, you moron? Haven't you learned by now that when you pick up cards after a deal you take more than there are players? What way is that to play cards? The French way? In any half-decent café they'd have kicked you out long ago! Who trumped?"

The room is painted milk-white with perhaps a pinch of ochre powder in the water-based white. "Cream," the painter probably said, "is chic," and he painted so fast that his ardor was consumed and he neglected to apply a second coat, leaving the rose-patterned wallpaper underneath to show through, because the roses were made with aniline dye, which water-based paint cannot cover. At the height of the upper edge of Verzele's bed hangs a photograph showing two young soldiers shaking hands. The bicycles in the background and beret-like headgear identify them as Ardennes infantry, which means they probably perished when, disguised as women, they shot from the attic windows at the first columns of German soldiers entering the village.

A vase of paper flowers with singed leaves stands on the night table separating my couch from Verzele's bed. The room has no window even though I wrote that the window was open. There is a band of mosquitoes suspended like a cluster of grapes in the open door, a thin cloud through which the light in the stairwell shone when Verzele opened the door and let me go in first, and their song followed us into the grayish, little vaulted room and went on long after I'd stretched out in my underclothes under a sheet reeking of ammonia. A bicycle rides past the inn's rear wall, its light shining, its dynamo whining. All I can see of Verzele are a shoulder and an elbow sticking out like a hill crest from under the stiff sheet; he breathes noiselessly between the bursts of storytelling. The only light comes from under the door, and motionless shadows lie over the foot of each bed, over the white of the walls and the duller white of the beds. The boy's thin, invisible head with its protruding ears lies on the pillow, and when I turn on my couch he turns in his bed the way my wife used to do many years back, though not entirely. Lying in parentheses we used to call it back then, two parentheses in the same direction. Verzele's thin voice rises and falls, expecting no response, so absorbed is he in his meanderings, and I dare not light a cigarette lest the scratch and the flame of the match disturb his drowsy, miasmal balderdash, and I listen to him enmeshed in his dreams. While downstairs the farmers go on with their weekly gab fest, I like a giant fish snap up the air that wafts from Crabbe to me in Verzele's narration.

"At the castle he was naturally boss the whole war through: they all had to bow and scrape to him. Even those who claimed he was a nobody, an asshole, a son-of-a-bitch, even they went to every soccer match he played, and cheered like crazy whenever he scored a goal. And when he wasn't there – because he had a meeting with Hitler or a battle on the eastern front – there weren't half as many spectators. He played the center forward. Naturally. Because what it took was a combination of speed and the ability to give orders. And to stand your ground of course. But the main reason Crabbe was a good center forward was that few of the men dared run into him and, believe you me, the few who did had scars to show for it: just ask. Anyway, after the match, when they'd won, because they always won, there were people who said that if the war lasted long enough we'd end up in the First Division, whereupon Crabbe would turn to the stands and raise his right arm the way the Romans did before being gobbled up by the lions. And in the locker room he put on his uniform, complete with revolver and boots, and went out past the waving crowd to Madame Harmedam's car. No, they did lose once, and to the second-string team of Standard Luik, apparently because it had a lot of White Brigade members. No matter what Crabbe did – he even kicked them – it was to no avail, and was he livid! The next day he went straight to the High Command and had six men on the team thrown in jail. Madame Harmedam came to the playing field every Sunday to pick him up in her car. She was a different person after he fell in action on the eastern front."

I: Who?

Verzele: Why, Crabbe, of course. My mother kept track of the whole story; she knows it inside out. She still has the papers with his picture and all. The men in his regiment they had to be one meter eighty – otherwise they wouldn't get in – and he fell in action near a frozen lake: the whole regiment was surrounded and the Russian fighter bombers had machine-gunned them into kingdom come, because when the first storm troopers, the Mongols, came, there wasn't a living soul left in the whole regiment. And my mother still has the picture showing him being decorated with the Ritterkreuz by Hitler himself and you can see the admiration on Hitler's face, and the reason for it is that when they were surrounded – near this lake that was frozen – and when the fighter bombers started shooting down at them, Crabbe suddenly stood up in his trench and fired his revolver – wait till you hear this – fired his revolver right at the fighter bomber's glass screen and hit the pilot smack in the heart. Madame Harmedam has shown my mother that same picture with Hitler, but in a German paper. There was a time when not a house in Hekegem didn't have Crabbe's portrait on display, and they're still talking about him in Brussels. He was a kind of Holofernes, you know who I mean, the man who fought at the head of the Jews, and one day when he was losing the war to the Jews he was riding through the woods and he was surrounded and it was bitter cold and he was very proud of his hair, you know the story, it was all curly and he spread butter all over it to make it gleam, and he was riding so fast on that white horse of his that his hair fluttered behind him and gleamed in the sun, and where the firs stand close together and their branches hang low he didn't duck down enough, and at that moment his horse reared because it saw Holofernes' mother sitting in the bushes, lying in wait because she knew what was going to happen, the bitch, and Holofernes was caught there, hanging by his hair and swinging back and forth like an acrobat about to fall, but he didn't fall, and his horse galloped off, and the Jews who were chasing him rode up on their ponies and they were all set to skin him alive when the Jewish chieftain said, Stop! This man has lived too brave a life. Let us take him to our city and show him to our people in a bear cage so they can all laugh at him. But the Jewish chieftain's mother slipped through the ranks and thrust a spear through Holofernes' heart with all her might. Well, Crabbe was like him, though his hair wasn't long, it couldn't be then, as you know, because in his regiment you had to cut your hair to the length of a match, and they even had inspections using German matches, and if your hair was too long you went, well, not against the wall but to jail. And don't forget the guy who had his hair cut off by his wife and whose eyes they poked out to keep him from bringing down the temple, that was worth the effort, that taught him to look at things with his own eyes instead of trusting in others. But Crabbe had his own way of looking at things. It's as plain as day! The same with Madame Harmedam. And when they found his clothes and medals in the mass grave over there in Poland near the frozen lake, they sent them to her, and from then on she was a different person, or so people say, real fat and all. The strange thing was of course that they didn't find a single man over one meter eighty in that trench even though Crabbe never made a move without two or three men from his regiment, which, as I'm sure you know, he called the Bluefooters. They had special permission from Hitler to wear a copper bird on their epaulettes, the Bluefooters, and the name goes way back, back to when the coastal people still lived in huts and painted their feet blue to mark themselves off from the foreigners (Jews and French sympathizers) who wanted to take over their land. They had knives made of stone as sharp as our bread knives, and when a bad wind blew in from the Baltic they went in the direction of the sun and sang songs to keep themselves angry and warm, and they had no chieftain back then because they were all soldiers together and marched along until they came to a row of bushes where the mothers of the Jews were hiding, because among the Jews it was the mothers who did the fighting: the rest of them stayed home and wove. Now the Jews had long since discovered iron but kept it a secret from everybody: the Bluefooters didn't find out about it until years later, and that's when the battle began. The mothers had the sun at their backs, so they could see better, and the two sides hacked away at each other, iron knives against stone knives, and the mothers kept winning and hacking the Bluefooters to pieces because no prisoners were taken, except for a few who *looked like* leaders and they were buried in the Jews' fields with only their heads sticking out and the Jews put railings around them so people could make fun of them for days on end. And that game went on until a Bluefooter managed to filch the secret of making iron from one of the mothers by promising to marry her, and then the Bluefooters built a chariot with sheets of iron and iron knives on the spokes of the wheels and drove it through the bushes and into the screaming mothers, who soon surrendered and wept bitter tears, and the Bluefooters lived happily ever after and did whatever they felt like . . .

(This while we are lying in parentheses at the level of the paper dahlias whose disfigured leaves give off an occasional tick like an iron fingernail running along a fragile glass panel, an unmistakable alarm rocking in Verzele's voice, a strangled, weary, reproachful voice hanging there in the room. And the room steps out of its hinges and bedding. My rubbery legs, seeking resistance in that enormous room where Verzele sings, travel for an unusually long time; my visor is screwed on tightly, and soon I will block the simple lamentations of the child's voice, which is turning into children's cries spread out over the summer evening in the port as they run or skate or ride their bikes along the esplanade, selling the special edition of *Ons Land, Ons Land* with the results of the tour de France, *olan, olan, withresulofthetoudefran.*)

The Statue Garden

When we emerged from the beeches, attracted by the cone of light from the terrace, we expected to see a lawn, a tennis court, an approach golf course, anything but that artificial wood surrounded by a natural wood with taller trees. The "trees" inside the circle of the more stately wood were stunted and blunt, the tarred piles of a breakwater, an orchard after the Rundstedt offensive in the Ardennes when the jagged trunks were licked smooth, frozen smooth by the frost. It was no great feat to decipher those columns of more or less equal height, tell them apart, put them in order. Someone had built them, as regular as trees in the ring on the surrounding grounds, to even out those grounds and thus annihilate them. The columns are identical, made of concrete and topped by an old-fashioned crown of braided leaves (laurel branches?), a bulging shaft, and a square base.

Mass production. From our line of sight (the boy, hunched farther forward than I, probably sees fewer of them) I can count sixteen, fourteen of which bear statues. Against the Ruysdael-like tapestry of birches and walnuts we see a field full of obstacles, the air above us, and the fringes of the park are too high, the light near the house too weak to reach the nearby figures, but I soon adjust to the darkness and after my initial surprise (not shock, it is not so much a frightening encounter as an awkward greeting on the part of a band of strangers on a playing field at night) I can make out the statues in the disfiguring darkness as the images of one and the same man. They are standing in profile, their heads all turned towards the house, in rows of eight, like pawns on a chessboard. The pedestals are alike and have not been adapted to the statues' various manners and matters, which are quite diverse, as if their maker had decided that the way to achieve a definitive likeness, to evoke most effectively the subject he wished to recreate was to use the most varied forms and approaches rather than make repeated, more or less successful attempts in the same style. Hence his portrait was fragmented and needed to be pieced together later under both closer and more global consideration with all the differences in place. There could be no doubt that the statues were all fashioned by one man: the same lack of finesse, the same lack of strength in approach was evident. Someone else had cast and placed the pedestals, after which the sculptor had populated them, this perhaps at the command of someone who had obliged him to look into diverse stylistic possibilities or provided him with a catalogue of figures enabling him to reproduce the Man as perfectly as practicable in all his variations. What man?

In the statue near the beech-lined path the Man is bald or has very short hair, the hair line indistinguishable because the head of the bust (which is more a torso truncated by its creator through the rib cage) stretches back as if in the throes of a cramp caused by a blow to the neck, the muscles modeled to look like ropes, the apertures of the nostrils blending into those of the hollow cheeks, the apertures of the eye-sockets into those of the forehead of this figure about to topple backward; the right shoulder is higher and bent inward as if to parry the blow to the neck; the left shoulder near the collar-bone is hanging loosely, like the side of a yoke; the ears are stuck too close to the jaw, making them look at first like outgrowths, protuberances on either side of the mouth, and giving the amorphous head an unremitting Neanderthal quality; the many wrinkles, naturalistically portrayed, do not so much make the Man old as indicate the ravages of misery and humiliation on a young face. Someone or something is pulling him back by the hair, and his right shoulder wants to defend him. In this congealed moment of gravy-brown bronze the Mammal, caught with his resistance down, is wavering. Later, the next day, I would see fingerprints on both torso and face.

Next to him, closer to the front of the zigzag formation (now I can see that the configuration is not one of a chessboard; what I picture now is something more like the branches of a family tree ending at the house), there is a bust that shows no feint or arm movement: the cylinder of the neck slopes gently into the shoulders, which start rounding before their ends (perhaps even before the shoulder blades) and are draped in a Roman toga whose stylized frieze of a border boasts various ski-sweater patterns. Elegantly carved. A figure not to be meddled with: a senator getting on in years, an ox in the field, formal, reserved. Not a bone, not a muscle in evidence. A nerveless block facing the terrace, where the weak yellowish light leads one to assume the existence of a house with a mansard; an elongated cranium covered with smooth hair clipped at the neck like an ill-fitting wig; a jutting chin likely to impress the senate assembly more by its dimensions than its shape. It is a neoclassical statue made for a city park and pigeons. The Man's life and illness are over; his memory honored in a bulge of sandstone, the middle-class ideology this Man defended dutifully delivering its admiration.

Behind these two – and between them, if one views them through a telephoto lens from the terrace – is a goblin of a statue. It is difficult to make out which profile in which direction is primary as it has multiple Janus heads. The homunculus, of lava or pumice stone – in any case a material with tufts, knots, and holes – is standing at full height but tottering on one leg and testing the terrain with the other like a soccer player preparing to make an instep kick, his arms with fleece for hands involved in another soccer maneuver: trying to keep an opponent at bay with two impotent defensive hooks. Spattered though he is with moss, coal dust, and dung, wobbling in the wind, the prognathous buffoon has nothing of the sycophant about him: he is as much a king as the two others if only for the inhuman brute force with which he raises his oversized head and balances it over his crustacean frame, bloated in the trunk and frail in the chest. Pride oozes from his pumice stone or whatever mineral the chisel scraped to create him. Between his nipples, illegible in the bright light, there are inscriptions, fillings, phalanges stuck on with quicklime. Or are they Roman ski-sweater patterns? And now I recall that the nearest statue, a Rodin-like bronze, wore a chain between the vaults of its rib cage and that a small container of shoe polish hung from it.

The wobbly king with the whelk-like head commands respect, even without inscriptions.

The first and third likenesses share an expression of impotence and brute resistance. The resistance is supple, as if the statues' maker were reproducing the stone marten in man, replete with claws and teeth, fighting its way back to its one-time unity and wholeness in an almost elegant lunge, an almost bloodless passion. We make tracks, the boy and I. And then, as if a slow-motion hinge between blind spot and facial nerve had held up what we had seen and only after our strenuous run under the trees towards the yellow glow emanating from the terrace and crossing the whitewashed wall alongside the house – the Almout house I had finally reached with the aid of my paladin

Verzele – let go of it, I see – while we are running, that is – the pales of a breakwater with other statues screwed upon them, like the ancient-emperor hedge that we clowns, Laurel and Hardy, were rummaging in not long before. And now in the glimmer emanating from the house and from ourselves a new field unfolds (the same but strangely altered, faded, broadened by our new position, a field we can see to the end, clearly delineated and complete). The statues are all subordinate to and grouped around one gigantic statue standing just before the staircase leading to the house on the line cutting the oval lawn in two, and as there is a gap in the hawthorn hedge surrounding the section where it stands, anyone sitting on the terrace can see it from head to toe. It is a copy of a Greek statue, but one whose proportions have not been maintained, it having been more or less adapted to the body it is meant to represent: the legs shorter, the shoulders narrower, the head too thin with too large a chin, the eyebrows growing together. The fig leaf is too big as well and has a dark rust stain on it; the leaf can probably be screwed off. The disfigured Greek is heroically brandishing a torch, and beneath his long-toed, athletic feet (made for soccer?) a bulldog is twisting its torso and grinning the grimace of death, which tautens its flabby cheeks. I would not have been surprised had one of the dog's front paws made a V-sign or stuck a cigar between its teeth. The hero is looking not at the downed British monster but at a future (waiting, flaming, on the maize-yellow terrace) that makes him part his arched lips, ogle like an idiot, and all but drool a marble drool. And there he stands, the Man of dead white drool and frozen semen, waiting for the word that will free him, torch and all, to make the decisive kick of the match.

Next to the giant – who, compared with the other likenesses seemed an object of abject reverence or a pipedream, a god made to measure for the middle classes in the guise of a fireplace set, and in the way the spectator had to pay his homage *from below* because he reached only to the monument's knees – is the portrait of a Mongol featuring all the traits I am by now familiar with: the high cheekbones, the single-line eyebrows above bright eyes curving up at the ends, the jutting chin – they are all assembled and jammed into a Russian winter cap or what I can only imagine Russian soldiers wore in their fields of snow, a variation on the leather motorcycle cap that I wore in my youth and that was lined with a short-piled silky fleece, riddled with holes (to let the air in!) and impregnated with the smell of sweat and leather (which I imagined then to be the smell of cowboys and cavalry officers), and that made my head gazing daily into the mirror look like the smooth, otherworldly glowing faces of the Stukka pilots gazing down at their instrument panels and standing next to the propellers or streamlined noses of their aircraft in the coarse-grained, offset-brown photographs in *Der Adler*. (Imitating the civil defense sirens on our way to school in the morning, we winged our way along the street, the terror of the neighborhood.) This cap, however, whose side straps hung down – ours constricted our hot and bloated faces – comes to a point, and the point, made of bronze like the rest of the statue, has fallen forward, as limp as a wet newspaper, and is resting on the bridge of the Man's nose. It is decorated with black buttons, with medals and warts; moreover, the same buttons run down the armor-like breastplate of the pilot's or parachutist's jacket that covers him to the chin. For the first time the hero of the many faces (disguises arising more from the capricious diversity of the materials than the conscious application of the laws that turn marble, bronze, and sandstone into a portrait) shows his teeth: he is laughing, and the stumps catching the light in his mouth and forming part of a bridle or jagged muzzle or dental implement are sharpened thereby, and even if the hero's mask, its chin resting on the breastplate and a pair of black goggles, does not belong to a familiar Fleming (Aryan!), a not particularly attentive or myopic or threatened observer – not I! – might presume that the teeth have been filed into points and inset with jewels for ritualistic purposes. (Not I, who suddenly hear steps to my right at shoulder level, feet shuffling on the terrace, and Verzele coming out with a trumpet blast.)

Further along the row of posts, which forms as natural a landscape as the vaster leafy one of beeches and walnuts: an iron construction representing only the framework of a man, the hair a comb with quills, the cranium a torture crown, the nose a blade, the whole a timid counterpart of a skeleton; and further still, a child in the more durable, less smooth celluloid, a cenotaph of Ancient Egyptian demeanor consisting of three superimposed heads (in alabaster?), a wooden figure sans face holding a wooden ninepin in a bended arm and resembling the statues of the Virgin Mary the peasants used to carve out of wood and hang in the trees to ward off hail and lightning.

Further: schematic, insect-like, inert fruit festoons, garters, garlands, blown-together seismographs made of metal and stone, market stands eliciting vertebrae and meat, cobbled-together attempts at using coagulation, plum reeds, bird's foot trefoil, corroded and concocted facial features and spiral springs and velvet sheen and perforated heraldic ornaments to fashion a likeness, though forever failing (not only because the corncob-golden light does not reach far enough from the terrace, no, definitely not, or because the observer's imagination is not up to filling the lacunae in the creator's imagination, no, even less, but because an overabundance of factors derails the search whenever one attempts to evoke a definitive image of someone, especially if that someone is the unchained Crabbe, that is, the unbound I), and suddenly there is nothing left near the beech-lined path but posts, pedestals overflowing into their statues, stone stumps with out-of-joint crowns in the yolk-colored light coming from the terrace and projecting an enormous magic lantern over the smooth grounds, stumps arrayed, arranged around the ludicrous marble giant glowing there . . .

The Giant shone. His name was Atlas le Cruel, the Largest Man in Europe, and arrayed and arranged around him was a group of smaller giants including a negro and a gypsy, the latter flexing his biceps in a pale pink leotard for the wide-eyed fair-goers. The gypsy was calling out that for only a thousand francs he would invite any of the onlookers to pin his two shoulders to the floor, the chance of a lifetime, to wrestle me, Zara le Gitan. The fierce-looking marionettes on the podium next to him waited, but as nobody took up the gauntlet the gypsy made another appeal to the diffident crowd. Then another strongman called out from his vantage at the cash desk, "How about you there?" He pointed. "You with your sweetie-pie at your side."

"He means you," said Elizabeth.

"Who?"

"The strongman. He wants to know if you'll fight him."

"Who?"

"You, sir. Come on, let's get out of here."

She said it on purpose to draw me out of my shell, and I was in no need of pity, not yet. She pushed her fragile body against me as if to defend her doll from these violent hunchbacked strangers, and I was the doll, de Rijckel-English-German, being threatened by a real man in silver briefs. How was I to react to her all but maternal concern? I am not only her lover; I am her teacher, her master, damn it! She put on a serious look and said, "I have no desire to see any more. Those men are so creepy."

"No," I said.

"Let's go, sir." But she didn't go; she just stood there, her filly hoofs planted firmly on the ground; nor did she hold me back when I raised my hand to take up the gauntlet. As for her quickly cultivated concern, it dissipated just as quickly when I called out to the gypsy, "You mean me?"

"Oh, the gentleman is Dutch. How nice. I'm crazy about cheese."

Howls, shrieks of laughter. Oh, the revelry of the fair! The revelers nod in unison. This strongman's got a nasty tongue on him. And Zara le Gitan, a.k.a. the Human Rock, carries on with "I'm a great Benelux fan, I am!"

Hooray!

"Step right up! Entrez! Come and see a true trial of strength for only one thousand francs. Children and soldiers half price. Step right up, ladies and gentlemen!"

The cackling crowd trundled up the slats leading to the entrance. She wanted to go with me to the side entrance and I thought, "Shall I push her away?" and made up all kinds of schemes with the three or four scandalous belch-born beings inside me, of which the first wanted me to dazzle her with a virile magnificence cultivated on the spur of the moment and delivered as a gift out of nowhere, just the kind of suntan-oiled strength displayed in the movie magazine I had once found in her desk (sniffing out her odor while the class was out on the playground and sifting through the school supplies in search of her childish personal effects – lipstick, Tampax, movie magazines, buttons, a nylon stocking, ribbons, family pictures – and furious to see she had all that: she was supposed to be my quarry, my property), and the second wanted me to kidnap her and lock her up like an orphan in my castle on the moors, while the third curled up as usual and shouted, "Home with you! On the double! You're trembling all over. Go while the going's good." And I managed to get her away, because Zara, the Human Rock, had perceived the despair with his schooled eye, having met up with my sort of hero at fair after fair, and he said that women were not allowed in the side entrance, so she went into the tent with the now thinning crowd, and he paid no attention to my whispered supplications, saying only that it was five hundred francs, the usual fee. So I nearly pinned him to the floor – or at least that's how it looked – and gave up only after a fierce, agonizing game, during which I almost came to believe in my strength, because so destructive was my lightest punch, so dangerous my elbow that no sooner did I touch him than he pulled the most heart-rending grimaces, made his joints crack loudly, and sank moaning to the floor. His skin was oiled and rubbery, cold to the touch, and while he clenched me in his arms I sought out Elizabeth, who was standing to one side and yelling, "Give it to him, sir! Pull his hair!" and I would hear it again later, when her embrace had become as distant as Zara the strongman's and much later, when she served me with the formalities that required us to go before the judge four times during the year preceding the official divorce. "Give it to him! Poke his eyes out!" And when, floored but cheered, I crawled off the stage, she was waiting behind the curtain outside and said, "You almost beat him, sir" and she knew about the money, because the children of the poor know "no money no game," no party, no victory, but she didn't let it show, and when I said I was totally done in she rubbed my back and smiled proudly.

This ludicrous Giant is made of marble, and all the juice has been sucked out of him, unless ice is juice. He is clutching the ice torch meant to deal with the ice wherever he goes. The empty gaze, depicted by the two perfect circles representing the pupils, is directed at the second story of the house, and someone in the house is mirrored in it. The curly hair – fashioned of the same ringlets as the hair in the armpits – and the lumps on the forearms, knees, and calves are oval in shape. A neo-Greek army in the nudity of 1900, when the desire for verisimilitude disrupted the eternal cannon. Flat feet. Had Crabbe had flat feet? It needed looking into, though the chances for a satisfactory answer were minimal. Mud-splashed, lifeless marble kept the man from coming through, and what was left was a hero, inert. Forget the giant.

Precious little is to be had from this description, Korneel's desires notwithstanding. I don't want to keep the statues, those half-baked obstacles, awake. As I see it, the reason Crabbe was portrayed in marble was that – like all the others in the ice field there, surrounded by the frozen lake, with only the Purifying Flame and their Honor to keep them True – he had to have been made of ice: only in a shifty mimicry of the sort could he have approached the life and world of his enemies, still rooting about as they were in the inert crust of the ice; and one night, during a wild eclipse of the moon, he would creep up close, and the marble torch – that is, the torch of ice – would burst into flame. Now he is brandishing it, motionless. The moon is shining. I am going to shout. Hold me back.

The Attack

At the very time he should have been reciting or dictating Eichendorff to his sixth-formers (reluctant to announce to the sleep-sick class that as far as he was concerned the sing-song rhymester with the smallest vocabulary of all the classics should be stricken from the curriculum), at that very time the teacher and the boy were back on the path they had taken the night before. Leisurely, like two Sunday hikers who, though out for the pleasure of it, have a certain number of the local sights to "do." The teacher wondered at the lack of new obstacles between him and last night's house. They proceeded unobserved, the village being absorbed by other worries. Had the teacher been less wrapped up in his Sunday-hiker role as he spiraled his way to his destination (the house, the woman), he would have been able to detect, investigate, explain the village's other concern, other passion, but there is no point in discussing that now. The boy had resumed his mute, solitary identity. Where, the teacher wondered, is the tension the beater on a hunt is supposed to feel when, striking the birch bark, he senses the moment when the game, surrounded by hunters in the vast trap of bushes, is about to soar up and away towards a misleading gap in the wood. The paths glimmered in the soon-to-be-midday sun, which was pale yet strong, and the teacher found his way this time, the boy not seeming to lead him, as if he had come to the realization that he had ceased to be the hound pulling the master on and was now as much a hunter as that master. The teacher cast an occasional glance at the boy, who did an occasional slightly lame hop of a dance step and mooed from time to time at nearby cows. The eyes of the farmers in the fields were inscrutable. A schoolmaster taking his class on a nature walk nodded to them, but the teacher's attempt to discern a hint of sociability in him was in vain. Other obstacles seemed unlikely. And then they reached the thick hedge and the elder trees and the tile-topped, whitewashed wall and the black-lacquered fence that gave them access to a broad lawn divided in two and resembling two lungs connected by the windpipe of a gravel path that led straight to the house with the mansard. The background, today like yesterday though broader and higher, consisted of the grounds, a wood. They stepped onto the gravel path in silence and moved in the direction of sounds from the stables and a child's voice singing a French song. The boy took the left-hand side of the path – which was shielded from the sunlight by the branches of the chestnut trees – hiding behind the teacher, who, having no sunglasses, kept blinking in the brilliant light. The boy said they had to agree on a pretext to present should someone come out of the house and ask what they were doing there, and just as the teacher was saying it was too late for that now, an old man emerged out of the darkness of the foliage near the door of a structure – half greenhouse, half shed – and made his way towards the visitors singing the final bars of a French song.

His voice was thin and pinched. He was very old and completely bald, and while his face showed not a wrinkle, there were bags under his eyes and his chin sank into a goiter. Passing without transition and almost without a breath from the song to his spoken voice, the man muttered something the gist of which the two visitors made out to be that he had been expecting them. For some time now. No, him alone. Who was the boy? The teacher explained that it was his son, whereupon the old man stroked the boy's shoulder and cried, "Goodness gracious! What next! Heavens above!" Waving an arm nervously like a bird with a wounded wing, he bade us walk on and said that the ladies would not wait forever and what wonderful weather they were having: you didn't need to go to the south of France to catch a peacock butterfly!

The boy threw the teacher a skittish look. There was nothing about him to indicate he had reacted either positively or negatively to the teacher's having claimed him as his son, but while they proceeded together in single file along the gravel path he stuck close to him, and for the last fifty meters, when it was clear that the old man, now sunk in thought, was taking them to a greenhouse near the stables, reached forward and took his hand. The teacher started at the sudden contact. The old man noticed and put on a broad grin. Just before coming to the brick edging that ran around the greenhouse, the man said that it was an honor for the house and the association to welcome so noble a guest and it was the first time, with the exception of course of the plenary meeting three years ago and the annual Association Ball at Ghent, that a foreign official ("if we may be permitted the term") would be taking part in the association's internal activities. It was a special pleasure both for him personally and for the ladies because we so seldom have occasion to see a new face. You understand, don't you?

When the boy scratched the palm of his left hand with his index finger, the teacher closed his hand over it. Fixing his myopic gaze on the teacher's tie, the old man went up to them, cocked his head like a swimmer letting the water drip from his ear, and remarked it was wiser not to wear the insignia, though some members insisted on it. The boy, in a playful mood, jumped out from behind the teacher (how did he enter so quickly into complicity with the teacher, so easily into the plot?) and lifted the lapel of his jacket to reveal a shiny metal button that elicited the old man's approval: he grunted, and when he went before them into the greenhouse he laid his small hand, manicured and too plump for the rest of his body, on the boy's shoulder. "Here," he said. The flowers and plants, which the teacher judged to be costly and well cared for, were placed mostly along the glass walls except for a conical vase with a number of varieties on a small, low table, clearly for decorative purposes. "Pansies and crown imperials, as you can see," said the old man, "and soon we'll be adding some saffron-colored crocuses." The teacher looked uncomfortable; the boy winked. "And things violet, if you know what I mean."

"Of course," said the teacher.

"The Chieftain's passion for violet and purple. Oh, the times Mother and I went into it – in private, of course. We explained it by his origins. You are not unaware of the fact – though you rightly make no reference to it in your biographical notes – that it was long rumored he was the illegitimate child of the Bishop of Bruges, the poor man, may he rest in peace. And that he therefore had a certain passion for the cowl, for ceremony, an inborn passion, as it were."

The boy burst out laughing; the old man smiled at him.

"I'll show you his pajamas and his dressing gowns – purple every one. And the clothes he took with him on the campaign, imagine that. And the bindings of his favorite books: purple. And here" – touching the petal of a pansy, the man went on in a voice neither emotional nor indifferent but as if he had said the words many times before with the same affection – "here he stood at the very end. 'Richard,' he said, 'I am going back, and we may never see each other again. Things are bad, but duty calls, and, Richard' – he never called me Rijkaard like some of the newly baked fanatics – 'if I do return, the face of the earth will have changed. The world,' he said, 'will show its true face.' And trembling, he raised his weak, childish chin and rubbed his cheeks. 'If I return, Father, you will see the light of the world in my eyes.'"

He stood with his back to the tower of flowers and repeated it, said it again like a stuck gramophone record, and the boy and the teacher stared uncomfortably at the trembling old man, who then cleared his throat and pinched the stem of a purple pansy between two fingers (and why did he call it a pansy and not a forget-me-not? The teacher also thought he could detect a French accent in his West Flemish dialect) and inserted it in the teacher's buttonhole. The teacher thanked him. The old man smelled of flowers. The teacher thanked him again and said that he felt strongly . . . He meant to say he felt strongly that a mistake had been made, but was interrupted by the man's – Richard's – bitter cackle: "Of course you feel strongly about the Chieftain. Who does not? But we must all of us keep that feeling alive. Keeping it alive is our most glorious task, that and doing what he so despairingly asked of us: turning what we believe into action. Isn't that so? Because otherwise it has all been in vain." He ran his handkerchief over his cheeks, did the friar, and then sprayed a blue powder cloud over the greenhouse.

Back outside, where the light was still needle-sharp and a hot wind of dust and needles had begun to blow, the teacher felt his eyes tearing again. The old man looked questioningly at the boy with his myopic gaze and halted. A superannuated harlequin, a terrifying puppet-show villain, he began to coo, but then a low croak emerged from his ribs, which he was clasping, and turned into the words: Precisely, just so, such is inevitably the effect the memory of Crabbe has on his followers. Dear me, dear me, he added, pressing down in the region of his liver, his voice dying away. The teacher wiped his eyes with two fingers (which he knew to be dirty) but got no help from the boy at this strange juncture: the boy just stood there smiling.

"Tell me, how are things in Holland?" the man said.

"Things?"

"The movement."

"Right, Father, what are things like?" the boy asked.

Furious, humiliated, the teacher shrugged.

"Precisely," said the old man, and the three set off towards the house, which had a French nineteenth-century look about it with a few barbaric restorations in the wings and a recently faced brick staircase leading to the front door. There they saw a young woman in a poorly cut pair of men's trousers. She was coming from the staircase into the sun and raised one arm to wave, as one might wave to call a group of playing children inside. She had had her hair cut since the day before. No, since the night at the Pavilion. The sunlight was ensconced in her powder, a thick crust of pollen. The teacher bowed. The old man said it was a great honor for the house, and the teacher – to avoid falling into the doddering role (of a stuck hurdy-gurdy cartridge) he had just played – hastened to introduce the boy as his eldest son. The young woman said, "My name is Alessandra." The teacher nodded but said nothing.

"I believe the young man here wouldn't mind something to drink," said the old man. "A hot chocolate?"

"A Coke," said the boy with a snigger.

The young woman went up the steps in front of them, her narrow hips swaying in the baggy, striped trousers, the straps of her bra showing beneath the white silk shirt, an ocher-brown neck, ears lined with black porcupine quills. And the teacher thought, No matter what, I'm getting closer, now, right now, mumbling it four or five times in dialect – I'm getting closer, even *moving fast* – because he wanted it to make it sound amusing to himself, unlikely and unworthy and grotesque, this long-awaited approach, but he failed, surrounded by guards as he was: Verzele and Richard were up to something he couldn't get a handle on, and so all he thought was, I *am* getting closer to my prey, my spoils. It's terrifying.

The room they went into extended the entire length of one of the wings and had a wall of narrow windows looking out over a lawn in whose left-hand corner – the farther into the room they went, towards a set of beflowered chairs grouped around a marble table – two, three, four statues of varying styles came into sight, standing out clearly against the leafy background. On the table next to a silver snuffbox stood a bust of Cyriel Verschaeve that had been made into an ashtray. It was the only out-of-place object in the room, thought the teacher, whose modest knowledge of period furniture enabled him to recognize no more than he did with the flowers, namely, that they appeared costly and well looked after. Eyeing a walnut, ebony, and mother-of-pearl backgammon table (like a farmer at the local magistrate's, as Sandra was to tell him later), he decided: Empire, Second Empire, the same as – wrong – the pendulum wall-clock with Minerva and the candelabra. The old man, whose skin shone as if he were suffering from an internal perspiratory disease, gave an animated tap on the bars of a cage and a parrot made a response (which in answer to his query she relayed to him, again later and with an embarrassed yet defiant smile, as "Du hast die Eier gefroren!" Your balls are frozen!), whereupon it fluttered somewhat lethargically about the cage.

The clock, embedded in a block of malachite with gilded bars, against which a timid bronze nude was clutching a laurel wreath, showed twelve twenty. Not the best time for a visit. The young woman brought over some sherry. While drinking, the teacher thought: Now I'm going to get hopelessly lost in a painful explanation, and be disgraced by the outcome. He had sunk deep into the sofa and was pressing his knees together. What could he make of it all? That they thought he was the Dutch delegate come to attend a nameless meeting whose participants included people he was presumed to know, like Kubrich, Normand, Unternährer, and Professor Huysentruyt. Most of the talking was done by the old man with the dewy peach-skin complexion; the young woman seemed to serve as a witness, against her will yet indispensable should the need arise to bring order and clarity to the confused and ever ramifying thoughts the man was delivering about the upcoming meeting. Richard – the old man, the father – said then how pleased he was that Mr. – or should he say Dr.? – Heerema ("As you please," said the teacher, who could no longer look the boy in the eye) had arrived on the early side – the other delegates were not expected until tomorrow – and that he could get to know the house, our house, better. The young woman started playing with a cigarette, and when the teacher (Dr. Heerema) lit it for her she inhaled and stared at him, without moving her cheeks. Daimon.

"Have you been in the country long?" she asked.

"Two or three days."

"Did anyone bring you here?"

"We came via Bruges."

"By car," said the boy, who was gobbling crackers with an indecent avidity and had placed an empty glass on the table for the second time. Then, after the old man had explained – because he too had been observing the boy – that although like Crabbe they were not in the habit of taking the midday meal, the visitors could easily find something to eat, the teacher said that they had just had breakfast, whereupon the old man stood and said, supporting himself with one hand while he ran his handkerchief over his pink bald spot with the other,

"Fine. And now I must leave you to your own devices. Duty calls. But you come with me. I want to show you some of my experiments."

"Me?" asked the boy nonchalantly.

"Yes," he said, taking him by the hand and pulling him out of the chair.

Now, so close, she was more distant than ever, and there was no Venetian courtier who sold Buicks for a living to connect them over that dense, torpid distance. A flock of screeching seagulls winged its way past the windows behind her, then turned back, diagonally, in front of the house, uttering love calls, children with amputated vocal chords.

"Love me," she said, switching to English. "I don't believe the weather will hold," she said, switching back.

"No," he said, "there's a summer storm on the way."

"These are the hottest days of the year."

"Yes."

"Why did you bring your son along?"

"He's been doing well at school."

"Have you other children?"

"No."

"You said he was your eldest."

His explanation was unsatisfactory: "My wife is expecting."

She was distant, a self-possessed upper-class woman elegantly turned out with a new hair-do of porcupine quills and pitch-black chrysanthemums, asking questions – knowing full well that the answers, no matter how indirectly, had to do with her and her alone – questions about Holland, about the repression in 1945, about his patients, and his explanations were unsatisfactory. And full of words like "bear the stamp of, economic factors, circumstances, reaction."

"I was a Catholic," she said. "Used to be. When I was twelve. Then came Crabbe, and wherever he sets up shop . . ."

The teacher was as nervous as ever, though less concerned about the possible consequences of his hoax. This is a moment of total purity, he thought; it will be gone before I know it, but it will have existed. And in his role of foreigner (he wondered why she, who spoke with a modified Bruges accent, failed to recognize his accent as that of a Flemish teacher of the language, that is, so-called Standard Flemish) visiting for the first time he asked: "Were you born here?"

"Yes. And I've lived here all my life. I've been abroad only once. I went to Germany in 1949."

Outside, a gardener with a halo of sunlight around his head was walking in the direction of the hedges with a clipper in his hands.

"I went to school in Bruges too. The Pensionnat de Saint-Joseph. To learn Latin. Then I came back here to live."

"There can't be much for you to do in the village."

She stood up, like a guide about to show the haunted Castle of the Black Knight to tourists, Americans with cameras dangling from their necks. The teacher dreaded taking a tour of the castle; he remained seated, the tourist who has paid his entrance fee and is waiting for the floor show to begin. She smoothed the bumps and creases in her baggy trousers but put off the departure by saying, "I do take an occasional trip to Brussels or Ostende. But mostly I stay at home. And wait."

"For . . ."

"Who do you think?"

"Crabbe?"

"Or somebody else." Her plaint recalled the remarks her father had made in the greenhouse, remarks trotted out and repeated many times before though not completely hackneyed. The avidity with which she displayed her mourning put him off. He wanted to keep her at a distance. She was and must remain a stranger. But she went on.

"Somebody else," she said, "though never . . ." And then she said, "Though never will anyone like him come to our house" (making "our house" sound like a trade union clubhouse). She seemed unable to stop. She had dropped back onto the sofa – they were sitting about a meter apart – and was spinning a web of ever more gummy threads. She was playing the child in Our House, the castle with the mansard and the immaculately smooth green lawn without a single statue on a post, and the pupil from the Pensionnat de Saint-Joseph during the Easter holiday in her blue uniform and gold chain and pendant sitting in the salon, listening to and gaping at the earnest young men in black uniforms and boots and wild young men in green battledress and helmets, and later, when they had all fallen or disappeared, she alone remained behind, anemic and timid and wild, prowling along the bookshelves, the beds upstairs, and here along the walls of glass, past the Minerva clock, the porcelain, crystal, silver, the glazed pottery in showcases, the pedestal tables of multicolored marble on bronze columns, waiting for the son of the house, who was not a true son of the house but a foundling raised to that rank on the basis of his gifts and his severity and wrath.

The teacher listened, sipping his sherry, an accomplice. And he thought: If she suddenly, now, stops mid-story for no premeditated reason – stop, Sandra – I will jump in and tell her, conscientious and precise, that I ran away from my school in a panic. Because I feared fear. Because I was divorced from my wife Elizabeth, who was my pupil, after a year. But for other reasons as well. Because I wanted to dissolve, like it or not, in a crystal-clear journey to something capricious and crystal-clear, which I know would not improve my condition in any way but throw some light on it, clarify it and – don't stop, Sandra, keep flying over my face with your dark, self-willed wings, and the teacher saw her pause when she realized he was no longer listening. She leaned back and crossed her legs, her ocher neck wrinkling in the silken man's shirt; she took off one of her coral earrings and played with it in silence.

"Heerema," she finally said, "a name foreign to our ears."

"My father was from Friesland," he said offhandedly.

"The Frisians go in for pole-vaulting, don't they? Over ditches?"

A scream filled the house. It came from the upstairs hallway – an old woman being strangled and resisting.

"I've seen it on television. Do you pole-vault over ditches too?" Her unusual, widely-set eyes would not let him go. The old woman's moaning ceased, as if smothered by a hand.

"It's my mother," she said. "She's not well."

"You can say that again!" he said, flushed, all but laughing.

"What's that?"

"What does she have?"

"Who?" (She, she? Who is that she? Is that the way they talk about people in Holland?)

"I mean what ailment is Mrs., uh (I must come up with her name), Harmedam suffering from?"

Aroused by the excitation, the heat, and the sherry, the teacher said to himself: If she dares to say intestinal irritation, I will race outside on the spot, and he wondered where that little bastard had got to.

"She has a cold in her neck," said Alessandra Harmedam, lying, and to change the subject she embarked on a story the teacher no longer remembers because it took an unforeseeably intimate course, one pursued again later in myriad variations, a temporizing, apologetic story meant to supplant her mother, and he pretended he had followed her completely. They were sitting together like two women in the cloakroom of a dance hall, and the teacher, begging the boy with all his might to appear, watched the old man – the father, the husband of the gagged, overgrown crybaby upstairs – back in the garden, walking along with the enormous open clippers in front of him like a steel phallus slit down the middle, and recited – it was a rude habit he had of exhibiting his love of poetry – the following as he pointed to the underage old man in the spacious sculpture garden:

"And ere they dream what he's about,
He takes his great sharp scissors out!"

The young woman half-closed her eyes and gave her pretty little mouth a twist of pleasure and disgust, and he, encouraged, was about to continue ("and cuts their thumbs clean off and then") when she said tartly, "Why are you speaking English?"

"Why shouldn't I?"

"Those are the first English words spoken at Almout for years."

No questions, thought the teacher; anything but that: I am the foreigner who knows everything.

"Sorry," he said lamely.

"I understand. The Dutch have a different attitude towards English. It's their second language, a bit like French for us . . . Still . . ."

He had made an unforgivable blunder. The little nursery rhyme was swelling up between them, spreading like a stain on his trousers.

"I realize it's childish," she said, trying to smile.

"It was a nursery rhyme."

"I don't understand English," she said. "Father studied it once, but he's a great one for systematically driving things out of his brain, so he's probably forgotten it entirely." She wiggled her wrists, waved to a child squatting nearby in the garden, and put on her sunglasses. "Oh, I've got some bits and pieces of it left from the year I had it at the Pensionnat, but when Father heard I was doing English – he paid no attention to my report cards – he wrote to the Mère Supérieure that he would take me out of the school if I went to one more English class. The war had just broken out. He wrote another letter to the Pensionnat when I told him – just to bait him – that we had more French history than Flemish and that the nuns had told us that there were almost no Flemings at the Battle of the Golden Spurs, that the French had been beaten by the Germans and Frisians. That was later, in 1944, and when Crabbe heard about it he wanted to go to the Pensionnat on the spot and force them to let him lecture to the entire school about the true significance of the Golden Spurs. Well, I was trembling with fear because who knew what horrors he would tell, but at the same time I was dying for him to come because then all the girls would see that Crabbe belonged with me, to me. Which is what I thought at the time."

She took her sunglasses off. They left a brown dash between her eyebrows, slightly higher than and parallel to the lowered, arched eyelids, and the teacher no longer recognized her: the woman who had walked along the esplanade or the breakwater with two breathless bloodhound ballroom dancers on her trail was now hiding in a schoolgirl's uniform.

"Sprange speaks English of course. And Mama too, ten or twelve sentences. During Crabbe's stay she joined in when they sang an ironic round of "Britannia Rules the Waves" after one or another *Sondermeldung* announcing a German victory. Crabbe read English books too. He once took a book by – I remember it clearly – Keynes, could that be it?"

The teacher gave a pedantic nod and bade her continue.

". . . by Keynes, then, and threw it at Sprange, and he said that the Leader, de Keukeleire, had recommended it to him but that it was more up Sprange's alley, because, he said, Sprange needed reasons to make a revolution acceptable. You can ask Sprange now. Have you seen him yet? I thought I saw him over there by the fence just now, but he's always disappearing." The teacher was unduly glad to note that she had not only switched to the informal *you* but was also slipping more and more into dialect, bridges to familiarity, affection.

Later they walked through the hallways shoulder to shoulder past walls hung with woodcuts depicting gape-mouthed medieval warriors shouting words that flowed onto a streamer and suits of armor and crossed lances and freestone shields. In the assembly hall, which is what they called a rectangular room with lead-and-glass windows and a refectory table, there was a reproduction of the Rodenbach statue at Roeselare: *Youth with Seagull*. Oak chandeliers, mock-leather wallpaper, a cracked windowpane etched with runes. Smashed in 1945?

"No, we never had trouble with the locals. Not a single stone was thrown at the house during liberation. True, there was a rumpus one evening down at the porter's lodge, but Mother made sure we had Allied officers billeted here from the start."

"I thought she had no English . . ."

"She could get by. Besides, the first ones were Poles, and Mama wound them round her little finger with her Polish . . ."

"She's not Polish, is she?"

"Not a Polish citizen. She became Belgian automatically when she married."

Scales that had recently been in use and polished they shone so; a picture of a rank of German soldiers at a field kitchen behind Almout House ("Boys from the Junkerschule Tölz when they were here in '43. Crabbe took the picture. There wasn't enough light, but it came out all right anyway, don't you think?"). The seagulls, so far from the sea, were making nosedives outside, and the teacher, sitting in a foam-rubber chair on the veranda, became aware that her exposition had grown less wordy, that she had practically stopped talking since they had taken seats there under the leafy trellis facing the grounds, the reason being that he had (naturally) failed to feed the conversation and rather than construct an elaborate, convoluted web of lies whose articulations I would later be unable to undo (and that there would be a later between them – definitive, detailed, and clear-cut – was beyond doubt) he had sunk into a crotchety silence. Though she had not pumped him for information (about his misdemeanor, his false position, for instance), presumably (no, obviously!) thinking that there was no need, that the lamb would hasten to lick the salt from her out-stretched hand. The teacher felt lethargic, excluded from the time that held sway in Almout House, smoking cigarette after cigarette while – nonchalantly, as if afraid of being spied upon by someone who might put a false interpretation on his trying to get to the bottom of the statues – walking at her side past the artificial woods, about which she had nothing to say, and an immodest late-Greek kouros with a torch.

"What would you say to a spot of tennis?"

He dared not tell her that fifteen years ago on his father's insistence and at his father's club he had taken ten or twelve lessons and shown a total lack of talent and go, as well as a certain shame for his body, the shame that had held him back at the dancing lessons the same father had imposed on him, and said instead, "I haven't played in ages."

"That's what they all say," she said. "Don't you want to?"

"No, I do, I do," he said, and appended a line from a cheap movie comedy: "I want to do everything with you."

"Or would you rather do a little pole-vaulting?"

"I would not," he said with dignity.

"I miss my tennis. I have to wait until Sprange is in the mood, and that's an exception: he's forever out in the shed, chopping, welding. But tomorrow I'll nab Professor Huysentruyt. He was once the champ of West Flanders."

"Then you should save your energy," the teacher advised.

"I'll be full of vim and vigor by tomorrow."

She led him (like a sheep, he thought) to the wooden shed, which smelled of animals and where he put on Sprange's worn-out, much too large tennis shoes. Sweating pathetically in his shirtsleeves, he hit every ball out of bounds, and she, after pretending to join him in the joke, overcame her eventual irritation and went over to his side to teach him how to serve, grabbing his wrist and poking him in the back. It only made him hit the balls further out of bounds, thinking: she's touching me.

Back on the veranda and sipping tea that, parched and exhausted, he would rather have swallowed in one gulp, the teacher told fictive stories about his youth in Friesland, then switched (what did he specialize in as a doctor?) to anecdotes from the autobiography of a psychiatrist he had read during study period a week before (was it really the week before? he pushed the massive, vexatious memory of the herd of schoolchildren, the Principal, and the Elizabeth who had betrayed him out of his mind), and she listened so greedily that he had to go into detail about the appearance and behavioral patterns of the rapist-murderer he had recently treated, which made her smile and ask whether that sort of thing was curable, the desire to annihilate the object of one's lust or affection or love, and he thought, She's swallowed the bait, the whore in novitiate's robes, she's biting, the Nun of Groenhout, Havermout, Almout, and said, "It is" and as proof listed a number of cases: they came up all the time in his practice.

The young woman had held on to a tennis ball, a soft, old worm-eaten apple of a ball, which she tossed up and down the whole time he was talking. When the teacher asked out loud where that boy could have got to, she said he was probably paying a visit to her mother. Father was in the habit of taking ev-er-y-one up to see her straightaway when she was sick in bed, which was often the case: it distracted her. When she asked whether he and the boy had any bags and he answered that they'd spent the night at an inn in the village she was shocked: it was a major gaffe. She bit into the ball, her broad taut lips and strong even teeth gripping its un-white, worn-down, hairy skin, then turned it in her long fingers, nibbling at it, licking it unconsciously and digging her teeth into its roundness, and when she started tossing it up and down again the ball was shiny wet in several places. The teacher felt himself unmasked and all alone in the house. Upstairs, behind him and to the right, an old woman's voice was singing a romantic song to a spasmodic, disjointed piano accompaniment.

The old man, the father – though it was improbable that this quivering, round runt of a man could ever have overwhelmed anyone to the extent that a child came out of it, let alone Alessandra, and the teacher did not even attempt to find traits or gestures common to the two – called to them from outside to say that he too wouldn't mind a round of tennis. The young woman called back in a shrill voice dripping with scorn (not for her father, no, for him, *him*) that the teacher was too tired. The old man was standing near a brightly colored, freshly painted garden statue, and the sunlight erased their differences, made them look alike. The teacher, unable to keep his eyes open from exhaustion and still perspiring, said he had to think about getting back to the hotel, but she paid him little or no attention: she was sticking her chin out at a man who had slipped in without a sound and, standing there in the doorway, may well have been observing the sweaty teacher. He had a rustic look to him and was wearing brown corduroy trousers and a light-blue shirt. His flaxen hair was combed down over his forehead, his alert eyes, immobile, trained on the teacher.

"This is Dr. Heerema. He does pole-vaulting too," said the young woman.

"Sprange," said the man, shaking the teacher's hand and sitting down opposite him. The teacher wanted to signal to Alessandra mutely, without even a gesture, "I've made it clear to you I want to get out of here. Don't be shocked if I up and run outside without warning," but Sprange, after pouring himself a cup of tea, sat too close to him and his feet, his powerful shoulders, all-seeing eyes, the smell of dust and stone in his clothing would not let the teacher go.

"I rode through all of Bruges," said Sprange in such a manner that the teacher could not help hearing him and might even comment, "and believe it or not only four of the people we were counting on for the day after tomorrow were in town."

"We've heard that before," said Alessandra. "They just happened to be out."

"Four," said Sprange, trying to get the teacher to respond.

"Don't get all hot and bothered," said Alessandra airily, tapping his forearm with her index finger, which had a long polished nail filed to a point. "When the chips are down, they'll all show."

"Want to bet the Bruges contingent will be smaller than last year?"

The teacher suddenly realized he had twisted his ankle while playing tennis, and thinking, I'm going to limp my way off the premises, he was overcome by a wave of sleep. The couple next to him on the sweltering veranda were going over the event taking place in two days, which they called a "social gathering," and the board meeting the next day, and going on about the number of members and their names and contributions, and the teacher's head started nodding, but then he noticed the old man standing not far off at the veranda railing – he too having made his way there noiselessly – with the shadow of one of the posts on his dented pink bald spot. He rummaged in his trouser pockets for something, pulled out a white handkerchief, unfolded it carefully, and spread it over his head, never deigning to give the party on the veranda so much as a glance. In the course of the conversation – which the teacher had stopped following: he was afraid they had put something in his tea, those two accomplices so near him, a powder that they were immune to but that had set his head a-bobbing like that of a senile glutton – Sprange had brought up the ri-di-cu-lous idea a man by the name of Baader had had of placing a crown before Crabbe's statue (as if there were only one), a crown in Flanders' colors, because it consisted of mimosas and black tulips grown by Baader himself

· 176 ·

specially for the occasion. Sprange vowed that if Baader took so much as a step with that monstrosity in the direction of *one of his statues* he would grab it out of his hands and toss it onto the manure pile.

"If the flowers were purple at least," said the teacher, suddenly awake. His remark hung in the air.

"You should know better than anyone that Crabbe was allergic to flowers," said Sprange wearily.

"But when I got here, your father . . ." The teacher wanted to bring the young woman into the conversation. Sprange gave a scornful sniff. The old man, not far off, did not budge, was not listening. "You're right," the teacher continued. "Besides, your sculptures are sufficient homage in themselves. They are like flowers."

"That was my intention," said Sprange.

The teacher thought, If it goes on like this – all buddy-buddy, let your hair down – I'll get to the bottom of things. And he had a presentiment of disillusionment, of an irremediable, dull and stupid impotence that would come with an elucidation of all the restless, nebulous activities that made them hustle and whisper and hatch their plots here at Almout, and he recoiled (as always) from the bright hole that would appear at the end of the tunnel full of ellipses and code words: he wanted to be stuck in the wet shaft with no outlet, in anguish and ignorance, and he stood up and bumped his knee – as was bound to happen in his attempt to avoid Sprange's knees – against the tea table and rattled the cups and spoons. Sprange raised a hand to parry a fall, a hairy, fleshy claw of a hand with truncated fingers and lunulaless nails, a tortoise paw, and the teacher grazed the hand in passing and, his fatigue having dissipated, stared at their wonder-filled faces. Sprange gave the young woman a telling look, then stood and said he would see the teacher out.

"Wait," she said and followed the two men with a lithe bound. But Sprange pushed her back or allayed her with a stroke of the truncated fingers, saying that he would be right back. She sat down again, spread her arms out at her sides, and waited for them to go. The teacher, who (once more he could not wipe it off his face) wore a sheepish grin, left the rusty old sad sack to his devices, turned back, and said to her already absent face that his name was Victor de Rijckel and he was a teacher at a school in the town just down the coast. She winked and said, "Right, right, if that's how you want it. Though you've got nothing to fear from any of our members. You needn't worry."

The teacher left the veranda with Sprange the sculptor, crossed the terrace past the immobile old man, and went down the freestone steps onto the gravel path. To keep calm, he forced himself to concentrate on the parade of misshapen graven images and refused to emulate the calm, confident stride of their sculptor. On they walked. Sprange, a tall man repeatedly wiping his hands on his corduroys as if the palms were clammy from tuberculosis, was telling him the frugally phrased story of his early life and how it had all changed with Crabbe's coming and how – he pointed to the head of one of the statues – if you wanted to show that your subject was blond you had to cut more deeply into the clay than if you had a dark-haired subject. The teacher let him go on: now that his explanation or rather his valiant attempt at an explanation had been, as far as he could tell, dismissed, all he could do was accept without hope whatever happened. And still no trace of the boy.

"People say, 'But the Jews, the Jews,'" said Sprange. "Well, let me tell you, Crabbe never killed a single Jew, not per-son-al-ly. Not even in Chernya, which you talk about in your book. No, it was the Germans there and the Ukrainians and the Spaniards, almost never the Flemish and definitely not Crabbe. You write that in Chernya the Jews were forced to replace the oxen and pull the SS wagons and when a Jew refused to salute they immediately strung him up in the street, which may be the case, but no Fleming ever did it. I'd like to ask you to look into the question again. And above all, above all to put more stress on the fact that it was the Jews and nobody else who forced Crabbe to leave the camp. They are the ones who made him into a – what do they call it? – turncoat!"

Things are getting all mixed up, thought the teacher and, turning his head as they rounded a curve in the path, saw the fuzzy, elongated figure of the young woman standing at the window of the assembly hall. It was distorted by a defect in the glass, the glass she pressed her face against, following his departure from the garden.

And when he turned back, he felt Sprange's luminescent, almost hateful gaze resting on his mouth (which he had always thought small and weak and which even now was curling down cravenly under that stare), and peering straight into those yellow, bloodshot, sticky-lashed eyes he saw Sprange more clearly than Sprange could ever see him, and thought, jubilant, This man is capable of any evil he desires, any evil he will do to me now that I exist in the garden of this house. He whistled "Malbrough s'en va-t-en guerre." Suddenly, a wind blew and shifted the shadow of the branches onto the ground. As they reached the entrance, Sprange slowed his pace, then stood still and asked how long the teacher was intending to stay.

"Here? Or in the village?" the teacher asked, thinking this would suggest he could count on help, reserves, and allies in the village.

"Here," said Sprange, indicating the grounds of Almout with his damaged hand.

"It depends on the circumstances."

"The only reason I want to know is that I need to get to work as soon as possible. You understand. Otherwise I wouldn't care."

The teacher wondered what he had done with his glasses: he suddenly felt encumbered by his nearsightedness and the house was off in the distance.

"I've got to get back to the monuments," said Sprange. "They've cost seven years of my life so far, and there's no end in . . ."

Just then – he could not see him but recognized the voice immediately and pinpointed it as coming from a window in the second story of the house – the boy let out an owl call. The teacher waved in his direction. Sprange made a peevish remark. After a surprisingly short interval the boy ran up to them, panting and sweating. Doing his best (unsatisfactory, four on a scale of ten) to keep his excitement under control, he cried he had just seen Mr. Harmedam's rock and butterfly collections, and rattled off – trembling, as if to hide how shocked he was – the Latin names of stones and insects, though it was clear he had no idea what they referred to.

In a stern voice more redolent of a schoolmaster's than a father's the teacher ordered him to greet the gentleman.

"Hello, sir," the boy said to Sprange rather casually.

"I've seen you somewhere before," said Sprange.

"Me?"

"I don't think so," said the teacher.

"You don't?"

The boy linked his arm with the teacher's and said, "Wait till you see the butterflies, Papa." The teacher blushed; the wind fell. There they stood, arm in arm, a united front against the petrified army of likenesses and the hirsute sculptor, turning their backs on the house where the young woman was still following their every move in a periscope and the voice of the old woman would resound again once evening fell.

My Notebook

A holiday. We're getting veal sausage and applesauce. Then chlorpro-
mazine. Synthetic molecules in the bloodstream to take care of anxiety. It's common knowledge. That's how (no sleep cures, no insulin
comas or metrazol convulsions) – that's how they get us to be all nice
and docile and in my case even to enlist talent and willpower and pride
to pin down the butterfly spots of the past, my two-bit past. But really,
Korneel, you should have known better: there's no clarity in criss-
crossy lines. You can't expect me to present you with a precise map
to be colored in: the why of my past. The lamp dims before my eyes,
and even the ink – "superchrome, writes dry with wet ink" – gums up
and my hand trembles and jogs up and down: everything's against me.
Just now I nearly fell asleep as I wrote. And of course I was writing that

the teacher fell asleep. There's not a soul in this dump. Nobody can whisper the answers the way they did at teacher's-college exams. The fastest years of our lives. Classes. Cheating, masturbation, pimples. Film. Over. So fast: a father, a mother, Elizabeth, the Principal.

She didn't want a child. Mostly finger fumble. A wife who still belonged in school. Criss-cross spider webs. Crossword puzzles. One day she crossed out the word "marriage" in nearly all my books. In red ink. Every morning she combed and combed her hair. Then she left me. No big deal. The first thing I thought was, I'm going to wallpaper the apartment to my taste. But she kept the apartment: her mother saw to that. The pattern on the wallpaper came from a junk shop: crinolines and fiacres from French woodcuts – that sort of thing.

I felt more at home in my hotel room. Anonymous as a classroom. I wish I could get today's paper. Or – I've asked that bastard twenty times by now – a dictionary. I want to dazzle Korneel (who will never read this notebook, may he die of cancer) with adjectives. I was good at composition. I once wrote a composition about spring. The teacher scolded me in front of the entire class for having copied it out of a book. I hadn't. But because I was afraid of him – it was my first week at a new school – I nodded yes. From then on I did copy whole passages, taking care to insert appropriate grammatical errors. Six or seven out of ten in composition. Good enough.

The men go to piss on the other side of the wall, behind my back, never alone, always in pairs at least. They take their time about it.

Tell stories. They're all buddy-buddy there behind my back. I'm getting eaten up in this place. For a long time now I've stopped taking my ritual all-day walks, door to window, back against the wall, never leaving the wall. It's possible. Tomorrow at dawn I'm going to start bottle counting. Sometimes – I can tell – one of the (at least) two men scratches my name on the wall with a nail or a piece of slate: I can feel it in the wall that is my back. In a little while I'm going to think he's writing my name again; no, I won't. I'm surrounded by a white shadow that, like the edges of a fading photograph, is devouring all – and I mean *all* – the elements, and the reason I know is that just as an old man is more likely to remember events from his childhood than the pap he swallowed the day before, so I lose words and gestures from the last few, no, from many weeks ago. I can't bear it. Bear with me.

(2 NOVEMBER)

Still dripping wet. I'm wearing somebody else's bathrobe. It wasn't washed, just machine dried, that's all. The sun has retreated from the small courtyard that houses the plumbing convenience. Not hungry, fortunately. I receive various manuscripts. Four. Oh yes, yesterday somebody monkeyed with my door and they grabbed him and beat him up. Not a peep out of me of course. Nor will I say anything: who knows what two-bit excuse Korneel will use to get me where he . . . to do what? He's supposed to be looking after me. That's his job. Or is it.

Slept. Head on arm. Sweat, hot cheeks, prickling eyes. Elizabeth occasionally slept with her eyes open, off dreaming somewhere, in the middle of class. Mostly on sunny days. I would watch. Her dull eyes in full sun. A mesmerized insect. Every once in a while she chewed on air with an intense, idiotic tug of the mouth, and the fantasy that she was thinking of me and what I did with her, that she had to turn away from the me standing there on the podium with an evil-smelling, chalk-infested rag and ruler in my hand to bring together the fragments and recreate me the lover – that fantasy flowed through me like hot water. There were times when she opened her thick lips, wide, and yawned, slowly, after which she immediately fixed her eyes on me and called out, "Sir! Oh sir!" (and by then she was calling my thing "Sir Junior"!), and I would have liked nothing more than to snatch her off the school-bench and race, with her in tow, across the immense skating rink of the playground, past the Principal's tower and its defense telescopes, and on to the esplanade, the breakwater. In time I stopped being a strange, dirty old man to her, which she regretted, and – unlike those sophisti-cated women, mostly in oriental lands, who are brought up in the art of pleasing men, keeping the ardor in them alive by means of absence, magnetism, imagination, and virtually imperceptible arousal – she had no tricks to keep the fire burning. No, our carriage and pair were no longer a team. Once everything was permitted (her mother and the dignitaries and the neighbors and the teachers handled our two-some in a *modern* way, if not accepting then recognizing the inevitable marriage that she later scratched out in my books) and we were sequestered in our own place, she switched from challenge to offer, from target to convenience, running bare-assed around the house, squeezing her breasts (so ripe so soon) together with her hands or sticking her tongue out or stretching like a slut – I swear she did. It was a daily regime of marital wares on display, which I, the teacher, was cowed into buying. And then came the tears. The reproaches. Grotesque, classical reproaches about how he, the teacher, I, that is, wasn't up to what a man should be up to. In other words, every day, forward march, lance at the ready. Though it was just as grotesque that he, who saw himself as the hunter, the deceiver, reproached her ignorance in these matters: she was eighteen at the time. The all-too-feminine sparkle she had copied from her movie magazines eventually took its toll, while I for my part sank into the (after all is said and done) luxuriant comforts of willing prey.

(8 November)
Elizabeth did the dishes (you can hear the tinkle of plates and glasses next door, *enchaînement gratuit*) once a week. She was the same Elizabeth who had dazzled me only a year earlier after German class (five ten said the clocks in the port-town living rooms of Korneel) when, after starting off with her classmates, she turned at the door and came back into the classroom, where I was reading the autobiography of a brain doctor, and when, hoisting herself onto the front desk and

swinging her legs in such a way that her kneecaps moved with them, and slowly raising one knee so that her low black-leather heel came up to the tobacco-brown, much carved and ink-stained edge of the desk, she set my eyes, unprotected by glasses, on fire. It was guile, guile pure and simple. She waited until I went up to her, and when I put my chalk-powdered hand in the fold next to her heel she said, "I'm in deep trouble" quickly and abruptly, as if she found the subject banal, vulgar. It would cost ten thousand francs, she said, and she knew a good doctor. I searched in vain for the cool, definitive put-down I had learned in countless pedagogy courses but in the end knuckled under. I, Victor-Denijs de Rijckel, said I wanted no part of it. It did not redound to your credit, Victor-Denijs de Rijckel.

She is in the room; she is lying on bottles of Harper's bourbon (Kentucky); she is sticking her basketball-shoed foot in the air, then lowering it to her face. "Sir." I tip her with the point of my shoe; she topples and flings her arms out, her oversized bra gaping from above. I kick her in the ribs; bottles break, roll away along the fringes of the linoleum; her ash-colored hair with its thick incrustation of chalk powder spread out over a bottle shard, her breath passing over the grit of coal and plaster on the floor, she does not sit up.

After I had done in Zara le Gitan, the Human Rock, we went on the roller coaster and other rides and then to Uilenspiegel Country, which consisted of a stink coming out of the walls and invisible holes, sinewy hands you could barely feel grabbing you by the clothes and dragging you along a floor that folded in two or three, flinging you against walls that spun like metal cylinders and down onto a moving band in the direction of an ever steeper slope, which seemed to end meters lower than the fairgrounds though you did not reach the bottom, and later the Caterpillar, Elizabeth by my side, invisible, hiccupping, seated in a chair festooned with wooden swan's wings, holding on to the strap and leaning forward to plummet into the tumultuous darkness when the giant wing came down on the seats and riders, increasing their screams tenfold and deadening them simultaneously, and holding her tight I bit into the purple taffeta ribbon in her short hair, and it was innocent.

I ask her, while she lies spread-eagled on the bottles, one foot dangling, the other hanging in a leather loop attached to the lamp cord: "Was I innocent?"

She laughs.

I push the point of my shoe against her chin and repeat the questions.

She giggles and the glass splinters sink into her skirt.

"You were starkers."

"Me?" (Me, a tortoise with no shell.)

"Yes, you." But what she means is stark mad, not stark naked. "It took three weeks for you to dare touch me even. And then, mind you, I had to ask. Three weeks long I had to listen to your German and

English drivel in that rotten, stinking class." And she sticks out her tongue, red, wet, a dog's tongue.

The taffeta ribbon was purple and had a meaning: it meant what la Dame aux Camélias indicated by wearing red camellias instead of white, and the girls in the class called one another Violet during their days of the month – she'd told me that. It could give rise to misunderstandings as well, as when the men of the Alliance, or so Sprange told me, would systematically paste the three-franc stamp of the king upside down on the envelope when corresponding with one another.

(8 November, 12 o'clock)
Elizabeth held English and German in contempt because they were something imposed upon her that she saw no use for, or simply because they were imposed upon her. Alessandra was repelled by English because it was the language of Crabbe's enemy and their allies. I – wimp that I am, with my all but sacral and oh-so-delicate feeling for language and words and sounds (or so I thought) – I was hopelessly helpless when confronted with their resistance: I would stand there speechless or with the tinkle-tinkle of Rilke's "Orphische" or the magnificent scratching of wing cases in Dickinson. Woe unto the fiancé who needs recourse to foreign tongues.

I must ask Korneel to stop the men from pissing against my back.

Despite the plaster and stone and wallpaper I can hear their stories. Every once in a while one of them is hauled away by three or four guards and he bumps against the wall, running his elbow along my back, or falls onto the tiles and bangs his hand against them a few times. Plus – at night, mostly – they light matches, and then I try to catch what they say: I breathe through my nose and lay my ear against the ice-cold crack under the door.

Yesterday I heard this: "The doctor I like best is the one with the beard. He gets all mad when I stare at it. 'What's the matter?' he says, and I say, 'Your beard, it's red.' And he says, 'What if it is?' And I say, 'You look like you've eaten your kids.' And he wants to be mad, but all he says is, 'Hm, hm' and writes something in his book."

And this: "Jante, he had four kids. And one day he's at the movies with his old lady and smack in the middle he says, 'I'm going home,' and she says, 'You must be crazy' and he says, 'No, I'm not. It's like God said to me, *Go home.*' And she says, 'Well, go if you're going, idiot.' So he goes and what does he see? His house in flames and the housekeeper clasping the baby and the other three dead too: first the smoke, then the fire. So back he goes to the movie theater, and the minute he gets there he passes out, and now he's been here three or four years. 'God will speak again soon,' he says."

And the response: "Well I never!"

. . . and I've stopped writing. Korneel keeps goading me. Two lines a day and we'll make it, he says. Frozen feet. Losing weight. Draw out vapors. This table was once used for cleaning herring; you can smell it in the wood. Draw out vapors. Write a fair hand, all curlicues and cues. I don't want this pen squirting shame on the paper; I don't want any regrets; the Past cloud sails past. Didn't I say they were spots? Like butterfly spots? I did. I sit.

I'm not writing at the table anymore. I've seen a fish scale – I swear – a flat, dry, silk paper of an eye, a round decoration as a gift from the spawning beasties. Calm.

I've got all the time in the world. Every day is like what used to be a day off at the beach. Bliss. No, more, because many days off used to come at the same time as the Teachers' Fund. I'm stretchable. Like any invention of myself.

Blah-blah, jingle-jangle, boo-hoo, wiggle-waggle. I don't recognize myself in it, but it's my voice. A bit hoarse, the way it used to get when I smoked too much. A wart in the throat. A split in the middle-skin. Internal gills, webs. Eighteen midget Brussels sprouts on the windpipe. Cancer on the vocal chords. This notebook is now – since I am a clerk, have been one, and once a clerk always a clerk – my text-recorder. Nothing else counts. The clerk himself? Don't make me laugh. Hair: thinner. Bags under the eyes, a pale eye-glass frame. Stomach: eructative. Toe- and fingernails: cracking. Wrinkles in the wings of the nose. The beast? Asleep. Sleeping like a clerk, Sir Junior. But no more shame, no regrets about any of this, not even the notebook. Luminescent, I scribble on, Korneel.

"Wir sprechen uns noch"

In the beginning – when the boy shouted it – I thought, trapped as I was in the web between the statues, I had seen Crabbe at Almout that first evening, but if that first time I had approached the house from the entrance, so that the light from the terrace was shining on it, I would immediately have recognized the figure – mostly by the bright-red, tomcat-like hair – as Sprange.

Now that night is falling and Almout House – which one of the farmers in the café called derisively Notatalmout House – is behind us, now that he sometimes comes so close I can smell his clothes, a smell of metal rather than slate and mixed with cold sweat, now he points his hook of a finger and says, "Very few, almost none of the portraits have been preserved. Every now and again somebody comes from the Foundation with a yellowing picture taken in Russia or Germany and says, 'Don't you think he looks like Crabbe?' but it can't be Crabbe because Crabbe was careful not to let his picture be taken. Oh I'm sure Sandra has a few stashed away in that little desk of hers, but does she ever take them out? . . . Not even if you begged one for, say, the cover of your book when it's ready. No, she's keeping those pictures to herself, and not for all the tea in China . . . So I have to fall back on my memory. And that's impossible. Because even back then he was constantly changing, and it wasn't only his posture or haircut; it was his face. No, no matter how you twist and turn it, the moment you try to pin down a memory of him something symbolic, something ritualistic bursts in willy-nilly to undo it.

"I formed no picture of him during his first days at Almout," he went on, "when his name was still Jan-Willem Crabbe. He was little more than a schoolboy when Richard took him in. He never said a word about his parents: he was a foundling or something of the sort, and while the Association has made attempts to throw light on his background I don't think it will ever be clear. We can go back no further than '39, when he came here with de Keukeleire and his guard.

"It was a time when many followers were leaving the movement because solidarity implied a pro-Belgian stance. De Keukeleire saw Almout as an oasis, a place to rest. As you must have read in the papers – *Branding, Onze Erfenis*, the Flemish supplement to *Signaal* – this was the time he put his hand on Crabbe's shoulder and said, 'Here is a man I can trust.' Shortly thereafter he must have made it clear to Richard that Crabbe was alone in the world. And Crabbe stayed on, that is, until May 1940, though again after capitulation he would return to Almout as if he resided here. On 20 May he was eighteen or so, and if we must believe him dead, his death would have occurred in '46 or '47, in other words, when he was about twenty-five. People say it was Alice Harmedam who kept him at Almout, but I don't believe it: he was no great lover of women . . .

"Sandra? That was something else. Pure love? Good heavens no. Crabbe was never one for trickery, for the visions that come from unsatisfied longings or physical needs. No, in his eyes Sandra was more the picture of nobility, an emblem of a caste, a duchess for our time, still tangible, as tangible as she and her sisters were in 1700 just before their scandalous disappearance into the rest of the world, before their defeat in the battle with the bourgeoisie everywhere, and that kept him busy, kept his imagination going, if not his body and emotions. Sandra will never admit it, of course. But that's the way I always saw it when they sat in the salon holding teacups – de Keukeleire in uniform, Richard, Alice and Sandra – only a child then, she and Crabbe chatted away. Crabbe was a slave to moments like those: they nourished the romantic nonsense that was churning inside him and later formed the basis for his ideology. It was then too that Crabbe took on de Keukeleire's ramrod posture, his military manner, his tendency to insert an abrupt remark into a long, convoluted story while the teller was catching his breath. He had de Keukeleire's training to thank for the old-fashioned, chivalric, ludicrously formal behavior pattern he held to later in the most dire of circumstances – and of which there were legion. Too often did I see him acting beast-like not to realize where it came from. He aped de Keukeleire. He was seventeen, eighteen, and de Keukeleire was an impressive man. Oh, I wouldn't go so far as some and portray him as a martyr; no, he died in the name of his personal principles and that makes his political principles somewhat suspect. But what made him so impressive was precisely his unwavering personal honesty in the face of the harm it might do to the cause he represented. Crabbe had a good eye for such things and was fascinated.

"He stayed on at Almout. Crabbe himself said it was because of Alice, and you can see why: Alice would have liked to have a son. And that suited Crabbe just fine: like all heroes and some pharaohs Crabbe had two mothers, the one whom he didn't know and who was possibly still alive, and Alice. He lived with the family the way some foundlings or vagabonds or wandering philosophers live with families in Russian novels: Pyotr X or Y has spent a good thirty years on an estate without the landowner's ever quite asking why or how. De Keukeleire was the god of Almout at the time. I can still see him, the martial head held high, the rather narrow chest thrust forward, and the white, hairless, delicate little feet curled up together in a washbasin of lukewarm water in the kitchen – it reminded him of the old days, he said, and the Harmedams, who had three bathrooms in the house, didn't dare express their wonder – and right there in the kitchen while we stood in a circle around him he chose to tell us of the new arrangements that would have to be made in the low countries, in which the driftwood of impotence and the love of luxury were everywhere afloat and the majestic channel of the soul obstructed. You will recognize the images Crabbe later arbitrarily used in his speeches. Of course de Keukeleire as much as anyone was a victim of his foibles or genes: he had an inborn puritanism – which doubtless predisposed him to exorcize the evil spirits of our people, a people of gluttons and spiritual sluggards – as well as a self-imposed austerity, which caused him to repress the degenerate, no, no, the down-to-earth element in him and also repressed a natural kindness, a meekness, with the result that people who didn't know him, a fortiori members of Parliament, took him for a Savonarola. By which I only mean that de Keukeleire refused to give in to the gulf stream that makes marionettes and men of us or indulge in the miasma of sensuality he so despised, and that Crabbe, who was prey to everything that touched him, troubled him, could never quite free himself from that artificially inherited puritanism . . .

"... and that, so to speak, a spring broke in Crabbe after 20 May, or perhaps the spring slowly unwound in the twelve days it took him to return from France, alone then, without de Keukeleire, whom he had followed at a distance of, say, a hundred meters in Richard's yellow DKW and whom he may have seen from a distance of only ten when they, de Keukeleire and his guard, emerged from the Museum basement on 20 May 1940 to be executed, which is when the spring broke, while we, all of us, were waiting here at Almout, waiting out the twelve days, sitting by the radio, hearing the officers billeted with us say they'd be strolling through Piccadilly Circus in a fortnight, and when the DKW, covered with children's scribblings and drawings and so caked with dust and grime you could no longer tell it was yellow, finally pulled up to the house, we saw no hint of what had happened on Crabbe's face as he climbed out and made his way to us, though none of us dared ask him anything: we'd heard the news long before, and there had been masses in the village in de Keukeleire's memory, and the only thing he did that day was to lock himself up in his room, where, as he told Sandra later, he turned all de Keukeleire's portraits and all the streamers with slogans to the wall, neither taking them down nor destroying them, no, simply tacking them back where they had been but with their picture side facing the wall, and they would have been there still had Sandra not taken up residence in Crabbe's room after the war . . ."

(He flips a hand, open and defenseless, in the direction of the porter's lodge as if brushing away gossamer, then makes a gesture with the open hand – a gesture that along the Mediterranean means "May you be cursed to the third generation" – and plunges it into the pocket of his corduroys, as if embarrassed by the outburst. There he stands, towering over me, brimming with revulsion and veneration and hoping to reach me, because he can't reach beyond his words and hazy feelings and knows he is all worked up and, in his haste, failing to convey his simple impressions of Crabbe, so on he babbles, using a stream of rapid sentences to achieve the clarity he so unquestionably needs, now, now. Yet in so doing he passes over the images that are *his* language. Or does he realize that the shadows Crabbe cast represent no language but that of art journals and the daily press? Try. Why not. What about the Rodin-like image of Crabbe absorbed in his death, fixed in bronze in a last-ditch attempt to rise to a life both grandiose and gruesome, a life he feels slipping off into a gruesome trap like liquid bronze about to harden. Or the Roman, the anonymous statesman Crabbe, or the administrator of a regiment of which the village cherishes a public memory, noble and weary, in a garden near the church.

Arno Breker is: the symbolic empty case, the plastic skull-and-crossbones doll of the Flemish Legion recognized as empty and superfluous. Next. The gnome: the glorification by modern means – namely, degenerate art – of a Third Reich maniac which ends by humiliating the subject and thereby demonstrates that Judeo-American art has triumphed over his ideal.

And what about the large statue with the torch? The fire battling the ice down through the ages, Crabbe in spotless marble that by way of camouflage has taken on the ice as weapon? Next! I refuse.)

". . . whatever Crabbe was up to with his hoplites – as he once, tongue in cheek, called them – it didn't alter the face of the war; it didn't even alter conditions in Belgium: with a few exceptions on the local level everything remained as before, a bunch of yokels who will occasionally vote if the press fires them up to it or the TV commentators instill in them a fear of imminent civil strife, but the Crabbe model has . . .

(The nun, the mad virgin, is staring down our necks. She is hiding in the assembly hall in the window's distorting image. Sprange launches into a tirade to the effect that Crabbe did not go to Russia so much to combat communism or consolidate Europe under the leadership of Germany – not that he had anything against that – as to discover something in himself, wake himself up, or find confirmation for something he had an inkling of on 20 May. Though everything Crabbe did seemed a pretext): "Then again, he maintained he had killed forty Russians at most while his comrades set the number at no fewer than eighty. How else could he have come so close to overshadowing the glory of le beau Léon, the Lion of Cherkasy? You remember, don't you, that they called Crabbe the hound of Kruskoe back then in Stemmermann's Eleventh Corps?

"We were surrounded, and from early January the Russians were out to *einkesseln* the whole Eighth Army. Thirty degrees below. It was clear that only Crabbe could bear it. And he not only bore it, he thrived! We had a man in the propaganda division by the name of Whitey Claessens. I can see him now, blue with cold, fear, and wonder that he could bring himself to say 'If we don't get out of here soon . . .' 'What then?' asked Crabbe, and spat a plug of tobacco on the ground, and this Whitey Claessens pulled his helmet down so far you could hardly see his eyes, and said not a word. Don't forget: that was a time when we too listened to the enemy broadcasts and we too read the propaganda pamphlets against Hitler written by the captured generals and how easy – and safe – it would have been for us to cross to the other side, and Crabbe just stamped down the ice under his heel, twisted his heel in the white grit, and said, 'We may not get out at all, but as long as I . . .' and, tossing his fur scarf, a gift from Richard, around his neck, went on, as much to me as to the propaganda man who had asked the question, who wanted to hear Crabbe justify his self-assurance, and was thus in Crabbe's eyes in a state of torpor, of less than full consciousness, 'Another word out of you along the lines of what you were about to say and I'll slice your eyelids off,' and off he went, dragging his feet somewhat as was his wont, away from the doubting sleepwalkers we were in his eyes, and not even I, who was Scharführer at the time, not even I could muster a clear statement or even just say what I thought, yet we all of us, all the hoplites, stayed, and he got us out of there . . ."

(Is she calling to us there at the window? Waving? I don't have my glasses; my ankle is aching, but I'm afraid to touch it; I do my best to beat an unobtrusive retreat from the Scharführer and that dangerous stretch of elms, but my bloody agoraphobia takes over: I shrink back, I can't move. What? Is she waving? She's chasing flies. Ha! She's catching them!)

". . . we had no proof he was dead when we heard it, but he wouldn't have let so much time go by before making his presence known, so she took over his room, sprayed it with Flytox for two days, plugged up all the cracks, chinks, and holes in the doors and windows, square centimeter by square centimeter . . .

". . . Crabbe often made fun of her, once because she was having her period and Alice had let it be known and called her 'Mademoiselle Indisposed' in my presence. She was thirteen at the time, I think . . .

". . . she never knew what Crabbe was fighting for, what kept him going; in fact, the whole political constellation left her ice-cold. It wasn't until a few years ago that she took an interest in it, though not so much for what is going on now as for what moved him to it then, as a kind of homage to his memory. No, back then she turned a deaf ear to the Almout discussions, just sitting there cow-eyed, and every once in a while he turned to her in the middle of the give-and-take – for a laugh at her expense yet actually as much at the expense of the whole gang and their ideals, regulations, and slogans – and asked, 'Don't you agree, mademoiselle, that . . .' something or other and she would blush beet-red, poor thing, though she was no less uncomfortable than the men in uniform surrounding him, by which I mean the priests, and Alice would say, 'Really, my boy, you're embarrassing her,' but he would ramble on – completely ignoring the incident and impassioned as ever, as if believing everything he said – about the Burgundian Empire and the evils of capitalism . . .

". . . she waited a long time for him. When Richard and even Alice had given up all hope and let themselves sink into the state you saw them in, pitiful, she picked herself up and telephoned the Ministry in German or went to the prison in St. Gillis to talk to the last people to see him (they said 'in Poland or Normandy,' making it up as they went along because they thought a noblewoman like her would be able to get them out). Then she gave up as well and moved her goods and chattels into his room, not letting anyone help her, and since then she's been driving her MG to Brussels and Knokke more often, supposedly staying with some girls she knows there. What was that? She went to a masquerade not long ago. Had you heard?"

(Seasickness, vertigo, agoraphobia. I still can't move. I shake my head and keep my face out of reach.)

"Well, bye for now, and as Crabbe was wont to say, 'Wir sprechen uns noch.'"

The Acting Director of "Winter Relief,"
Richard Harmedam

It was the time of day when one could see a full moon and the sun setting in the heavens, the fourth day after Liberation. The path of the Liberation, which was likewise the path of the traitors, ran principally from the bridge in the Hazegras district (where four days earlier three young men in white overalls had been gunned down) to the marketplace. That is why it was lined by the town's inhabitants, not one of whom of course had said to the barber, "Say what you will, the Germans have discipline," not one of whom had cursed the English bombers, not one of whom had received a Schein for extra rations of gas and food. We had come together, all of us, and the young people with white or tri-colored armbands who were helping the local police to keep the peace were looked upon with envy by the eldest and youngest among us.

It was the fourth day we had toasted the health of Montgomery and Stalin and treated the Poles and Canadians to the geuze we had laid away for so long. Our town was liberated; three young men had sacrificed their lives for it; God had shown us mercy for once. Then a shiver ran through the crowd that had gathered along Leiestraat, Marnestraat, and Oudemannenweg, and people left the sidewalks and pressed on as far as Bennesteeg because the open truck that had been requisitioned from Haakebeen's Lumber and Furniture Center (Haakebeen had helped to build the Atlantic Wall), the familiar truck that had until now, during the last four days, followed the path of the Liberation from Hazegras to the marketplace with four of our boys in white, pistols at the ready, and two gendarmes on the mudguards, its back filled to the brim with Black – that is, collaborationist – rabble, pale and trembling on the sawdust-covered floor, our traitor-truck, had suddenly, unannounced, driven from Rolstraat to the market-place, and what were we doing there beaming along our jubilant streets with the pathetic, rotten fruit we'd paid an arm and a leg for in one hand and a cobblestone in the other? Was that what we wore the yoke for these four years? The people pushed forward to see. A ripple ran over their heads, as Poseidon ripples the wine-dark sea in his displeasure, and voices cried, "Harmedam is with them!" "That's why they took another route. It's Harmedam." "Powerful traitors have powerful friends!" "They're taking him straight to the POW camp!" Those of us who during the occupation had lain low in our houses (because after ten you couldn't go out into the street), steered clear of *all* politics (just you wait! just you wait! when the whole thing is over, we'll see who laughs last!), and kept to ourselves (what could we do to defy the Werbestelle, the Kommandantur, the SS, the Black Brigade?) were nonplussed: this anonymous hypocrisy, this perfidious violation of justice within our own, newly liberated walls – we weren't having any of it. After them! cried a jeweler. Don't let him get away! a member of parliament commanded. And we ourselves closed off the marketplace before the vehicle, our own truck, the truck we'd commandeered from Haakebeen's Lumber, could set out. The enemy in the back of the truck was under control.

The enemies of the town were all there, pale as could be, hiding under their jackets. They were protected by the gendarmes – four for this special convoy – and a couple of police officers and a lieutenant from the Independence Front. It goes without saying they were lavishly recompensed by the families of that scum, but they succumbed to our righteous anger when we shouted at the top of our lungs, "All we want is one! Harmedam!"

We didn't see him at first, didn't discover him until the others had climbed down among the gendarmes to reveal a long canvas sack painted with khaki and brick-red zigzags. It was trembling. Only then did we realize that even Harmedam's comrades had left him in the lurch. The day of reckoning had come. We parleyed for half an hour – nota bene, we didn't touch the truck, let alone storm it – after which the official representatives and people charged by the people with executing the law reached an agreement.

The remains of a rainbow stretched over the Town Hall and its headless statues of guild dignitaries. A breeze came in from the sea. Then a cheer arose and continued as the trembling sack on the truck was opened and out crawled Richard Harmedam. He stood up and smiled. This greatly intensified our rage, and there may have been those among us with enough gumption, too long suppressed by the Germans' Feldgrau, to lunge at the smiling man, but others, the majority, announced that Harmedam was going to pay his respects to the monument to the fallen soldiers in public. That mitigated our rage, and the cursing and grumbling ceased.

The monument was located at the foot of the Belfort, which houses Janten and Wieze, the giants we carry in our annual procession. It sports Greek goddesses crowning a fallen warrior with laurel wreaths, this before a simple cement wall that bears the gilded names of those who fell for their country in 1914–18. The monument is known to one and all. Many a prominent official and even a general or two had placed flowers on it. And who of us at that hateful hour known as closing time, who of us had not made water at the threshold of the Café Français or La Taverne Brueghel in the direction of the constable coming to warn us and thereby incurred a fine for insulting a representative of the Authorities while on duty, a fine for offending public morals, and a fine for desecrating a grave and disparaging the armed forces, because by aiming our tools in the direction of the constable we were aiming them in the direction of the monument, which lay behind him. But we are not here to make pleasantries, so let me repeat: the monument is known to one and all. And although there were no trumpets, no bands, no ribbons or wreaths, our hearts were gay and we felt it was a solemn occasion when Harmedam, Richard was lifted out of the truck and led to the shrine by the gendarmerie. The rest of the traitors, trembling, were watched over by the White Brigade, but nobody cared about them: battered by our fruit and stones, they would be brought to justice like the others arrested in the past four days. Harmedam was wearing a Prince of Wales suit, which we saw as a provocation, wondering at how well it set off his sausage-like build.

None of us had noticed before how short he was. By the time he stood in our midst cowering, his gray-blond hair was disheveled and his odious face had lost its smile. We waited; some children booed. Then, to the tune of an earsplitting "It's a Long Way to Tipperary" coming from La Taverne Brueghel, an honor guard of local burghers was formed around the two gendarmes supporting him because he seemed to have trouble walking, and these burghers marched (as they had had no opportunity to do since 1940) at attention, several with their right hands between the third and fourth button of their jackets, in rhythm, in step, and he, the sausage, got out of step (though he had marched perfectly well, mind you, at the funeral of two slain Flemish guards in 1942!). Harmedam stumbled when Sjef van Roeners stuck a billiard cue between his legs. What a laugh we had when he lurched forward and managed to keep from falling only by grabbing the belt of one of the gendarmes, and the man thought he was trying to unsheathe his revolver and gave him a sudden swift blow in the neck with his truncheon, and Harmedam landed in the gravel on his two hands with his face in the hyacinths planted in a round bed around the monument. Did we roar! *Kyrie eleison*, cried Octave van den Abeele.

"Kiss it!" our women shouted. "Make him kiss the monument!" And several workers among us rephrased the demand with characteristically smutty humor and made the maidens blush. Though truth to tell and between you and me, this Canadian period left precious few maidens intact.

Then the gendarme who had hit Harmedam took him by the scruff of the neck – though some say by the hair – and pulled him to his feet. While we held our breath and the traitors off to the side waited for the buzzards to swoop down and sweep the guilty off to justice, Harmedam, glancing right and left, went up to the first sandstone step and knelt cautiously out of respect for our martyrs or to spare his Prince of Wales suit or in fear or because of his age – somewhat hesitantly, in any case – then bowed his head and, yes, kissed the booted foot of the dying soldier of 1914–18, at which point an old woman pushed her way through the still ungratified crowd, yes, a raging buzzard, and before anyone could stop her she pounced on her prey, lifted her flowery skirt and gave his neck two stamps of a flat-heeled shoe. Under everyone's eyes his mouth cracked down hard on the stone. The old woman, in whom we recognized Tjampens, Cecilia, housewife, sat down next to him and observed him with interest while we all stared at the three teeth lying on the ribbed sandstone and a young man, a student we never saw again, gathered them up and tossed them high in the air. The younger among us leapt up to catch them. And that was pretty much the end of that.

The dapper clown we had seen till the previous month strutting around this very square as director, if you please, of winter relief and heard barking his Teutonic orders – "Here the soup, here the vitamins, here the zwieback for women over sixty-five" – as if he were the only one who knew where the needy lived – this man was dragged off, mewling like a child, and hoisted onto the truck, and the others, already there, trembling and white as chalk, thanked him, probably because he had served as a scapegoat, by wiping his mouth and stroking his hair. It was the time of day when one's shadow is longer than oneself, when a detailed discussion of the incident at the Café Français would not be amiss because the war wasn't over yet, mind you; on the contrary, the enemy under the command of von Rundsted was back at our gates, in our Ardennes.

Sandra

The tennis court was made of red clay, my clothes stuck to my skin, and the wide tennis shoes made me slip. "Service!" you shouted, Sandra, and you jumped to the side, and I leaned back and hit the ball – even though I threw it to the proper height just over my shoulder – with the tip of my racket and cursed my father for ever having made me play the game, and just as I was about to hurl the racket at the fence you came running over and grabbed my arm: you'd realized I was hopeless on the court.

"Your stroke is off," you said as if it were news, and gave me a demonstration. Three fast balls skimmed over the net, a fourth fell on our side, and you smelled like a multitude of women. Where were my glasses? You showed me how you pivoted on your left foot to meet the ball, at the same time twisting your hip and holding on to my sacroiliac with your soldier-like hands. Then you sat down in a garden chair and dangled a foot and looked at me for a long time while I tried to guess "What is going on inside her? What is she after?" But you hadn't a clue, you still thought I was the Dutch delegate of your girl-scout fantasies about the dead-and-buried Crabbe, a light-haired doctor who had written an article on Flemish national socialism containing references to Crabbe, and this doctor didn't seduce you – though your ever so blasé expression gave me to understand there was a chance we might some day (like the first men on earth, stark naked, pure-blooded) couple, but what you saw was the doctor, not the teacher on his wild goose chase, and what you wondered was, Why are all men shadows, sketches, études of my never-to-return beloved? It was something I had seen before, Sandra, to wit, in hopeless amber eyes rounder and lighter than yours, Elizabeth's, when of a rainy day she sat in her chamber, our bedchamber, where I had entrée whenever I pleased as a guest of the resident snake-charmer. Absorbed for hours on end by a childish pleasure that curled her tongue over her upper lip, she would clean the teeth of her comb with a needle, wiping off the gray grime on a white handkerchief, and as she gazed at her handiwork I could read in her face, Why aren't you somebody else? Why are you the double of someone who loves me passionately and would pull me through life?

You picked up the tennis ball in your right hand, spun it with the tips of your fingers, then sank your teeth into it, and it was all white and hairy like a bunny belly and (not yet thinking of Crabbe visiting the German extermination camps and the possibility that he could have met Banach there – he died there – the Banach who discovered the paradox that an apple [a tennis ball] can be cut into pieces and put back together in a ball smaller than an atom and larger than the sun) I thought, She's getting her claws into me by biting into white hairs decked with bits of red clay. No matter how hard I probed, how hungrily I watched, I found nothing in you of what I remembered from the White Mouse Ball: you were somebody else. To my unreasonable, totally unjustified pride. In the house resounding with your mother's song you parried and attacked with bromides culled from etiquette books: you said, "However a woman helps a man to find himself, she holds him prisoner," by which you meant, "I couldn't do anything for Crabbe; he still holds me prisoner." When the red-haired sculptor sat down at the tea table and it slid back and forth and I was stuck between you, the room shrank into a cabin floating above Almout's vast grounds, and I was an astronaut, hunching, untrained, and you saw me floundering in the net of ropes that hung from the hooks of the round cabin and crisscrossed my body, dividing me into segments with no tangent plane so that I could swell and contract to sun and atom, and then your tennis hand squeezed my knuckles, and you were hunger and sweet satiety in one, you bitch, I could see your teeth and you shook your short – you had cut it short two days before – hair. One of these days I'll break out of this room, Sandra, have no fear, I'll stop visiting you in Almout House, where you keep all those barking dogs, there's no sound more ghastly on earth, it's absurd, it's excruciating, I hear them in room after room, they're driving me crazy with their barking and they . . .

Occupation

They did not get away from the house because before the teacher could ask directions of the boy bobbing at his side, which he had meant to do with a stern countenance like a father left in the lurch (as the boy could tell: the teacher had started wearing a hangdog look and proffering mendacious explanations), they were stopped at the porter's lodge by the voice of Sandra's father calling out, "There you are at last!"

The boy darted off to the side, seeking shelter in the bushes, but the old man nabbed him by the jacket. "You little rascal, you!" he shouted. "Trying to weasel out of your promise, is that it?"

"I haven't had time to ask him yet," the boy said.

"I see!" the man cried triumphantly.

The boy – on the heels of the man, who was signaling to them – whispered something the teacher didn't catch.

"No time, my foot!" said the old man, bending forward as he passed under the alder branches. A wooden structure attached to the porter's lodge came into sight. The boy gripped the teacher's forearm. His roguish face did not bode well.

"Let me go," said the teacher and removed his hand.

"Wait," said the boy loudly and gave him a reproachful look as if to say, "You were keen on, insistent on seeing the house up close. Well, I'm helping you."

Once inside – while the old man went on about the mess, which they'd have to overlook: it was the way an artist worked and besides he knew exactly where everything was, it was only when the cleaning lady tidied things up that . . . – we saw that the ambiguous space he was waving his arms around in with such satisfaction was a photographer's studio-cum-laboratory equipped with retorts, distillation tubes, grated boxes of guinea-pigs, a dissection table covered with blood-stained towels, sextants – you name it. In front of a silver-white screen stretching diagonally along a wall that had once been a fireplace we saw a woman.

"Madame Harmedam, née the Duchess Miësto," the old man said, bowing in her direction.

The woman remained motionless. She was naked and painted white and engulfed in a netting of metal wires that made her pinched skin puffy and chalky. The only thing she was wearing was a pair of gold lamé skittles that had been pasted onto her nipples. Her face was made up immoderately: false eyelashes, mascaraed eyebrows, and phosphorescent lips topped with fine, wispy, red-brown hair that stuck out of the shiny meshes in places. The wires ate deep into her skin, and she was kneeling in an uncomfortable position: heels – their dirty, chapped, paint-smeared edges plainly visible – pressed against calves, arms drawn backwards over full thighs. Five meters away stood an old-fashioned camera: the torso was being photographed. She was not smiling and aimed her wide-open, brown eyes at a point behind and above the teacher, who thought, "That eye color doesn't exist; the eyes are painted too. The whole body has been tampered with, doctored, or else she has eyes yet sees not," but then Madame Harmedam began following the movements of the boy, who sat down on a box that had rustling and peeps coming out of it.

"I was just focusing," said the old man, who had ducked under the black cloth that lay over the camera and, chattering away in a muffled voice, elbows flying, recounted how the studio had belonged to his brother, whose works they could admire on the walls, and there was indeed a profusion of photographs tacked to the hardboard on the wall. They were pictures of children. Ten- or twelve-year-old peasant girls with runny noses and rumpled hair, occasionally daubed with soot or in tears, had been placed against an idyllic background of weeping willows, mountain peaks, a lake. Even more prints – disparate in size and hue, gigantic, buckling – were piled in a corner. Over and over the teacher recognized the grounds of Almout behind one or another village child: the beech-lined path, the lawn (statueless).

The old man was having trouble with the camera: several times he crawled out coughing from under the dull black cloth, squinted at his model, adjusted one of the aluminum spotlights, and disappeared again. Eventually he gave up, probably under the pressure of the visit, and offered the teacher a chair, perching with one buttock on the windowsill and resting a foot on a wheelchair. No one spoke. The old man found the silence intolerable. He said he was sorry the teacher had never met his brother, a remarkable man: they would have got on like a house on fire. Before the war at least. Because the war had left an ugly mark on him. He had ended up . . . well, let's just say he came out of it somewhat damaged. One day, about a month before his death, he wanted to have all Alessandra's teeth pulled.

"And have dentures made?" asked the boy.

"No, my lad. No, no. To keep her from being a flirt!"

"And she wouldn't let him?" asked the boy.

"No," said the old man, indignant. Not that it was so foolish: Didn't the bushmen chop off their fingers as a sign of mourning, and wasn't it true that we were so out of touch with our bodies that we to-tal-ly ig-nored the corporeal? Though it may be, he babbled on, that his – yes, well – eccentricities stemmed not only from the bestial treatment he was subjected to in the Ostende marketplace, after which he lost his hair, for one thing; it may have started much earlier with the fumes from the mercury he used in his experiments.

The teacher was tired and in constant pain because of his ankle, which was pinched by the shoe. The old man, having set forth a variation on the theme of maiming he deemed a propos – namely, that in the Middle Ages a man "known to give false measure his thumb was wont to lose" – came out with a cackle of a laugh and, reverting to the childish voice he had used when welcoming them to Almout, sang a ditty with a mixture of Italian, French, and Spanish words. After it ended, in a goat-like bleat, he explained that it was his brother's favorite hymn; he had even taken it upon himself to copy out the words and sign it with the name Scardelli. "And I'm not ashamed to tell you that the song was as idiotic as the bacalà-bacalà Louis XVI was in the habit of singing." This reminiscence broke the dike, and out came one after another. And as the time slipped by and he occasionally slipped off the windowsill, the old woman, her costume-jewelry eyes fixed on the boy, breathed with increasing difficulty.

The boy, who may well have found all this as irritating as the teacher, banged the heels of his shoes against the box he was sitting on, fiddled with an exposure meter, and peered through the viewfinder of a camera that had a zoom lens. Meanwhile the old man quit his windowsill with a sigh, asked for silence, and disappeared again amongst the folds of the cloth behind the monstrous apparatus. There were mosquitoes. A hairless rosy hand emerged from the folds and pressed a rubber pear, after which a deep-red Richard Harmedam emerged, stretching. "And perhaps you've heard how he behaved towards the end, in the garden. You haven't? He had himself rolled into the garden in his wheelchair, and after an hour in the sun he thought he was a tulip and asked Sandra and Alice to water him! What a blessing he soon went to his Maker!"

The room was silent again. The old woman, drenched in sweat, belched, and the teacher, who had risen, tried to stand on his painful foot. Nearly falling against an enlarged photograph of some bushes, he noticed that the edge of her heel was painted and, bending over, that the sole of her foot was lacquered scarlet, and he thought not without self-satisfaction that such was the custom of Cretan priestesses, who were forbidden to touch the earth, the ground, outside the temple.

Her chalk-white face kept the boy in its thrall and then, an event: her right eyelid sank with excruciating lethargy over its eyeball. She had sat as motionless as an owl one fancied stuffed, and suddenly this sluggish wink. Was it meant for the boy, a signal? The woman's hoarse, cracked voice said, "Scoundrel."

Angry, the old man responded that he needed absolute concentration at this point and had called for silence three times. Had she quite finished?

"Bastard," she said.

"Will you please shut up, Madame," he shouted.

Madame – one eye a perfect, unnatural purple jewel, the other invisible under the light blue integument – replied that this house and the three villas in Blankenberge were her property. That stood the old man for a time, and he tinkered with the lens of the colossus next to him.

"Did you promise Mr. Harmedam anything?" asked the teacher.

"That I would introduce you to Madame," the boy said tetchily.

"Well," said the teacher, "that's done . . ."

The boy got up off his rustling box.

"I'm as fed up as you," he said.

The teacher bowed in the direction of the salami-woman and whispered something in the frightened old man's ear about circumstances that obliged him to leave, and after a few exposed, unguarded, dangerous steps towards the door he left the couple in an odor of dissolvent, perfume, and acid.

All the way to the dusty village street, accompanied by the boy kicking a milk-carton soccer ball, he said not a word, wondering as he was at the events of the day. He consulted the bus schedule at a café in the marketplace, but as he had feared, no, damn it, hoped, there was no bus to the coast until the next morning at eight.

The innkeeper was waiting for them at the door. He failed to respond to his lodgers' "good evenings," and when the teacher made to enter he did not move out of the way until the last moment. He followed them and put his hand on the boy's head and asked him what his name was. The boy ducked from under the hand, smoothed his hair down, and said it was none of his business. The innkeeper laughed a slightly lascivious laugh; the two young farmers in overalls sitting over by the jukebox slapped their thighs in merriment, and one of them opened his mouth to reveal a paste of chocolate and neighed, "God damn! 'It's none of our business,' he says. That's a good one, eh, Pier?"

The other suddenly stopped laughing, but his mouth retained its sneer. "He thinks we're a bunch of assholes, like in the city."

Humiliated and dead tired, the teacher took a seat and massaged his ankle. There were public auction posters spread out on the table in front of him.

"So you won't tell me?" said the innkeeper. He drew a glass of beer for himself and swigged.

"Verzele," said the boy. "Albert Verzele."

The two young farmers nudged each other and crowed.

"I knew it!" the innkeeper cried. "I said to myself, Pier, I said, there's something fishy going on here! You've got to have a nose for these things." He downed the rest of the glass and exhaled. "And if I may say so myself, I've got one." He turned to the teacher. "Not a pretty business," he said. "Not at all."

The teacher nodded. The innkeeper, taking this as a ruse, said in a nasty voice that the rate for their room had just gone up considerably and asked if he was willing to stand the Vermast brothers to a drink.

"Of course," said the teacher.

"We've heard about your kind. Right, Bernard?" said one of the Vermast brothers, the elder one. "Well, that may be all the rage in the city, but not here, pal. Not where we live!"

The boy was seized by a sudden fit of laughter, as if affected by their spirit, and asked, "Hey, what's the matter?"

"Don't bother your head about it, Albert Verzele," said the innkeeper, setting two beer glasses a quarter full of cognac before the brothers. "Cheers," they said. "Santé."

Before the next round they toasted the teacher, then the boy, then the innkeeper, then the local soccer club. The innkeeper pulled up a chair next to the teacher and sat with the back between his knees. He said it was time for them to come to an understanding. The world is full of all kinds of things, granted, and God keeps track of his own, but some things go too far, right? And too far is too far. Not that he or the Vermast brothers or anyone else in the village had anything against the teacher. No, damn it. But if the transgressions went on in his inn, then he was partly responsible, damn it.

"And not us, right?" said one of the brothers.

"Shut up," the innkeeper commanded.

"What?" cried the brothers.

They began arguing over which of the three had first heard the crime reported on the radio and finally agreed they had all three heard it at the same time, on the one o'clock news. The announcer had even hesitated when he came to "thirteen years old" and – remember? – cleared his throat in a meaningful way when he came to "accompanied by a man of about thirty-five with light brown hair." They toasted the announcer.

"That's all well and good," said the teacher, "but I don't see . . ."

"He's blind," said one of the brothers.

"As a goddamned bat," replied the other.

The boy was digging in his nose to hold back an irrepressible snigger. The teacher got up for the umpteenth time and walked over to the door next to the taproom without looking back to see whether that traitor of a Verzele was following him. He was, as was the innkeeper. At the stairs the innkeeper made the "Psst!" used to call a cat or a child. The teacher, jumpy, was caught in the trap and said, "What is it?" and thought, "Should I tack on a 'goddamn it' so he . . ."

The innkeeper asked if he could give him the bill: it was five thousand francs plus a thousand francs for each of the Vermast brothers.

"I haven't got that much on me," said the teacher.

"But you can get it or have it brought to you."

"Don't," said the boy in a loud voice. "Don't let him take you in."

"Perhaps I can send you a check," said the teacher.

The innkeeper shook his head, surprised. The red, furrowed face of the younger Vermast brother appeared around the corner of the door. "You're not going to try and get us to pay, are you, Pier?" he said.

"Shut up," said the innkeeper.

"I know you, Pier," he said. "You've double-crossed me before."

The boy was impossible: he burst out laughing again.

"Perhaps I can give you half the amount now," the teacher began, but the young Vermast cursed violently and said who did he think they were, your city assholes? It was getting awkward there at the staircase (and yesterday I dreamed about it: the staircase was pliable, rubbery, and the stairs were human limbs excreting a liquid that drenched my trouser legs, and I cried out and Korneel beat me and gave me a shot).

"I'll see what I can do," said the teacher, to which the innkeeper replied, "Good idea."

"Don't let him pull a fast one on you," said Vermast, slurring his words.

Back in their room the two travelers mulled things over. "I've had it with this dump," the younger of them declared. Then, without consultation, they started packing, which meant the boy stuck the underpants he had forgotten to put on that morning into his pocket and the teacher gathered up his cigarettes, a handkerchief, and his fountain pen and dropped them into the briefcase with his pupils' uncorrected homework. Only then did they consult. The boy wanted to climb out of the window, but the teacher knew he couldn't because of his ankle. "Okay," said the boy with a laugh, and shoes in hand they descended the stairs, and though nothing creaked, the teacher was trembling from head to foot, and when they reached the side door that led out to the courtyard and the vegetable garden and the wheat fields beyond they were met by the innkeeper, who said, "That's no way to act."

The teacher struggled on with his shoes, after which the three of them – the two prisoners pushed forward by the innkeeper – entered the taproom, which had filled up surprisingly in so brief an interval. Their pitiful position was known to all – there could be no doubt about that – but the cardplayers who had spontaneously materialized – whether out of discretion, a sense of fair play, or connivance – behaved civilly: they asked how the teacher and the boy had spent their day in the village, whether they had found it to their liking, whether they had seen the bronze plaque commemorating the sojourn of the Leader, de Keukeleire, in the village just before he was taken away, on 8 May. The two of them answered the questions in a dull, dispirited voice, and the villagers soon went back to their own conversations and their cards. Yet the eye of the village kept them in its thrall: every once in a while the teacher felt a malicious, minatory, or inquisitive glance trained on him, and he was conscious of an unbroken link between the whist players and the innkeeper, who was keeping watch at the bar behind the chocolate bars, wafers, hard-boiled eggs, sausages, and the picture of a missionary priest. The teacher drank a glass of English stout, the boy a lemon crush. Then the boy got up – under the innkeeper's spell? – and, after following a card game with a yawn or two, went over to the bar, and whispered something in the man's ear. The man shook his head. The boy then spoke urgently into the motionless red column of his neck, and the man, chewing on the match in the right-hand corner of his mouth, nodded. The boy went back to the teacher and told him they could stay another night, maybe two. In the wake of the boy's calling out and receiving animated "good nights," the teacher, cursing God, made his way once again, yet again, to the door leading from the taproom to their room. "Don't go looking for trouble," said the innkeeper as they passed him.

In the hole buzzing with mosquitoes the boy witnessed the teacher cursing his lot, striking the bedside table, and helped him, once he had calmed down a bit, to undo his shoelaces. He told him the innkeeper had forbidden him to sleep in the room and he would have to spend the night in the little room on the landing. The teacher shrugged. "I'll be glad to be back at school," said the boy and was gone.

"Shouldn't I have said good night or made a cross on his forehead?" thought the teacher. "What do fathers do when they send their children off to bed?" He was so tired, Victor-Denijs de Rijckel, English-German, that he all but collapsed. "Is this diabetes?" he wondered. "I'm completely helpless."

Undressing, he realized that he too was looking forward to school: he would have been only too happy to be walking around the playground the next morning or telling his spirited class anecdotes, for the most part invented by himself, about Goethe. He fell asleep. Towards morning he dreamed that Alessandra Harmedam's father dressed in dripping-wet clothes was sitting in a wheelchair on a soccer field trying to look at his brain, which made his eyes shiny and round, and nearby, legs spread wide, a nun was stretching convulsively to do up the zipper at the back of her habit. Then the boy, who had slept in his clothes, was standing pale and unwashed next to my bed. "I've been up for hours," he said and took a seat on the bed at the teacher's feet. The sun was blazing on his face, and he shut his eyes and would have fallen asleep again or for the first time had the teacher not given him an uncharacteristically rancorous kick in the knees.

"So you didn't sleep?"

"No, I did. What makes you ask? Maybe *you* didn't."

"Have you seen the fellow?"

"Yes, he says we can stay as long as we like."

"And what would you like?"

"To get going," said the boy, walking up to the basin and splashing water over his face, smoothing his hair down.

They took a long time over their breakfast of bread, butter and cheese and coffee, and the innkeeper, at his post behind the taproom counter, did not seem to mind. The teacher, having curtly turned a blind eye to some of the boy's more outrageous remarks and gestures, read the local newspaper and the *Ciné-Revue* while the boy made a paper airplane out of a refrigerator advertisement. Then the innkeeper put a coin in the jukebox and announced the three titles of the records: "Heimatland," "Du bist meine Sonne," and "Heute wollen wir marschier'n."

The boy listened, head on arm, right ear bent forward, eyes closed, singing along from time to time. He got the endings wrong and the rhythm. The teacher asked for *Het Laatste Nieuws*, but the innkeeper said that all they had was *Het Volk* and that he needn't worry: there wasn't anything about them in it. The ice-cream man pulled up outside, and the boy went out and bought one. The sun grew warmer, and the taproom filled with noise from outside: chickens, cars, bells. Farmers were coming in. All of a sudden the innkeeper cleared his throat, wiped his hands angrily on his undershirt, and said something through the door. The teacher followed his gaze, and just as he caught sight of the low, hideously purple sports car with Sandra at the wheel a horn with two notes rang out. "The mistress from the Castle," said the innkeeper, and the boy raised his chin from his elbow, shut his eyes again for a second, then jumped up.

The young woman burst out laughing. Had he (the teacher) slept in the cornfield? He looked atrocious. Had he forgotten their date? She was lying and he went along with it. "Of course not. I've been expecting you for at least half an hour. And" (while on his way outside) "it was the frightful incertitude of whether you would come or not that made me look the way I do!"

He turned and glanced at the boy, who was standing in front of the open, hammered-glass door with CELTA PILS in slanting white letters on it, and he was about to ask, Are you coming or aren't you? (Are you, my guide, leaving me in the lurch? Or do I have to leave you, my sleepy paladin, as security?) when he said, in the shadow of the innkeeper's giant figure, "See you soon."

"Soon?"

"Yes, I'll join you when I can. I can't now."

The car set off.

She drove with a free, easy hand, looking occasionally in the rearview mirror and moistening her lips. She kept up a running commentary as they passed the convent, where only rich, young, clever, elegant nuns lived, and the farm where – no one had ever learned why – the son had slit his mother and father's throats. The car hummed along past youths in corduroy shorts with flags and rucksacks, past families that had set up tables and chairs to eat lunch under God's own sky, past filling stations and villas called Bonanza and Mon Coin Perdu, and when she got to a wooded area she swung onto a side road and braked. In direct sun. She made a forty-five degree turn in his direction and, resting an arm covered with tinkling coin bracelets and chains on the steering wheel, said, "Hoo? Ha?"

The teacher thought about movies where this kind of thing happened – American movies in cinemascope with deep blue skies – took a deep breath, and stared straight ahead, a close-up, in great anguish but as handsome as they come.

"I could hardly sleep last night," she said. "And you?"

Not bad as gambits go.

"Did we really make a date?" he asked, coward that he was.

"Yes."

"Then I forgot," he said. The charms on her bracelets were making a racket: she was chasing away a fly. "I'm divorced," he added, and thought, What's come over me anyway? Can't I ever stop being the schoolmaster?

"For how long?"

He was making his way along wobbly boards beside a raging sea.

"A year."

"Was she pretty?" (Was she as pretty as I am?)

Yesterday she looked at my ring finger, he thought. "I thought of you last night, Alessandra." That was safe. Shallow water. Then, ever the schoolmaster, he embarked on a broad plain full of convoluted sentences and mysterious turns of phrase, declaring, for instance, that he had never felt so strange and had seen himself (was it because he had read that movie magazine in the café?) as a dirty old man in technicolor next to an eager teenager, and he turned in the plush seat, bumped his painful ankle against the handbrake and his mouth into her chin, and slipped down into her warm, moist neck. "Hoo? Ha?" he said.

She looked in the rear-view mirror and arranged her prickly hair around her small, red ears, and as the coin bracelets slid tinkling down her arm he wondered impatiently what pet names men used at that precarious stage, but there was no whoop of triumph, no sense of victory welling up in his being. She trained her eyes on him. Arms thrashing on his raft, he said with more malice than he had ever before mustered, "Do you still expect Crabbe to return?"

"No," she said, leaning back, pressing her body against the seat and positioning her white, low-cut shoes on either side of the pedals. "That's over."

What? The moment, now? Had he missed something, let something slip through her wet fingers? "What's over?" he asked nervously.

"*That*," she said. There were tears trickling down her nose. She licked them off with the tip of her tongue and waved a hand towards the dark green woods and golden countryside in the light caught by the window with the registration and Touring-Club stickers.

"I was a girl of eleven at the time, and whenever he came to the house I was sent into the garden and told to play with Berthold, the dog, because Tania, the porter's daughter, had a rash that year. My stepfather was doing arithmetic and geography with me, and I was to start boarding school soon. My mother slept all day or ate chocolate in bed; the only time she left her room was when the Leader came to call, and that happened less often than was later reported in the literature. He was a slender man who stuck his chest out and his chin, and there was always a ruffle of skin above the collar of his uniform. He would kiss Mother's hand – or, rather, her palm, as if wanting to taste the chocolate – and stroke my braids, calling me Nele, not Sandra: my Nele. When he was in uniform, he never leaned his back against the wall, never crossed his knees. When he was out of uniform, he often wore white socks, which was not the fashion at the time: our Anglophiles, who later, during the war, as you'll remember, used white socks along with wide jackets and plus-fours as marks of identification, would have wondered at it had they known. What else? His hair was short, and he smelled of expensive soap. Mama's gift. But I wasn't cross at having to leave when he came: they would go on about incomprehensible things like the State and the Folk and the Community. The place I most liked to be was my stepfather's studio, where I could play with his three old-fashioned cameras, though of course I also enjoyed an occasional dig in the wardrobe where Mama kept her costumes, forbidden though it was, and once I came up with some baby clothes. The other place I liked to be was the chapel in the afternoon when it began to get dark, and I would kneel by my seat, which was up front, next to Mama's, in a side niche, and stare at the colors in the glass – which then grew brighter and gaudier and I nearly fell over if I watched them for too long – or the white glass with the sun and our coat of arms ablaze and the endless grains of dust twirling around them and I, I was one of them, and then I'd fall asleep on my pew and wake up at twilight, after which I genuflected once on the marble step in front of the gospel and once on the wooden spiral staircase leading to the pulpit and once in the confessional, and then, the last, in the middle of the chapel between the first two pews reserved for visitors. It was my own chapel: my name was sculpted into the wall and on Sunday mornings when the giant white-headed bird preached it was for me alone, because Mama and my stepfather were in a state of mortal sin, and the tall priest in his habit was all mine, my slave, there to open the path to heaven for me, rub it smooth, make it accessible with his prayers day and night. I was crazy about the old priest. When Mass was over and I had to kneel before him to receive his blessing, I would see the watch on his wrist and his bare brown arm and look for signs of the flagellation that Tania said he and the other priests underwent on a daily basis as penitence for our sins, Tania's and mine too, and I loved him because he was so concerned for our future bliss that he was willing to suffer great pain. I was never told when he was replaced or died, probably because Mama wanted to spare me, but his successor was fat and bespectacled and he spoke a lot faster and in complicated sentences and with more gesticulation, and I started going to chapel less often. This was around the time Crabbe showed up at our place one night with the Leader. Anyway, I had a dog and his name was Berthold and he was exactly my age, as they never tired of telling me, and although they explained twenty times over that the age of a dog has nothing to do with the age of a human I couldn't help wondering why he was unable to keep up with me when I ran fast, why his long red tongue would immediately hang out all the way to the ground, and why he was such a coward, because whenever a cat arched its back and hissed, there he'd be, rubbing up against my leg, and even if he was covered with warts and pustules I could have kissed him if Mama hadn't expressly forbidden it and said it would make me look like a dog, and that far I was unwilling to go. Berthold would spend his evenings curled up in a corner, and that night the thunder made him terribly scared, and when Crabbe came in with the Leader and I curtsied Berthold came over to say hello or enlist my protection, and when I went back to my chair and the Holy Scriptures he curled around one of the chair legs and laid his head on my socks. The Leader and Mama and my stepfather were talking about what everyone talked about then, the war and the like, and Crabbe was silent. Or was he? I can't remember. Every once in a while I looked up from the Burning Bush or the Golden Calf and glanced at Crabbe and he glanced at me, and each time he was the first to lower his gaze, and I could have laughed, so proud was I that I could outstare those yellowish oblong eyes in their up-slanting pods, but I didn't laugh, and once when Mama served Crabbe a cognac, because that was the Leader's drink, he held out the glass in my direction and said, 'Your health,' and I, as if I were the one who had drunk it, began to choke. The Leader, whose story had been interrupted by my coughing, stood up and gave me orders: I was to lift my hands in the air while breathing out, but it didn't help and I kept hiccupping even after Mama gave me a sugar cube, and suddenly I saw a bestial face, Crabbe's, looming no more than a meter from mine – the sharp, uneven teeth jutting out at me and a silver statuette of Our Lady of Beauraing wrested from its home on the fireplace waiting to be flung at me – and heard a piercing, female shriek. Mama cried out, the Leader barked 'Crabbe!' and Crabbe set the statuette down. I didn't budge, didn't peep, but suddenly all the blood seemed sucked out of my body and I ran weeping to Mama, who comforted me. 'See?' said Crabbe. 'She's stopped hiccupping.' But because in his West Flemish dialect the word for 'hiccup' and 'sob' is the same, in other words, because he had ordained that I should stop sobbing, I started bleating with everything I had in me, which brought a growling Berthold, who had been following everything, to Crabbe's heels. Crabbe stretched a hand out, and Berthold snapped at it, though half-heartedly, and Crabbe shouted, 'Get back in your corner, you mangy cur!' his yellowish eyes – dog's eyes, I suddenly realized – shining, and Berthold panted his way back to his corner by the window, away from me. The Leader apologized for Crabbe, and my stepfather said, 'But it did help: the hiccups are gone, aren't they, Sandra?' But when I tried to get Berthold to go for his evening walk, he refused. And when Mama poked him, he just lay there, ears drooping, eyes shut. Crabbe stayed with us from that evening on, and the next day Berthold was still in his corner and would drink no water, eat no food. That afternoon I had to go to Bruges with Mama to try on my Communion dress, and while we were there we saw *Fra Diavolo* with Laurel and Hardy, and by the time we were back Berthold was no more: he'd gone mad while we were away, said my stepfather, and they'd had to shoot him. 'They' were Long Mittens and his sons, who were known for things like slaughtering hogs and taming and shooting dogs. A week passed, and I still didn't understand. Good old Berthold mad? The closest I could come to a mad animal was Mietje the goat the time he gobbled up all the geraniums, and no one shot him for it! They wouldn't shoot him even if he bit you. I hated Crabbe for having brought it on Berthold. Besides, I was just then beginning to sense how arid and false my life at Almout was. True, when left to my own devices, in the evening, in the bushes, I would subdue and tame: any number of weird animals that had retained their ice-age identities, the rustlings in the branches at twilight, the buzzings of the whole nocturnal world out to trap me. I gnashed my teeth, I wept, but I refused to give in. I mastered my anxiety, believe me, but I'd had it too easy, and what I had tamed and subdued was mine in the way the chapel and Berthold were mine: I was a part of it all. But now Crabbe was out, excluded. He was a monster and had nothing to do with the garden, the animals, the branches, a monster that had assumed human form, a soldier out to get me. In time I grew up and wasn't entirely helpless, though Mama and my stepfather abandoned me every day, she to her mirrors, he to his studio, where he lured the village children with sweets and ribbons and shooed them away once he'd finished with his picture-taking; no, I was always aware of being stronger than the people who gave me orders or petted me the way you pet a dog, and I grew up and made it into National Socialist girls auxiliary, the Dietse Meisjesscharen, and it wasn't long before they appointed me leader, because the girls were so ridiculously tame, but what was I to make of the marching orders: collective love for Folk and Fellowman?

I mean really. I was perfectly willing to give in and sink into an anonymous solitude, but it wasn't anonymous, it was all group, and a pitiful group at that, hustling and bustling not to be alone, not to be afraid. That was the period when Crabbe was at the house every day. He was there every day and I had no one else, Berthold and the emaciated old monk being gone, and though I did all I could to resist him, that vigorous, dangerous boy who drove dogs mad, a week later I loved him as I'd never loved anyone."

The teacher, who was more comfortable now, the sun having gone behind a spreading beech tree, asked whether it had lasted.

She had never betrayed him, she said. Not even now. Though there had been men, she said, men, conjuring up an illusive group with laws, flags, and slogans, but she had never let them near her. Well, almost never.

The teacher nodded and raised an eyebrow the way he did when he saw a lesson convulsively recited by heart grinding to a halt for want of comprehension.

"I swear," she said.

"That's not necessary," said the teacher.

"I can prove it," she said, her elbow grazing his chest as she pushed the glove compartment button and extracted an envelope from among the gloves, chocolate bars, and maps. It was stamped with an eagle and Gothic lettering. "There's a ring from Crabbe in here, and I've kept it all this time. The day I let a man come near me I'll put it on."

The teacher took the envelope – she made no attempt to stop him – and tore open one end. It was a rubber ring wrapped in cellophane. "Bravo," he said.

"I didn't think you'd open it," she said.

He gave the thing to the young woman, who put it back in the open envelope and stuffed it into the glove compartment. She then turned the ignition key, and they rode off in the direction of Almout. As they approached the castle, they could see ten or so people through the spikes of the high fence. They were standing by a ring of cars. "The guests have arrived," said Sandra.

"I don't want to go in yet," he said.

"I don't either," she said.

"Keep driving," he said.

For a moment or two she sat helpless in the rumbling car; then she stepped on the gas, drove back into the woods, and stopped. There was no one in sight. A jet fighter zoomed past overhead; a peacock screeched. He watched her looking out of the window even as she spoke and gesticulated frantically and whispered meekly, and he admired the cool, the air-conditioned room she maintained in herself in a sweltering city, yet said nothing but "Yes, Sandra. Right," and when her head, of which he could see only the coal-black chrysanthemum-cum-prickles and the net of specks formed by the white needles of the skin, came to rest on his belly, and her fingers, cool and thin, groped and dug, he sang; he sang while she silently performed her skillful job of love, her hand- and mouth-job, a mere game, and he sang "All the way to the cerebellum, Sandra" and pressed against the head as it moved, and pulled the finest hair in the world. With the leaden eyes of someone who has just looked into the sun and perceives everything as monochromatic and lacking in outline he saw her bewildered face again. Her mouth was making gluttonous noises, and she cleared her throat and rested her neck in his lap, her thighs crushed together, as if maimed, gazing up at his wonder-laden face. He placed his hand on her lips, and she chewed on his index finger. Shall I say thank you? he thought and, The first one to speak after sex is a moron, and he turned the radio on and started looking for a station, but she said "No," sat up, shook her head like a poodle in a drizzle, and ran her palm over her lips; then she looked in the rear-view mirror, smoothed her eyebrows with a wet finger, bared her perfect white upper teeth in a smile, and scratched her jaw with two fingernails, making a sound like a beetle in a matchbox.

The teacher, who felt no affection for her and could muster no tenderness – they were as distant as if she had been the central attraction at a masquerade ball for which he happened to have bought a ticket – said "Thank you" and watched the distance between them increase, the mist, the bad air thicken, and thought, *She is a stepping stone, a springboard to someone else*, and *This wasn't what I had in mind three days ago when she was standing there facing the sea*, and he realized that when she had bared her teeth it was not in a smile or even the liberating yawn-smile that follows a hard day's work. It was a stranger who, tense and reserved, went into reverse, made a U-turn, and headed back to Almout. Was he carsick? The chassis seemed to be shrinking, the steel plates coming closer; he even had the feeling that the unbreakable triplex-glass windshield had begun to melt at the edges. His rib cage swelled, then collapsed, then filled with water. The fields spread out like bumpy billiard-table-cloths that he was certain the car was going to slide off any second.

"I've never done that before," said the young woman.

He was on the point of saying It's about time, but pushed down on the seat under him instead and leaned his elbow against the door.

"Do you believe me?"

"I believe everything you say, Sandra. Always."

"That's nice of you," she said. And fell into thought. She waved at the passing farmers, tinkling the metal at her wrist. Then the car speeded up and he plunged both hands into his lap. Glory hallelujah! Sandra, Sandra!

"I loved Crabbe, and the things I did with him are of no business of yours. It made me stand out among all the goody-goodies at the convent school in Bruges. And when I had to stay home because of the bombing, I didn't know what to do with myself. I bit my nails and combed my hair in my room for hours on end; I listened to the Sondermeldungen with Mama and my stepfather and ran to meet the postman, but in vain. Then he was granted a special Urlaub because one of his friends had been shot down by the White Brigade and they hung the body on the Town Hall fence with a note pinned in his ear: 'A Kamerad of Crabbe's.' He was a different person. He would pace back and forth in the anteroom as if bees were after him, and cry, 'What can I do? I can't send them all to Germany, can I? Line them up against the wall in the marketplace? What do you expect me to do?' And I said, 'They're Walloons or Russians or Poles who've been hiding in the Ardennes and have just been rooted out and sent here.' Which is what I'd heard in the village. Ha! he laughed. Just like an old woman. He came back on three more leaves, and the last time he didn't say a word about the Ostfront no matter how much Mama and I pumped him. We had to watch what we ate when he was with us, because he was a stickler about rationing, and the time Mama served us ham and blood sausage from a clandestine slaughterhouse he refused to eat it and nearly bawled her out. On his last visit he had pimples on his eyelids and didn't say a word until the next to the last day, when he lit into Sprange, who was his batman, and we thought it was because he knew they couldn't hold out on the front much longer, and that was part of it, but the real thing was that Crabbe couldn't hold out against Crabbe. Was it his faith? In what? No. Crabbe had long since lost his faith in the Order or Flanders or the Third Reich, call it what you will, it had all kinds of names at the time. No. What Crabbe lost then, I think, was the thing he had always been, and that happened almost by chance and nobody could help him, I least of all: what did I know about him then?

He treated me badly, like a child you want to hurt, and when the last time he came I screamed and begged, 'Take me with you. You can say I'm eighteen and the leader of the Dietse Meisjesscharen and I want to be a nurse,' and he sneered and didn't say anything for a while, but then he took hold of me, bit me in the ear, and said, 'You know nothing, Sandie, nothing.' After which we lost him for good. The reports about the last days were far from pretty: Mr. Crabbe took it upon himself to defy Providence, or that's how I see it, the Providence that had allowed de Keukeleire's brain to be shattered in a little town in the north of France because a French officer had had too much to drink, that had allowed him, Crabbe, to execute women and hostages in the name of something he didn't believe in, something he alone had the weapons for, when he no longer knew what to do with himself, and nobody knows how it ended."

There were about fifteen men standing on the lawn, chatting in groups of three and four, waiting for a signal, and when the teacher and the young woman headed for the kitchen entrance they all looked in their direction, and one man moved away from the others and was about to speak when Sandra gave the teacher a poke in the back and they went through the kitchen – where two girls were quarreling near the sink – along the hallway with the woodcuts, up the stairs on the runner of wine-red coconut matting, past the life-size bronze statues of saints and militiamen, and into her room. They stayed there a half hour. The teacher awoke to her licking his neck, pushing the hair up with her tongue, and he stretched and watched her getting back into her clothes, jauntily, like a girl on the beach who feels the eyes of a group of sailors on her but has no wish to hide anything, confident as she is of having taken their breath away with such shameless beauty.

The twenty or so delegates downstairs had been moved to the veranda, and the teacher, who was introduced to them by Richard Harmedam as Dr. Heerema (doctor of jurisprudence!), shook hands with each of the moderately well-dressed gentlemen of forty-five or fifty, all of whom had the same well-trained grip. A somewhat run-down specimen with overly long hair claimed to have met Dr. Heerema in 1942 at the Kesterheide meeting, and when the teacher nodded nonchalantly the man gave an account of the extraordinary flag-waving ceremony that had taken place there. They all went into the assembly hall, the teacher in the wake of Richard Harmedam and Sandra. They all took their seats. A peasant girl, her eyes on the ground as if she had been ordered not to recognize their faces should she see them again, poured coffee.

Don't let me down, Sandra, I begged.

Sandra sat next to the teacher and kept her eye on him just as he kept his on her, and together they listened to the first speaker, a man with an artificial leg, who read out a list of statistics. Applause. The roll was called, and each man jumped up and said "Here" when he heard his name. Neither Sandra's nor Dr. Heerema's name was called. Then the smokers put out their cigarettes and a man with thick spectacles, a doctor (medical doctor) by the name of Dieter de Walsere, gave a eulogy, which everyone stood for. The doctor declared in stentorian tones that they had come together at the place where people still believe Flanders' fate was not completely sealed and that he was proud, as proud they all must be, that none of the faithful was missing – apart from Marcel Goossens, who had been recruited as an advisor to the Greek Army – and that this was a glorious occasion – sad, granted, but uplifting. The doctor's intonation was plaintive, and the teacher wondered whether he had composed the eulogy in blank verse. His attention wavered – the man in question had sacrificed his life that we might live – when Alice Harmedam came in. A corpulent woman getting on in years with short gray hair and purple eyes, she sat first on a chair by the door – which meant that the teacher could see only a third of her because there were three erect, soldierly men guarding it – then, as the doctor paused to take some newspaper clippings out of his briefcase, slipped between the chairs up to the front row and took a seat on the edge of a chair Sandra had saved for her. She did not recognize the teacher. The clippings that the doctor, Dieter de Walsere, read aloud were about the arrival of American tanks in the Dolomites, and the reader supplemented the brief, chronicle-like reports with remarks about Crabbe, whom he variously called He, The Commander, Our Comrade, Our Dearly Departed. According to him Crabbe had last been sighted in the vicinity of the Sindlsee when he was trying to blow up a number of boxes containing confidential documents and works of art hidden in a salt mine with bombs he had intercepted from the American Air Force. When he failed, because treachery and cowardice had everywhere gained the upper hand, even amongst his most trusted intimates [*sic*], he used flame-throwers to set fire to the paintings and sculptures of our age-old European legacy that had been placed under his protection, so that the victors found nothing more than five hundred gold napoleons belonging to the security division and (the audience had a good laugh) a receipt indicating that the general funds belonging to the intelligence and police divisions had been handed over to a salvage commando under the leadership of a major and a captain. The bespectacled doctor concluded his speech with a lyrical encomium for a man whose example and whose future must never die in our memory, and intoned "Farewell, My Brother!" The teacher sang along for the first four lines but did not know the rest of the words.

The coffee was cold by then. The teacher – everyone else was drinking it and mumbling to one another – was in good spirits. True, certain problems had raised their heads – where the boy had got to, why twelve of the twenty conspirators, veterans, trusted comrades, had been maimed in one or another fashion, why Sandra had jumped up in the middle of their foreplay and sat as if insulted on the edge of the bed, her chin resting on her collarbone like a rabbit whose neck has had a taste of the ax, meditating, trying to dredge something out of her memory, but he thought, "Later, later. I'm alive. There's an almost tangible faith in hope and love present at this gathering. How wonderful!" But the man who had provided the statistics raised his artificial leg, which as far as the teacher could tell was made of nickel or aluminum, and said glowingly that it was a nearly perfect piece of work and that it was only the Germans of course who could have produced hinges with the requisite flexibility. In all these years he had not had the slightest trouble with it.

The teacher replied that there were times when a person had to make sacrifices for an ideal. The man nodded and cited a few more statistics: the Fund had provided four wheelchairs, seventeen artificial arms, and eight artificial legs in the previous year, and year by year perceptible progress was being made. Especially in the pharmaceutical department.

"In the Netherlands," the teacher said, "we are still far behind in terms of solidarity and mutual assistance." The bespectacled doctor entered the conversation with a bitter remark to the effect that these were unsavory times. When the hordes were at the gate – when the time was right – no one had appreciated the sacrifices they'd made. And since then they'd been pilloried. Hadn't the Europe Ball put on by the Flemish Legion in Ghent last year been scandalously sabotaged by the authorities?

"You needn't be so bitter," said the teacher.

"And think of all those maimed where nothing shows!" whispered the man with the artificial leg.

"And the children," said the doctor. He raised his coffee cup as if it were a wine glass and pointed it in the direction of Richard Harmedam. "To our host!"

"He must be the one who suffered most," said the teacher, and the doctor recounted how Harmedam had been confined to a dog kennel at the entrance to the White Brigade's barracks for an entire week, and the guards would kick into the kennel, and after that Harmedam suffered from a split personality ("to use the medical term in vogue at the time").

"His brother?"

The doctor nodded. "His brother, a twin, died when he was eight months old. And he turned up again after all those years."

The old man, who was standing next to Sandra, gave them a smile: he knew they were talking about him. His wife held his hand between hers and was rubbing it warm. She was short and round and wore her gray hair pulled back: a kind schoolmistress presiding over a school dance. Only the purple irises bespoke a life beyond the banter of the salon. Had she taken tranquilizers? Definitely. The teacher sensed Alessandra Harmedam making an occasional attempt to catch his eye, but he had ruled out all contact between them: he had only a few minutes to determine what had upset, disturbed, disconcerted her before he fell asleep in the four-poster bed with the satin sheets.

The old man came up to him and said, "Are you ready? Everyone is very curious."

Jubilant, the teacher watched himself, a man of ice about to toss a torch onto a field of ice men, take a last gulp of coffee, stand deep in thought, and, after a few moments, raise his head and say a silent "Yes."

"Excellent," said the old man, and clapped his hands. Amidst the scraping of shifting chairs he announced that Dr. Heerema from Groningen, who had made the trip to Almout just for this occasion and who, as they all doubtless were aware, had published an extremely well documented work on the Pan-Netherlands movement in Holland and Belgium and was soon to follow it up with an essay dealing primarily with the Leader and Crabbe, would now say a few words about this new project. Applause. Silence. They coughed and sat waiting. Crossed their legs. Looked up at him.

What was the boy up to in the innkeeper's tentacles? The teacher, with a hint of panic in his eyes at the thought of what the boy was going through as a result of the totally futile adventure he had dragged him into (forgetting that the opposite was actually the case), glanced over at Sandra, who may have recognized his indecision and interpreted it in her own way – What had wounded her? the teacher wondered – and speaking for the first time, which caught the audience, obviously unaccustomed to hearing her voice, unawares, she said, "May I propose that the talk be postponed until after dinner?" and smiled an artless smile at the sight of their wonder. "It's my soufflé," she said, turning to feminine wiles. "I'm afraid it will fall, and I've spent the whole day over a hot stove."

"Why of course," said the old man. "Gentlemen . . ." But his voice and superfluous explanation were drowned out by the reactions of the hungry men: "Good idea." "We're in need of a break." "Then we don't need to . . ." "For a soufflé I'd be only too happy to . . ."

The teacher (saved? no, annoyed) could think of no excuse to have the boy called for, and while members of the Association swarmed around Sandra she, as if having expected him to grovel at her feet in gratitude for having delayed his humiliation, turned the now familiar vertebrae, folds, and birthmarks of her back on him. He stood there listening to a man who introduced himself as van de Walle, Third Army, for life, who promised to send him the records of his regiment: they might come in handy.

Fredine

(18 NOVEMBER)
The man who gave me his jacket out in the field when I had that cramp, he knew what he was doing, friends: the elbows have worn thin and the pocket linings are torn to bits. Or didn't he think about the fact that he was giving away a threadbare jacket. Why did he do it, the good Samaritan? I'll never know. Would I give my jacket to a naked, shivering man? Half my jacket, like Saint Martin? Yes.

There's a pisser with prostate trouble behind my back. Pain, grimace, pressure, feet shuffling off. Never have I been so dependent on others. Who aren't even others. Because the voice I hear calling out to the child, "Soup's on, Ka-rel-tje" is mine. And I'm the one dragging my feet and applying pressure and pumping that stinging thing over and over. I'm totally ensconced in my soledad sonora. I buzz, a wavelength. And meanwhile I turn my lens on what my tale is meant to be, and in fact a story complete with adjectives and choice illuminations is emerging. The story was not like that. From the outset I was surrounded, beleaguered by the mastiffs strategically positioned for battle, and from the outset I was in the position of a hedgehog without quills except for my arms, which I kept stretching in all directions while they, the dogs, yelped and snapped though they remained invisible to the end.

There's a woodworm in the room. And two gray flies. They shove their tiny proboscises into my jacket sleeve. A rat – the worst creature on earth after man – I have yet to see. But something rat-sized must be lurking in the airshaft or between the shaft and the drainpipe to the right of the wall bed: there's an occasional scraping noise coming from it. Unless Korneel has set up an observation post there. I haven't spoken in forty-eight hours. One can probably forget how. Or is the crocodile the worst creature on earth after man? I'll have to look it up in the teachers' library, in the *Larousse illustré*. The pink pages I used to read. With their Latin expressions: *Quis poterit habitare de vobis cum igne devorante?* What were you thinking? Just now. That your notebook was full and you'd submitted it to Korneel, which meant your file was closed and you'd shake hands and could go back to the teachers' library? Well, that's what Korneel promised. Something of the sort. Wh

Half an hour ago the electricity went off. What was *Wh* going to be? *Wh*en? *Wh*y? *Wh*ether to stay awake? The whole damn place was in an uproar. Moaning and groaning. An old man on the second floor shouted, "Not again! They do it on purpose!"

She came in after scratching on the door panel. Even with my eyes shut, in the dark, I recognized her by her metallic smell. The old biddy wasn't carrying a lamp, no, or food either.

"They're making some repairs. Korneel thinks it's a general black-out."

"Oh."

"Right, and he says to me, 'Go and find out.' Well, I don't give a hoot, as you see. He'd have a fit if he knew I was here."

"Oh."

"What's wrong?"

"Nothing."

"You didn't even say hello when I came in. It's not nice."

"What have you come for?"

"Hey! Where's your manners? (Gently chiding): You're not going to get rude on me like the others, are you? They think they can push me around 'cause I haven't been to school like the rest of the staff, but I've got as much say as them, believe me. (Gentle but malicious): One word from me to Korneel and you're in for it. That you're jumpy. Or you kicked me. And bam! you're on the scrubbing toilets list. Or the shock list. Wouldn't want that now, would you." (Electrodes on temples. Three tenths of a second, if they get it right, twenty volts through the brain, and suddenly you're comatose. Then thirty seconds of convulsions. Then you just sit there, dazed, and ten minutes later you're still out of it but blissful. And a half hour after that you could eat a horse.)

"No, Fredine."

"That's better."

"It's darker here than anywhere else in the building. Do you like being in the dark? I do. But you're just like little Willy, who starts screaming as soon as it gets dark."

"I don't scream when it gets dark."

"No, but you do scream. And you know it's forbidden. They've told you, all right: 'Start in again and it's under the shower with you.' And you keep doing it."

"They don't put little Willy under the shower."

She laughed. "But they will a grown-up. (Suddenly serious): Not that I don't understand why. Still, you better watch out."

She was sitting by the window, no light, curled up, knees tucked under. A dark smell. She went to the door, locked it.

"What's wrong with me? How could I have forgotten?"

"I'm not running away."

"No, but just in case. Who'd pay for it? Fredine. No matter what happens, it's always my fault."

"If I ran away, I'd phone and say you had nothing to do with it."

"Good." She stroked my hand and leaned her stomach against the table. She stroked my hair the wrong way, back, in the security of the dark.

"You have such gentle hair. Feel mine. Hard, eh?"

"Yes."

"What are you laughing for? It's nothing to laugh about."

"I'm not laughing."

"Yes, you are. I can feel it. Don't think I don't know." Her finger ran along the corner of my mouth, along my laughing lips. "See?"

"I was laughing because I don't even know your last name." (Because I had so many names – at school, with Elizabeth, at Almout, and none of them was mine.)

"Van de Sompel . . . You still laughing?"

"No."

"Yes you are. I can feel it . . . You're not from these parts, are you. You talk like my sister's husband, and he's from Limburg."

"No, I'm from Roeselare."

"Your card says Waregem."

"That's where I was born, but my parents were living in Roeselare."

"What do you think of me? Tell me. Don't I do a good job? If I didn't say so just now, would you know I never had an education?"

"No."

"Do you realize you couldn't say a word when you came here?

Korneel says you're a school teacher, but he's always making things up to keep us from getting close to the guests. Are you a school teacher?"

"Yes."

"So it's true. And in the middle of class you began to scream."

"Who, me?"

"Yes. And your wife just happened to be at school. On the playground. She's the one who brought you here in a taxi. But she hasn't once come to see you. That's odd."

"Yes."

"You're so quiet. I like it when people are quiet."

"Tell me more, Fredine. What did she say, my wife, when I came here?"

"I don't know. I don't know. That's Korneel's business. All I did was bring you in, wash you from head to toe, comb your hair, give you a shot, and talk to you. But after a while you started shouting off and on so we brought you here, because you couldn't afford a first-class room and all the other rooms were occupied."

"Are they still?"

"No." She pushed her groin against the table, very near him, and scratched her head. There was electricity in her hair. Her hard hand – it was cold and seemed made of rubber yet also of wood – strayed into my collar and over my shoulder-blade.

"You're trembling."

But it was her voice that was trembling.

"It's awful being here all by yourself for days on end, isn't it? Look, don't be so shy. I won't eat you up. Don't stop me."

I knew for a fact that the reason she was talking so loud was that Korneel was there between the airshaft and the drainpipe with his tape recorder. I didn't stop her.

"Nobody can see us. Isn't that nice? Nobody in the whole place."

I wouldn't touch her as long as the room smelled of metal. Then there was a knock at the door, at the height of the middle horizontal board.

"Hey, anybody there?"

"Yes," I said.

"Where's the key?"

"Isn't it in the keyhole?"

"No."

There was a fiddling in the lock.

"You by yourself?"

"Yes."

"Seen Fredine?"

"No."

"Don't move. There's a blackout in the street. There's no reason to . . ."

The voice trailed off.

"I better be going," she said. "I'll come back. If you want. You do, don't you? You see? I thought so. You're all the same, you men."

"Then don't come."

"No need to get all hot and bothered, but it's true. I'll put the light out when I come back. Okay?"

"It doesn't matter."

"Yes it does."

The light has come back on, and I'm back at my word games, a silent, deserted, immobile country fair. No circle ever gets round this way. Even if you stand in the center and draw crisscrossing spirals, nothing radiating from that center is anything but suspicion and loss. Her voice in the darkness was awkward, hard to take, different from the cheerful, hearty voice she used when bringing me my coffee and bread every day. It is still brooding in the room, ready to soar.

I've got to get out of here, Korneel. To the city, the Hazegras with its sailors and women, the man-of-war *Antoinette*, the bustle in the cafés, the jumbled streets of a below-sea-level port, a Belgium under the radar, under spinning comets and satellites.

Outside, Elizabeth is walking a terrier on a leash, talking to a woman about a tailor-made suit, unaware of my existence. Should I have bought her a television set right after we got married? Heavy winds.

(STILL 18 NOVEMBER)

An alarm clock has gone off. Everyone hears it; no one is immune. I can hardly read the paper anymore. The headlines run together. Induction, Eduction, Education. And I am too rushed to describe things, Korneel, too wound up to note things. Forgive me. I am not a shed that buzzes softly, infrangible, immobile, like a shed under a pylon: no entrance. I would like to be such a shed with instructions nailed to the wall and all kinds of apparatus, useful, used. But I am a man who has embarked upon a journey and wishes to give an account of it, a man who is in my way, he and his journey: a fifth wheel. Nor am I the car any longer, though I keep rattling on. This rumination on demand, Korneel, it has gone too far. This supplicatory twaddle will no longer do. In due time. Always: in due time.

The odor of boiled cabbage wafts through the corridor and under my door into the hole.

Her voice (recognizably West Flemish, peasant class, poor peasants who complained even when during the war they bought four or five pianos and hid twelve radios and twelve fur coats under the bed) jerky, hoarse, as if about to bark: "My sister was like your wife or you, I don't know which; anyway, she didn't want children. But whether she did or didn't, she had to because her husband was home all the time. Because he was on the dole and she took in sewing. She was good at sewing. She'd been at it since her days on the farm. But she was always behind: it was her three kids. It's as plain as the nose on your face. One day she showed me her stomach. It was all blue. Sometimes it went up to her face too. It was all those days at the sewing machine. But she said to me, 'Fredineke,' she said, 'the baby' – it was her last – 'is dead inside me.' 'You really think so?' I said. 'I'm positive,' she said. 'Come to the doctor with me.' So we go together, and the doctor says, 'You're crazy.' And four weeks later she says, 'Come with me, Fredineke,' and we go back. 'Don't be silly,' the doctor says. 'I know better than you, and I tell you there's nothing wrong, not with you or the baby.' 'But I'm positive!' she shouted, and the doctor shouted 'No!' much louder, but then he said, 'All right, I'll tell you what. Come with me.' X-rays. And two days later when the plates were developed, you know what they showed. You should have seen his face. 'Yes, Madame,' he says, 'you're right. The baby's dead inside you.' What do you think of that? She was glad, of course, but sad too; I guess she didn't know what to make of it. Well, he gave her a shot and out it came, and guess what: it had no arms or legs. Right. It was all those days at the sewing machine: her arms and legs moved the most. 'That's got nothing to do with it,' the doctor said, but it's as plain as the nose on your face . . ."

Silence. Stop it. I was afraid the light would suddenly go on and I would see her face, the face of an ancient storyteller. I said that Korneel was looking for her; she said she would be back soon and turned the key in the lock, on the other side of the door this time. I'm safe and sound, once more in the saddle, at the table with the fish smell. Everything can happen to me again. I've scratched out the label on the notebook for the umpteenth time. The last was: A Tale. Modest, pleasant. Simply: A Tale. The first was: This Is My Notebook.

I've pasted a new label on it. Blank. My name below: Dr. Heerema. In a handwriting I wonder at recognizing.

Up on the wall behind me and to my left the name of Crabbe appears twenty-four times.

Once for each day.

I wish they'd finally give me today's paper. I keep trying to get it. Things are happening, and I'm left out. I ruminate. Even while grazing, while my life as Dr. Heerema was taking place, I was ruminating. Each move I make is considered, each word noted the moment it escapes my cork palate, read out as if from a blackboard.

Somebody sneezes and at the same time I hear the snot drop onto the floorboard, and if I write down: onto the floorboard dropped . . .

We left Haakebeen's Lumber Center that evening feeling guilty under the sodium lamps that gave us guilt masks, and she stopped me and said, "Not so fast, sir," and pointed to a stripe of congealed blood running along her thigh and looking like a fat vein. And we went into a café in the Hazegras district, yes, at that late hour, a teacher with a pupil, as everyone could see, and everyone meant sailors, all with identical brutal faces, just as the Canadian soldiers had identical faces when they descended on our city and sold us chocolate, condoms, capstans, and blankets (which our womenfolk used to make into coats). Unrecognizable faces leaving no trace on the memory. After cooing in the overwhelming odor of the wood for half an hour and luring me into her absurd game, she was now giving me light-hearted, breezy, treacherous smiles under the eyes of collusive sailors just as she gave me a defiant smile when she got an "Excellent" on her German exam and an embarrassed smile the next afternoon when we ducked into a house under construction and climbed over the loose beams and the freshly laid brick walls, squatted amidst the detritus, fell into the piles of Rhine sand, lay against the sacks of cement, and when I asked her to marry me she gave me a nasty bite in the upper lip "so I can see it tomorrow, in class."

It is not out of the question that Sandra Harmedam will have a child by me. Je sème à tout vent. First of all, up in her room she was playing with a rubber she had extracted from a torn envelope with sealing wax and a stamp and then from its cellophane wrapper. She'd had it since just after the war. She asked me whether I thought it was "dead," and we finally blew into it and tossed it into the wastepaper basket, where anyone could see it – the chambermaids and maniacs waiting for us downstairs at their meeting. Soon she'll be having a child by me. It would make me happy, I who have no watch, no glasses left, who can't even get today's newspaper; it would be something tangible, something of myself and of an other, something unruly but not so ephemeral as this notebook, something like the tennis ball, soft and frayed and threadbare, lying here on the table before me, its nap like fur.

Rumors

The boy who is my messenger and guide, who has led me from disgrace to scandal – and how eagerly I trod the path from my room in the hotel to the siege by hairy, bare-teethed hounds – expects nothing as he stands there watching till I'm wide awake, his hands pressing his buttocks as if to hide a hole in his trousers, and says reproachfully that he's been awake for ages. We've got to go downstairs, is what he means. That bastard of an innkeeper is waiting to be paid. "How are we going to pay him?" I ask.

"We're not," says Verzele. "Not a sou." He has a scratch on his right cheek, pointy ears, straggly hair. "Nobody in this backwater shithole can lift a finger against us, believe me, because they know we're expected at the castle and Madame Alice runs everything. Isn't that great?" He grins: never having heard of trust, devotion, governance, laws, or services, he is unscathed, he spins his own webs. Though untouched by strontium 90, he is a child of another race than the teacher, a mutant. True, the genes are still fermenting in his blood and he has no gray hair, no eczema, but that comes later. In *his* children.

He outstares me, just as he has throughout the trip, waiting until I tire of looking at him, just as in class I get sick of keeping my eye on the beasts and gaze out of the window, soiled by playground dust, at a solitary sparrow, a branch waving in the wind. Smelling of the clammy handkerchief he's just wiped his forehead with, he tickles my feet. As we go downstairs, he shamelessly pokes me in the back, keeping to himself what he's thinking: What can a person who can do everything and a person who dares do nothing have in common?

At the table, spread with a red-and-black-checked cloth on which the innkeeper sets out his cheese and jam sandwiches and glasses of milk and cups of coffee, Verzele crosses himself and starts eating without waiting for me and with a voracity I find alarming. When the innkeeper goes down into his cellar, I whisper, "Do you think he'll just let us go?"

With a mouth so full his cheeks were round he said, "Sure, of course."

"Why?" No, I don't ask that. "Are you positive?"

"I just told you so, didn't I?" he mumbles impatiently, and then louder – I have no idea how he has the nerve to snap at me so nastily, so indignantly; I suspect some sort of ruse, a stratagem to slip away – "Hey, what's up? You scared?"

"No."

"Oh yes you are. I can see it in your eyes. You're scared shitless, Mr. Lard."

"What?"

"What are you calling him now?" the innkeeper asks, content.

"None of your business."

"Tsk, tsk, tsk," goes the innkeeper, all smiles.

The boy is on his guard. The innkeeper goes over to the jukebox. A German operetta aria starts playing.

"Lard?"

"I'm not the one who says it; it's the others, the classy people. It's the classy people who give names, and they call you 'lard' because you're as smooth and sticky as lard spread on bread."

"Me?"

"Yes, you."

I nibble on a piece of bread. Some jam drips onto my hand.

"You're scared," says the boy. "Du hast die Eier gefroren."

"He hasn't got any balls to freeze off," says the innkeeper.

"If you got a slap in the face, you'd keep your mouth shut," says Verzele.

"Just you try, Verzele," I say hoarsely. He shrugs.

"You're strong in school because there you're the boss . . ."

"We're not in school now."

A German march. The two of them sing along. What's this game they're playing? The innkeeper makes the next move or, rather, series of inter-related moves designed to strengthen the web.

"There was an article in the paper about this artist who took a boy to Italy. They were gone four months."

"Didn't see that one," muttered the boy.

"Got eighteen months, the artist. Because he kidnapped the boy, the paper says. He was trying to clean the boy's father out with the ransom."

"Clean him out?" said Verzele with a sneer.

"Right, snotnose. That's what it said in the papers."

Some farmers come in. "Hello, Trach." "Hello, Bertrand." "Hello, Bogger." "Hello, everybody."

The ice-cream man blows his horn outside. I give the boy some money. He licks, I lick, the innkeeper licks.

(The splendid, splendiferous counter was made of nickel and marble and had a molding of ochre and moiré and light blue. No one was allowed to come too close, let alone leave fingerprints. My parents are sitting in the burning dunes, which the ebullient sea so pummels, assaults, and invades with its foam-capped waves that it will soon reach and devour all human life ensconced there, including my two younger brothers – spades, cherry-red paper hats, and all. The sound of the sea enters a place where so much ice cream is sold that the entire population is well supplied and licking away. "Be quick," said Mother, "and don't talk to anyone." The place is an amusement park, and everybody wants more ice cream. Why didn't my father come with me? He didn't feel like it. I can't see him anymore from this gigantic glass cage, but he's still there behind the tops of the shore grass with his trouser-legs rolled up over his white legs and his fiery red hair. Six girls on roller-skates have stopped in front of the counter and are stamping their dangerous metal feet all around me; they are much bigger than me and waving their arms in the air. The counter is level with my eyes. I lift my hand, which is clutching a one-franc coin, over it. If you put a piece of paper over a one-franc coin and rub a pencil over it, you get a picture of two black snakes, and then you can easily cut around it and paste it in a notebook: I've got pages and pages full. The woman behind the counter doesn't hear me.

"One, please."

"Just a second, little boy."

Everybody's got an ice cream but me. That big, scary woman is spreading the yellowish, sugary, lickable, cool, sticky, gooey ice cream over checkered wafers for everybody. Except me.

"One, please, ma'am."

"What size?"

"For one franc, ma'am."

She makes unround balls with her spatula and presses them between the wafers and hands them over my head to someone behind me. The roller-skaters are gone, and a fat policeman is licking his four-colored treat.

"All right, now, little boy. What size?"

"For one franc, ma'am."

She's wearing ice-cold clothes, and an ice-cold wind is blowing from behind the counter, and she has ice-cold red fingers, and looking at *me and only me* she rattles off something in a language I've never heard before: "Polonaise vanilla chocolate sherbet pistachio meringue strawberry."

"I don't know, ma'am."

I'll never understand that language, so I just point to a dome-like green mass in the container, but she starts in again in that language, and I run as fast as I can through the wide-open door into the boiling heat of the out-of-doors, bawling.)

The farmers Trach and Bogger ask after our health. I say it depends on how you look at it. The boy has fallen asleep, his head on his forearm. The innkeeper says through the marches that they'll be staying for some time in the village, the friends of the castle. Bogger or Trach says there are a lot of people at the castle, more than last year maybe. And what for? For a man as dead as a doornail.

"For all I care they could have strung him up in the marketplace. I wouldn't have taken my eyes off my cards. After all the misery we went through with that bastard."

"You don't know shit about politics."

"Cut the crap, will you? After all I did in forty-five. I hid at least ten Blacks on our farm!"

"'Cause you were scared they'd set it on fire if you didn't!"

"So what. Did I help or didn't I?"

"True."

"Crabbe and his ideas about how people would change! Well, have we changed or haven't we?"

"We have."

"But not because of him."

"Those 'three classes' of his! Blind as a bat he was."

"The nobility, the clergy, and the bourgeoisie."

"No, Roland, you've got it wrong. The Party, the Army, and the Workers Front."

"What about us? Didn't we have anything to say about it?"

"The 'new spirit.' He couldn't see farther than his nose, that Crabbe. What was it he said? We were the laborers of the earth and the world was a machine marching forward, something still in need of shaping and forming, but not for us, no, for the future. What a load of crap! What he meant was we should slave away and give up meat not only today and tomorrow but for years and years, till we were ready to drop."

"Right. Remember? We were going to turn into a whole new caliber of men. Revitalize ourselves. Remember? For the Promised Land . . ."

"No, no, Roland. For Pie in the Sky . . ."

"And work ourselves to death for it?"

"Ha."

"That's not what he said. Listen, damn it . . ."

"No, no, no, you two. You're going too far."

"Look, sir. Here you are, going to the castle like it's a funeral or something. What are you after, anyhow? You want us all to follow the priests and give up this life for another?"

"He's not saying."

"He's right."

"All we want is peace and quiet. We seen it all, been through it all. Don't worry. The priests will tell us how to save our souls. So what if the country ends up in the hands of the Americans? Rather have the Russians?"

"Six of one, half dozen of the other."

"Stop this."

"And you want to play the martyr? Fine, then pay the consequences. Crabbe wanted to be a hero. Well, now that the worms have done their job on him he is one. The end. Fini la musique."

"It's all well and good for the castle people: they can talk their way out of anything; they can win elections and make fortunes. But what do we get out of it?"

"And if it's not Whites and Blacks, it's Blues and Reds. There'll always be different opinions, sir, don't you think?"

"He's not saying, Trach."

"No, he's not, Bogger, and he knows why."

"Luckily there are other people with other ways of thinking," said the innkeeper, "right here in Hekegem."

"Thinking? Thinking what? You saw what happened. The Leader thought for us, instead of us, and what did we get for it? Go on, say it."

"Nonononono."

"Yes."

"You know what you sound like? A puppet of big business."

"Cut the crap, will you?"

"I can just see you when it starts in again. Coming to my farm for a kilo of butter or a ham!"

"You've changed a lot since you went hawking *Volk en Staat* in your black boots after Sunday Mass."

"Yes, the gentleman here belonged to the elite, the ten percent."

"The ten percent with the power, authority, and money. And we had to kiss their boots."

"Everyone had to toe the line, everyone," said a farmer with a gray, bloated face and small mustache, "and if you didn't you kept your mouth shut. Everyone was in on it."

The jukebox was roaring. The boy failed to wake up; the teacher failed to brighten up. Then Sandra blew her horn outside. I abandoned the boy: he was clever enough, I thought, to keep from giving whatever it was they expected of him.

The boy, who'd said before heading off that night, "I'll be glad to be back at school," said later, sitting on the bed with the creaky joints, then lying with his head slightly lower than the pillow and looking anxious and infantile: "Madame Alice married the old man because she was blinded by his financial schemes. And because her father looked up to "the man from the castle" and made her. If she'd known what he was like, she would later say, she'd have beaten it to the mountains. Because even now he made her fast and she was forbidden meat and had to look upon Crabbe as her son. Understand? And having Alessandra didn't make him the least bit happy. Until she told him, which was true, that her real father, the man who made the child, was de Keukeleire, who was murdered in France. Then he cheered up, the old man. And now that the people in the area don't dare send their children to Almout anymore, she has to be his model and let him take pictures of her. There's nothing she can do about it, she says, and letting him take pictures of her every day is like letting him suck her backbone dry. But she can't run away from Almout: she's too old and she's got no money and she's lost her nerve. She was game once, when Crabbe swore he would take her with him, away from Richard, because when they won the war Crabbe and all his officers would be given an estate the size of a province and he promised her he would choose the estate in Poland where she'd lived as a little girl, and they would cordon off the whole province with barbed wire and run it all by themselves, and she would live with him there as if she were his birth mother. But nothing came of it. The last time he was in Flanders he was half his former weight, and he wasn't heavy to begin with. And he swallowed pills all day long and couldn't stop trembling. Couldn't sleep either: he told Madame Alice he had seen hell, the gates of hell had opened, and he would lie there weeping in her lap, in the lap of Madame Alice.

"The shock of it did her in, because all of a sudden he was another man, a Crabbe no one had ever seen before, a Crabbe who could hardly keep on his feet. What had he seen? Hundreds of children dancing around a wooden tower with glass windows, and the ones who weren't dancing were sitting on wooden horses that couldn't turn because they had no motors. And when Crabbe and his officers walked past checking whether the Red Cross nurses were doing an honest job of distributing the hard biscuits, they saw the children fighting over them, but they didn't stop dancing as they fought because somebody high up had ordered them to dance and they turned and turned till they dropped before they could bite into their biscuits. Because they weren't allowed to until later. Then came inspection and they helped one another up and pushed one another into line, and they all had to wave their biscuits at Crabbe and his officers and shout Auf Wiedersehen. He went back three days later on his own, Crabbe did, and he said not a single child was alive, and it was after that he couldn't eat, he could only take pills." (The boy had a tic that made him laugh soundlessly: the left-hand corner of his mouth would go up, his left eye stretch to the side, and his jaws chew on air.) "He couldn't keep anything down, poor thing: whatever he ate those first few days came right back up. Even his officers noticed. Madame Alice had forced him to go back to the Eastern Front that last time, but she got five telegrams asking where he was and they never saw him in Russia again. He had deserted, but they didn't dare make it public at the time, of course: the White Brigade propaganda machine would have gone to town with it. Where he disappeared to, God only knows. Madame Alice says the shock did her in, seeing him that time, the man of iron who mowed down Russians without a second thought. "He'd faced up to it" is how she put it. Anyway, she had Sprange summoned to the castle, but he refused to say a thing about Crabbe because the war was still on and he didn't want to snitch on his comrade and fellow officer, and after the war he held his tongue because the concentration camps were all over the papers and he was sure he'd be implicated, and then, by way of atonement, he made all the statues in the garden. It took him seven years and set him back half a million, people say. Alessandra is the only one who believes Crabbe is still alive, says Madame Alice; she's as stubborn as a mule organizing those yearly meetings and ceremonies at the cemetery, and what can Madame Alice do but atone and let Richard take her picture. And that's only right because as a mother, I mean, being a mother, she's had such troubles, if you know what I mean . . ."

Then I went into the house with you, my stubborn beast of a Sandra, up the steps and not on tip-toe, no, in the sunlight, in full view of the delegates mumbling to one another on the lawn. You walked ahead of me though your good upbringing should have taught you otherwise, given that a gentleman is then obliged to keep his eyes on the lady's legs, but that new taste in your mouth made you impatient, and I followed you, with a lump in my throat, that globus hystericus that holds back tears. For me too it was so long ago. Your room was mine then. Approaching Crabbe, I wandered through his belongings; following Crabbe (and preceding him, in case he should turn up again), I fondled your buttocks under the silk's peacock eyes. There was a flag with the lion of Flanders standing in the corner and a pennant of Verdinaso tacked to the wall above the wardrobe whose mirror contained two strangers, a slender woman with red cheeks and a teacher I could not see clearly without my glasses. They were clutching each other's hands, like hostages before an execution. You were taller than I even though you had kicked your shoes off by then; your shoulders were as square as mine though higher and narrower. You kept staring at yourself while I knelt, and I could hear your teeth clicking against one another, chattering, and see your face in that treacherous spy of a mirror, the close-set eyes, the cold, hungry look. Say "Crabbe" out loud, I ordered, and you repeated it several times over. I underwent a metamorphosis. A quadruple seagull cry filled the hollows of my brain, my ears shrank, the lobes sank, and a bar took shape in my eyebrows, a bar that neither weakened nor wrinkled at the bridge of my nose.

The corners of my lips are turning down. I am becoming Mongolian, and I bite.

In the Rapeseed Field

Remember that at the time in question the countryside is completely yellow with rapeseed and not a single farm has a television antenna. The anti-aircraft artillery has been dismantled, though now and then a farmer is surprised to come upon a lone machine-gun that had been mounted on one of trucks accompanying the retreating army. The young men hide in the rabbit hutches or chicken coops or in the ditches while the rest of the population watch the last of the Feldgrau soldiers pass. They are mostly amputees or Slav auxiliary troops and all but weaponless. They have our farm horses, and some are riding tireless bicycles. Look, Grandma! There goes one in a beach cart. Peddling gaily. They beg for and are given bread and fruit. Nobody knows whether the Atlantic Wall will hold, but everybody hopes it won't: we've had enough of the invaders, and as soon as the dust settles behind the army trucks tricolors start hanging outside the windows. A distant thunder clap, an eruction from Heracles' stomach, announces the first Allied tanks. Our snipers are audible as well. Tak, tak, tak – their stengun bullets hit the birch trunks. Naturally there are bottlenecks at the bridges, and most of the bridges have been dynamited, but we're not afraid our village will be cut off from the rest of the world; no, damn it; even after four years we've got supplies to spare, believe you me. Now you see that young man with the long curly hair who's suddenly our center of attention, the one standing in the middle of the street hugging another young man who's also wearing a woman's wig and white overalls, well, we've been liberated, and they – Gustie Zeekers and Poepe Lammers, as anyone can tell – were in hiding right here in the local orchards, and we didn't even know. See? They're disappearing again and we're cheering them on. Oh, they're going back into hiding because, alarm, we've been too hasty with our cries of victory; quick, quick, pull the flags back in: new regiments of the retreating army are passing through the village, younger soldiers this time, but crack troops; quick, get indoors. And when we come together on the playing field to talk over the situation and what to do about it, the notary shoos us away: "It's too early. You'll have plenty of time to celebrate. Our tanks are khaki-colored, with a white star. And don't you forget it." So we run home, and only one person lingers along the railway tracks: a nun. She has hollow cheeks, and if we saw her up close, we would realize she has powdered them. Her gait, while not brisk, does not drag: she takes broad strides, and suddenly – we have a good view of her from our windows – she is moving along wondrously fast for a nun, even one in mortal danger, and before we can say "Why, it's a Sister of Charity!" she has disappeared. Later a Polish soldier peering out of his tank turret sees her running through the grain and makes a friendly remark, to which she raises the hand holding her rosary and blesses him like a priest, and he crosses himself and sets his colossus, an armored toad with two trunks and a single bronze hair, back in motion.

The nun is resting behind a hawthorn bush. She soaks her callused and blistered heels and hairy ankles in a pool of stagnant water near a stream. She pays no heed to the mosquitoes. She dries her feet with grass. She has a scratch below her left knee, and she dabs it with the tip of a handkerchief monogrammed A.H. A while later she pares an apple with a silver dagger decorated with Oriental motifs. As for us, after throwing the fugitive head teacher's bookcases, wardrobes, buffet, mattresses, and family portraits out of the windows of his house and putting a match to them, we are dancing around the fire. The nun is sighted for a moment in the flames but then forgotten, so quickly does her apparition dissolve. Our bedrooms shake in the thunder of the giant tanks, and we are happy for the next few days. Our radio crackles away, and we see Hitler – now that a caustic pen is drawing him in the one-page newspapers with new names circulating among us – being torn to bits by the Bulldog, the Cock, the Bear, and our own

Lion. Someone points out to the nun that she has passed a convent without crossing herself. We learn to make omelettes out of powder. The new warriors' melodies are crooned and sweet. The warriors themselves are loath to salute their officers and saunter through the streets with their hands in their pockets. One night the nun breaks into the house of an old woman living alone – Tjampens, Cecilia – and steals a rabbit, six eggs, and an umbrella, after which she disappears from our midst like a bolt of lightning, but the vice-chairman of our Carrier Pigeon Association is out in his jeep one evening near Bruges on the route to Knokke, and what does he see in the light of his head-lamps but a skinny, dirty woman in rags that the vice-chairman claims put him in mind of a nun's habit. The woman stops the jeep and makes to climb in the back seat, but just then a gust of wind tears off her kerchief and out come wisps of gray hair half a finger in length. The woman gives a start and after a moment's hesitation runs off through a stubble field and behind a farm.

We hear the names of the members of our new government and think them worthy of office, rationing will soon be lifted to the regret of those who live off it, there are squabbles among the various factions of the Resistance – all this takes some getting used to. We're doing our best. At the same time we hear – and the oral testimonies of eyewitnesses reach us faster and in greater detail than radio reports – that in an apple orchard near Heernem a raggedy old woman has been struck by lightning, which was probably attracted by her zipper, and it turned out, when they took her to the shed put up on the school playground to serve as the Heernem prison, that she was a man. What we don't know is whether she was Crabbe, because the face was burnt to a crisp. And the next day the body was hauled away by two New Zealand soldiers, or at least two men dressed as New Zealand soldiers.

Crabbe's Presence

Sprange, who came up to me when we were heading for the kitchen door and had waved while standing among the delegates as they discussed the reason for the interruption of his story (Sandra and me); Sprange, who after five steps realized we were ignoring him, and paused by the rose bushes under two identical round heads, like garden statues in living flesh – Sprange had lied: he had not known Crabbe before the Westphalian army camp. That is what Richard Harmedam said.

"Then what was he going on about when he said he saw Crabbe come to Almout after his trip to France?" I asked impatiently.

Richard Harmedam scratched his crotch for a long time and said, "The lad does nothing but lie. From the word go. Believe it or not, he told us he'd studied under Kolbe and Arno Breker! And we fell for it!

I don't know how interested you are in sculpture, but the moment Madame Harmedam and I saw Sprange's first maquettes we realized what was going on. Breker, Kolbe! I mean, really! He's not fit to lick their boots!"

Oh, the perfect, matte-shiny forms of the Aryan man and his woman embracing, the sparkling aura around the waists and profiles hacked out of marble and then rubbed and polished; oh, the stability of that life-size, lard-slick, blubber-slimy couple; untouchable, unticklable, they had no exhaust pipes, no backbones; they were one, totally absorbed in each other, Aryan white and divinely immaculate, and opposite them, on the right-hand page of *Signaal*, squatted two degenerate gawkers, damned and oppressed by heredity and barely reclaimed from the dusk, with coal in their mouths for teeth and holes in their ribs, with ghastly masks!

"Lying is like breathing for him," said Richard Harmedam. "But what do you expect? He was schooled by the Jesuits. Doomed! And though converted, you might say, by Crabbe, he retained something of the early, insalubrious fever: sin, if you know what I mean, and fear and a certain thirst for an ideal that one awaits around every corner. There, right there."

Old baldy – with the high voice whose infantile quality he could turn on and off at will was now serious, which made his noisome baby face even more devious-looking – held out his hand towards the grounds and beyond: gardens, woods, cities. "Now we, you and I, my friend, who have studied the Greeks and Romans and tried to identify with them because they bore their lot nobly, we could smile at such vulgar convulsions and their very different goals, could we not, yet we must nonetheless recognize that this unhealthy schism in man can have its consequences. What was that? Oh. I thought you said something . . . Anyway, once the traitor of Tarsus came on the scene and spread his poison dust and made sin a possible plus for the hereafter, what remained for us, the likes of you and me, I mean? A smile, right, irony. But that was insufficient. We knuckled under, we Greeks and Romans, when Christianity came along. And you know what pains me the most, my friend? That Crabbe was poisoned by the dregs of original sin, because in the end it was compassion, something nobody needs, that brought him low."

He was seized by a sudden bout of coughing and hunched forward, but I didn't dare slap him on the back. Then we went into the garden – the second part of the meeting was about to begin – and stood by a cone of gravel. "As if consolation, when you need it the most, could be sought elsewhere than in the disconsolate lives of others." He sighed. "All that hope!" And sighing again, he cast a remarkably lucid glance through the low-lying branches to the castle now in shadow.

"Hope?" I asked.

"Yes," he said, and I thought he meant the hope he had nurtured all his life, but then rejected the idea: it was the futile millstone people burdened themselves with, a humiliating heat that made them seek the refreshing mud in which they could wallow like . . .

The old man picked up a hose and, aiming it at the gravel pile, doused it with water. I helped by holding it, steadying it, at chest level. The water made a clear sound and shifted the gravel. Suddenly Crabbe was standing next to me. Here it is, Korneel! If you could read this notebook instead of the other story I'm writing on your orders, you would have to put an x in the margin at this point! All I knew of Crabbe's physical appearance I knew from the way the statues portrayed him, but he was standing next to me and I could feel his breath on my neck when he cried as a seagull cries or a child whose vocal cords one has tried to destroy chemically without complete success. I gripped the hose more tightly and saw it rise, because my back went stiff, my face grew hollow – someone had sucked my cheeks in from inside – and an iron belt stretched tight around my midriff. Someone was chewing, my jaws were grinding, and I fell. The stream from the hose splashed all over the place, spattering me as I lay there, my eyes wide open. Richard, mumbling something friendly, helped me up, but by then Crabbe had disappeared. As imperceptibly as he had just violently forced himself into my frame. I smiled back at Richard and was a different person, a ball-less storyteller and voyeur no more. Richard turned the hose on me in jest, spraying my shoes, and I smiled away, now with my own mouth.

In the distance we heard the delegates gathering, calling across the grounds to one another by their first names, and I headed for the dark castle where Crabbe (who had indulged in the most capital of sins, as Richard put it, self-destruction) resided no longer, because he resided in me, practicing destruction by splitting me in pieces, tearing me apart. Sprange came up, saying something about me to the man at his side, but he could no longer humiliate me – then – and I smiled and joined him with my sopping, squeaking shoes.

Flight Without Defense

The teacher sat in the first row among the delegates. Just in front of him, between him and the speaker, was a small round table strewn with books, which, judging by their titles, had been written by those present: *My Life Under the Belgian Terror*, *Problems of an Outsider* by XYZ, *Towards a Planned Economy*, and several issues of a journal whose title he could not make out, though the back covers contained the publisher's advertisements for *To Die and Then . . .* by Father P. Telder, *Mother and Her Spouse* by Dr. J. Waterink. For a while the teacher had noticed a musty, smoky odor, but he ascribed it to his extraordinary sensitivity to smells (he always felt nauseous the moment coal fumes entered the classroom, while the hale and hearty herd fairly thrived on them) and forced himself to ignore it and concentrate on listening to a man in a tweed suit and climbing boots Sprange had introduced as the thinker and poet Bert van Wageren read an essay on Willem van Saeftingen, a monk who left his monastery to fight the French at Groeninge. Madame Alice had disappeared after dessert.

Sandra did not listen, nor did the elderly man sitting next to her, who had a withered carnation in his buttonhole and was fast asleep. From time to time a trickle of blood emerged from his nose and he snuffled it back. His elbow was resting on Sandra's hip, which did not seem to bother her.

Van Wageren was tall and reddened by the sun, he rolled his r's in a most un-Flemish manner, and his text abounded in mutually contradictory adjectives. Having evoked the Battle of the Golden Spurs, he drew parallels between 1302 and today to prove that the struggle was even more necessary at present. The teacher had, for the past hour – that is, approximately from the time he had talked to the old man and helped him with his watering – been feeling under the weather. It was absurd, of course, but the atmosphere of doom and the memory of doom and the glorification of Crabbe's demise reigning in the House of Almout had affected his limbs like the early stages of a flu, and he caught himself – perched on that hard, neo-Gothic chair under the clear eye of Sandra and her cronies – imitating somebody, perhaps even Crabbe, avoiding contact with the back of the chair, keeping his torso as straight as an arrow, and thinking, That is how the menfolk behave when the lights go on after a cowboy movie and they saunter out to the street, a nonchalant hand resting on the hip where the holster should be.

He was then only mildly surprised when Sprange announced that the bard and thinker was to be followed by Dr. Heerema, the eminent historian from the Northern Low Countries, from Holland, whereupon he began to speak in a voice that had nothing of the long-suffering or condescending professor but was clipped and clear. While the gentlemen looked him over and the old man with the carnation petals strewn over his lapels, now awake, shifted to the other buttock and away from Sandra and Sandra threw him (the teacher) a malicious glance, he announced that his talk (he wanted to outdo van Wageren) would deal primarily with the uprisings along the coast in 1340. He watched with glee as van Wageren took out a notebook and licked the point of a tiny pencil. Then he saw Sprange wink at Sandra. The teacher leaned against the marble mantelpiece, rested a heel on the wrought-iron bar running around the fireplace, and looking out at that riff-raff in their Sunday best, those campaign survivors willing for the sake of a defeated, destroyed, definitively missing Scharführer to sit through bad verse and keep their resentment alive with excuses, palliative fallacies, differing little in their essence from the arguments that held his Principal's Party meetings together, looking out at Crabbe's inquisitive, overwrought admirers ready to interpret each of his utterances as a revelation about their ruler and to replace the coast, when he announced the topic of his talk, in their imagination with the steppe and the Cherkasy swamp they had once been entrenched in, surrounded by Konev's Second Ukrainian Front and Rotmistrov's Fifth Guards Tank Army, looking out at them the teacher felt (renewed) wonder. I may be in Crabbe's clutches, he thought, but I'm no longer him, not now. I'll even make him forget and, despite the trace of shame he felt about the whole stupid affair, he plunged in, immersed himself in the moment, set to, and persevered.

"The County of Flanders, in the territory of Ancient Friesland from Kales to Walcheren and as far as Zeeland in . . . a string of islands presented as a gift by Charles the Bald, feudal lord, to Baudouin, man of iron . . . a campaign against the Normans . . . on the cusp between the Germanic and the Roman . . . the hereditary stain (some call it the glory) of his feudal military origins . . . Flanders was offered to Rollo, but he was already there and would have none of it: he found it too swampy and preferred Normandy . . . our wretched matrilineal laws of succession that encouraged foreigners to marry into . . ." and he had only just begun, had only laid a bridgehead from which to launch his screed, a personal diatribe, which was meant to be vexing, crushing, incriminating, and it was about to take off when he stumbled over the word "foreigners" and ground to a halt, the word getting stuck, causing unintended damage, and when he saw it run rampant among them, those lily-white, true-blue, racially pure Flemings, saw it raise their hackles, he could not go on. He stared over at Sprange until he looked away and said something to Sandra. The room was silent. The teacher imagined Sandra on her back in Crabbe's room, running her fingers over her thighs and pale, yet visible, vaccination scars, scratching her head of soft, curly, dyed auburn hair shaped like a comb, then sitting bolt upright with a snarl on her lips, the word "foreigners" casting a shiny nylon net between them.

"Excuse me," he said, and pointed to something behind him, just behind him, the fireplace, whose flames were emitting puffs of smoke and all but singeing him.

"What's the matter?" asked the carnation man.

"We're on fire," said the teacher.

"Who? Where? What?"

"Scheisse!" shouted tall van Wageren.

And in fact the smell the teacher had noticed for some time and taken as one of the pipe-smokers' revolting tobacco was rather a nearly colorless cloud rising from between the cracks of the parquet floor, at first concentrated at his feet and in a semi-circle around the fire but then – because the audience had become aware of it, jumped up, and caused currents? – growing thicker and darker, curling and spreading. The delegates pressed together, trying to see, but soon dispersed, because by the time windows were opened the smoke was billowing dense and black. Some, though their eyes were watering, did not budge from Richard Harmedam's side as he issued hesitant, irresolute orders in French, and this and the shuffle of feet over the fuming floorboards had gone on for quite some time when Sprange picked up the pitcher of water that had been set out for the speakers but remained unused and poured it over the floor. The smoke grew worse, then dissipated. The air stank. Hurrah! the delegates cheered, and the carnation man, still coughing, was led out into the hallway. The prim servant girl appeared with a pail of water and started mopping. Sandra then explained that a piece of the embers must have got under and between the floorboards and smoldered there. "Perhaps we should take a break," she said, and, turning to the teacher, added, "Don't go away."

"Good idea," thundered Bert van Wageren, heading the gentlemen through the French doors onto the veranda.

An athletic-looking near-sighted man asked the teacher to sign the artificial-leather guestbook. Opposite a page with "He who dares not shall fail" emblazoned on it in Gothic script the teacher wrote his name in a punctilious, schoolmasterly hand to the disappointment of the man, who had expected an adage or line of verse. Bringing the book up close to his eyes, the man read out questioningly, syllable by syllable, "Vic-tor-De-nijs-de-Rij-ckel?"

"That is the name on my passport," said the teacher, a bit jittery.

"Oh, I see," said the man. "In any case, it's not for me; it's for my boy, for later."

"That's all right," said the teacher.

"Thank you," said the man and, after shaking the teacher's hand, tickled his palm, a sign.

Proud of having inscribed his name in their midst and ignoring Sandra and her request, no, her order, the teacher walked outside, listened with one ear to the break chats, made a vain attempt to find Richard Harmedam, refused to think about how to resume his talk, and noticed that his confrères made a point of not disturbing his concentration. They were recalling their feats on the battlefield. Then Alessandra Harmedam appeared on the steps and called out, "Oh, doctor! Dr. Heerema!" and at first he thought someone had been hurt, but it was clearly her voice and did not sound the least bit anxious; no, it was more peremptory and aimed at him. She even made a come-hither motion with her finger and then with her hand, called him over like a servant, and he went and followed her into the room next to the kitchen, all ironing boards and tables piled high with washing. She leaned against a shelf containing folded shirts and towels. The room smelled of burnt linen.

"Come closer," she said. She bit her lower lip, then a fingernail. "What are you going to talk about?"

"What I've been talking about all along."

"Flanders?"

"Right."

"What do you know about Flanders? Do you know what Flanders means to these people?"

"All too well."

"Ha ha." It was a bad imitation. A boarding-school girl's attempt at acting. She fiddled with an iron, held it up to her cheek; she kneaded a skein of wool into a tiny ball. "Are you satisfied with yourself? Are you happy?"

"Yes and no."

"Shut up," she said. "Good God! For heaven's sake! Are you satisfied with what you've done?"

"I haven't ever . . ."

"Ever what? Ever what? Did you think you could keep it a secret? Did you think we'd never find out how you stopped Dr. Heerema at the border?"

I scarcely recognized her as she stood there, arms stretched back against the shelf, veins blue and thick. She was panting, her narrow chest with the inch-wide cleft between its vaults heaving like that of a ballerina who is keeping her stomach immobile, a column with a torso pivoting above it. She was livid. I made to go up to her, but she lifted the iron and pointed the blunt end of the unwieldy thing right at me. "Is it true what Sprange says? That you're not even Flemish?"

"Who? Me?"

"Are you Dutch or are you not?"

"No."

"Not even that! So it's true what he says." She would have liked to turn and press her grief-stricken face to the wall but was afraid to expose an unprotected back to me, so she restrained herself, and two ropes came jutting out under the skin of her throat. I thought everyone was eavesdropping in the hallway. "Well, don't think you'll get off scot free!" she screamed. "Nobody can do this to me! I'll cut your throat. I swear!"

The teacher looked at her as if she were a stranger. He told her he was Flemish and taught German and English, but she threw her prickly black crowned head back and laughed. "Don't you think we know that? We're on to you, all of you, you small-time informants! Your Sûreté Générale aren't the only ones who keep files, you know. So you've come to spy on us. Of your own accord. The men out there don't know yet. Only Sprange and I, but . . ."

"How does Sprange know?"

"How does Sprange know? Ha ha!" She turned suddenly ugly and burst into tears. "He can smell it on you! You people smell, you know that? It's just like the Sûreté to send a Jew to do their dirty business for them. And I . . ." Her shoulders were heaving.

"You didn't smell anything," the teacher said sweetly.

"I saw it, but I thought it was from an operation. I didn't dare think . . ."

"I am circumcised," the teacher lied. "Like all the men of my race."

She screamed a long, protracted scream that must have been audible throughout the house, and he roared with laughter. But not for long: he heard voices in the hallway and forced himself to stare at the creature before him, at the twisted face with the lower teeth exposed, the hands trying to protect and pacify the sullied organs, and flashed her a winning smile. "And here I thought it was my being a Jew that aroused you so, Sandra, my being a Jew that made you so submissive afterwards, my angel." He was disgusted with himself for twisting the knife round and round in her as she stood there nodding stiffly, maliciously, her misery a lump in her throat, and thinking That face is in the process of dissolving; how strange: it's different, he handed her a checkered, newly ironed dishtowel from the pile in front of him. It had an overpowering smell of starch. Dumbfounded he watched another face taking over, a face he had forgotten under the Almout attic roof – the mask she had put on for the car dealer in the gazebo of the Pavilion a few days before – and recognized the slimy madness, born of stupidity and despair, emanating from it.

"I am Crabbe," he said to the face and slapped it right and left with a rock-hard hand.

In the hallway he found fewer délégués, calm or anxious, than he had expected – they were simply standing there, herded together, looking a bit lost, experiencing their senselessly interrupted commemoration of the dead – and, his back unprotected, he ran along the hallway, through the lobby, and out of the door. Sprange was nowhere to be seen, only vague figures wandering among the cars in the garden twilight. Having passed the greenhouse and the abandoned porter's lodge – who was the porter here? – he came to the beech-lined path and the bushes where he had squatted with the boy when he still believed Almout could be taken. The bushes did not part easily, and he thought he heard noises behind him, someone or some people striking the trees as if trying to flush out game, but he did not wait. A donkey started braying not far off and he set off at a run along the path leading to the village.

When he sighted the inn, the street looked quiet, but as he drew nearer and began thinking with a guilty conscience of the boy he had abandoned, he realized that a number of people had congregated at the open door of the inn. When he was even closer, he saw that they were neither villagers nor farmers: they were young men in blue tracksuits, the two teams of the local soccer league. He hugged as close to the row of houses as possible. The young people seemed taken up with something exciting they had observed and were discussing. A lone shop bell rang, a dog barked, somebody cleared his throat, and then he heard a radio broadcast of a soccer match and saw that there were men behind him, on the other side of the street, and next to him, all moving in his direction, that they had taken cover at the entrance to the Rode Hoek and were accompanying him back there. He moved out into the road and a few younger men came up on either side, keeping pace, backs straight, but aloof, not even looking at him.

Then a few of the soccer players noticed him and poked one another and called to one another over the din of the radio and flowed out onto the sidewalk, where they formed a group. The sports announcer was giving the names of the players as they took possession of the ball; the fans were screaming, waves of rage running through them; the teacher headed straight for the noisy crowd, and the soccer players, a few of whom were shouting "Now we've got him, the bastard!" broke rank and formed a semi-circle around the door. The teacher put on his stern playground-face and was about to cross the threshold when he saw Alessandra Harmedam's low-slung sports car, top down, behind a heavy-set man in a tracksuit, and at the thought that she was waiting for him inside he stopped short and was going to walk past the soccer players to the side entrance in an attempt to slip unseen into his room (his room! without a single piece of his belongings! where he had slept for two nights!) when suddenly, who should he see in the inn, right in front of him, in his line of sight, but Sprange holding the boy by the wrist. His tone was cautious but firm, and he was saying that no harm would come to him so long as he came along with him to the castle without resistance. The boy's mouth was open, whether out of surprise or a dislocation of the jaw. He was shorter than the teacher remembered him, and was leaning meekly on Sprange as the latter moved forward, so that the teacher now saw him as a catamite who gave himself to whoever happened to be the strongest. It was a painful thought, and he felt like boxing Verzele's ears to put his jaw back in place.

After Sandra's violent farewell the teacher felt physically aroused, vibrant, intoxicated. "But of course, cher ami," he said to Sprange. Surrounded by the male contingent from the village – new, tight-lipped groups kept emerging from the side streets, having stood watch there until now, until this triumphant moment – the three of them went out to the sports car, where a flaxen-haired soccer player leaped out from behind the steering wheel and cursed when the heavy-set man in the tracksuit told him off. The innkeeper – arms crossed, ruddy and self-assured – was standing by the headlights, chatting with a village constable, and when, still flanked by the crowd, they reached him he held up his hand like a traffic policeman and declared in a voice loud enough for the entire village to hear that this was all well and good but he wasn't going to leave it at that. The two guests, he said, had a bill to pay. Sprange walked past him without listening and, fixing his eyes on the mudguard, frowned at the sight of a spot or dent.

"Tell me, Sprange," said the innkeeper, "you're the one I'm talking to." Sprange raised his head and nearly bumped into him or at least gave an odd swing of the hip – the way in a small circus that makes the rounds of our province the ancient clown expresses his scorn for the bespangled and bepowdered Gaston, the troupe's musician, behind his back, thereby sending our children into gales of laughter and setting our embarrassed young ladies to licking their ice-creams assiduously – leaped over the streamlined door with a dexterity one would not have expected from his rather coarse build, and settled in behind the wheel. Suddenly the constable placed his truncheon, a rubber truncheon designed to cause subcutaneous bleeding, on the teacher's solar plexus, keeping him at a distance, among the villagers. The insufficient lighting from the two streetlamps, the grocer's display, and the neon letters of the café reminded the teacher, caught in this bizarre scene, of an illustration in a German reader of his father's in which amidst a landscape of rocks and edelweiss William Tell was making an appeal to some mountain dwellers, and now it was the innkeeper who was appealing to the soccer players and local burghers: Once again the castle had turned against the village; how long was this going to go on; once again a criminal had escaped justice; what were we, men or mice? But his speech – was it too emotional? too flowery? – was met with morose grumbling: the castle sports car had a more powerful, more direct effect, and once the innkeeper realized this he lowered his voice and ended with a timorous phrase or two, a peep, a sigh.

Out of sympathy or a sense of fair play Sprange stood up in the car and, leaning over the door, patted the innkeeper on the shoulder. "Now, now, Pier," he said. "Don't take it so hard. If it's the money . . ."

The innkeeper moved up closer, and they discussed conditions and amounts. Meanwhile the boy did something quite unexpected, something unthinkable: tearing himself away from the teacher, he turned to the crowd, which recoiled, and began shouting in a shrill voice, "They grabbed me, and Pier put his arms around me in the inn! I want to talk to the priest, I want to confess!"

The villagers were taken aback, but the teacher caught on in a flash, and joining him in his simple, ingenuous yet successful boy-scout-like ruse – the boy had deflected the attention of the smoldering crowd, which was now thronging around the writhing, shrieking five-foot epileptic, and the constable was trying to get to him – he took a deep breath and raced off through a sparse group of nearby bystanders, who, wonder of wonders, stepped aside to let him pass. Loping with kangaroo strides away from the noise into the dark of the village street, he came to the village church after about three hundred meters. There was a small electric light shining above the massive, richly sculptured door.

The door was shut. The teacher tugged on the artfully worked wrought-iron handle. He could hear moans and hoarse cries coming from the crowd, girls' screams too, and then, near the ceramic tiles of the public urinal by the church, where he saw an old woman carrying a broom and a bottle of milk, he slipped, grazing his calf just above the injured ankle on the iron railing that ran around the urinal, and bumped into the old woman but pushed her out of his way, and the next thing he knew he was in a side aisle of the cold, whitewashed, incense-impregnated church. He dragged an oak bench to the side door he had entered by, sat down on it, and exhaled through his nose. He rubbed his calf. His hands were shivering, and to warm them he mindlessly rubbed them against his nylon socks, which, he thought, let no sweat through. Then, out of the blue, the front door opened, the key in the well-oiled lock making not a sound. The darkness inside the church, to which he had not yet grown accustomed, was pierced by voices, men dancing and cursing their way down the nave. The teacher dropped to his knees and – while the men doubled back, hounded by a high-pitched, admonitory, irate voice calling out that this was God's-Very-Own-House – crawled, unheard and unseen, until he reached the carved wooden lectern behind which the dignitaries of the church-factory sat every Sunday at ten o'clock Mass. There he sank to the ground, leaning his elbows on the velvet rug covering the parquet floor and pulling in his still wet feet. Thus curled up like a fetus he prayed for peace. His prayer was heard. The irate voice, a priest's voice, steeped in wine and daily commandments, grew louder, more urgent, chasing the unclean from the temple, and another voice, that of the constable or soccer coach or construction worker, untainted by reverence or piety, lent its assistance. The men talked back but returned to the evening streets. The church fell still.

The teacher did not move. I want to stay here, he thought, stay a week and not budge. He felt an artery throb in his throat. His temples too. Somebody sighed; shoes shuffled.

"Yoo-hoo!" the boy called out, and the priest's voice said, "Where are you? Come here immediately."

"Do, sir," the boy whispered, "do."

The teacher remained where he was, next to a ticking wooden figure. Later he thought it was because he was afraid that Sprange had hidden in the church and that he was ashamed of the visible erection his fear had induced. Irrational as it was, he obstinately held his breath and said to himself, "Find me. Look."

The two of them moved stridently, scraping nail-shod chairs, going up and down the rows. "Sir," the boy whispered. "Sir." And then: "How about turning the light on?"

"No," said the wine-steeped voice.

There was a candle burning near the image of Saint Rochus, and the polychromed saint, heaving slantwise into the curled-up teacher's field of vision, raised his cloak to bare a knee while an elegant Egyptian greyhound stuck out a golden tongue level with cloak's hem. The teacher groaned. They found him.

"I can't move," he said. "I'm lame."

The priest was very young, a curate. His vestments did not fit him: they drooped on his frame like a rented masquerade costume. "You must," said the curate. "Try. You can't stay here. Under any circumstances." He pulled the teacher by the arm.

"I can't."

The priest knelt down and, extending his arms into that narrow, shadowed kennel, massaged the teacher's neck and shoulders, and the teacher, feeling the boy tugging at his legs after a while, began to laugh.

"That's better," said the priest.

And the teacher thought, "Everyone, Sandra – these two here amidst the incense, Fredine when it's dark, even Crabbe – they're all out to get me; I don't touch them." And he was just feeling a certain confidence flow back into his limbs – the broad, expansive vaults of the church's ceiling were no longer so intimidating – when outside, right next to the choir, a girl or a man able to make his voice very high gave a scream. Immediately thereafter one of the windows was shattered and a stone hit a wooden bench and bounced over the tiles.

"Billions, billions!" shouted the priest, and gathering up the skirts of his cassock he ran to the entrance, threw the door open, and delivered a string of maledictions in dialect from the threshold to the church square. The teacher crawled out from behind the lectern and made his way across the smooth tiles in the candlelight. The boy helped him, if roughly, to his feet, and he sat on a prie-dieu with a copper plaque on the back: NOTARY VERKEST. Next to him, in painted relief, the second station of the cross. The priest joined them again, shaking his head. "Unbelievable," he muttered. "How are you doing? Better? Probably a bout of arthritis. My brother's got it too."

"No, pure fear," said the boy. "He was so scared he nearly . . ."

"Sh! Quiet."

They saw the old woman who had tried to block the teacher's way at the side door shuffling through the church with her broom and bottle of milk, in tears. Seeing them, she said, "How could you let it happen, Father? It's all his fault," and, when the teacher tried to get a word in, added shrilly, "Yes, your fault, you crook! They'll tear down the whole church before you know it, those socialists!"

"I'll send you a check," said the teacher to the innkeeper, to Sandra, to the priest.

"For how much?" asked the old woman, spraying him with her saliva. "Have you any idea what it costs?"

"Leave us alone, Jeanneke," said the priest.

Her mouth foaming, she pushed around the chairs, inspecting the stones, the slivers of glass. The teacher's teeth started chattering. He placed his fist under his chin, and it shook in rhythm.

"Man can be a beast to his fellow man," said the curate. The teacher meant to respond but was unable to make a sound and thought, There must be some unconsecrated wine in the sacristy. I'm parched.

The boy yawned a nervous yawn.

"Haven't they learned a thing from the horrors of recent years?" he said, his voice stern and older now, though still wine-steeped. Behind him two evangelists were propping up the prie-dieu.

"Could I live here till I was old and gray, singing psalms in peace and quiet, doing good, leaving the adventures of flesh and spirit far behind, gazing at an image, believing, trusting, content?" He stood. "Reverend," he said, "could we (he, the anonymous narrator, and his wily errand boy) possibly spend the night here?"

"No," said the curate.

"But you can't chase me out. The Church is holy. It says so in the capitula majora of the Lex Saxonum."

"Don't you think I know that!" the curate countered, whereupon the teacher took the man's warm, dry hands in his and said he would send him a check for whatever amount the curate saw fit.

"It'll take forty thousand at the very least, believe you me," said the old cleaning lady.

"You must be off your rocker!" said the boy with a sneer.

The priest frowned, thought a bit, then muttered, "Right, in that vicinity. Forty or so. We'll see. Give us a ring in a day or two." He took them into the sacristy. While the teacher and the boy waited amidst chasubles and books, lace and linen, collection boxes, prie-dieux, candlesticks, pails of holy water, and halberds, he looked through the window, disappeared, returned from the impenetrable darkness, and whispered, "The coast is clear."

"Look to the right again," said the boy.

"No, my boy. The street is deserted. They're all at the front door."

The priest made a cross with his thumb on the boy's forehead and said "Good-bye for now" to the teacher, who was standing in the doorway in the evening air.

"Where are we going?" asked the teacher.

"Take it easy," the boy snapped, and the teacher, after holding on to the frame for a second, pushed away from it and set off as fast as his legs would carry him along the churchyard wall, across a cypress-lined path in the grass, into a sunken road smelling of ammoniac, and up the gravel alongside a railway track, and to his joy and wonder the boy easily caught up with him and ran next to him, breathing through his nose. A whistle blast rent the evening air behind them, and through the night came the clomping and wheezing and shouts of their pursuers.

The teacher, who had intended to follow the track, changed his mind when the boy grunted something into his ear, and at the barrier he shot after Verzele's dancing feet past the house of the barrier guard, huffing and puffing in time with the snorting in front of him, his throat dry, his ears ringing, but the rhythmicity of it all kept him going, and they eventually came to a dirt road with deep furrows. Here and there a false step sent a darting pain through his ankle; the wheat swayed in a copper gleam; they ran through a cloud of mosquitoes. Far behind them the villagers were spreading out over the fields. The teacher was sure the soccer players would catch him, and for a moment he reproached himself for not having listened to Elizabeth years before when she tried to get him to buy a Renault Deux-Chevaux, but his pursuers had lost track of him or quarreled over the course to take and had scattered into a large semi-circle, nothing more now than spikes against the horizon, treading the oats, rye, and wheat.

A rind of moon came into sight and dimly lit the countryside and the wriggling men caught in it and defending themselves on all sides. Suddenly he could take it no longer: he had to stop. The boy turned and cursed.

"Spleen," said the teacher, gasping for air and bringing up a mouthful of gall.

"Fuck!" the boy shouted. And pushed him down and dragged him into the grain. There was a car up ahead making two long and three short beeps. It was answered by hoarse, fragmentary commands in German. Lifting his throbbing head over the low, uneven line formed by the stalks, the teacher saw bent figures advancing from the west. The commands in German were now perfectly understandable. At the spot where the boy had ducked down next to him onto a sparse bed of crushed stalks the teacher was kneeling with his fingers in his ears, yet the new sound went straight into his head. The soldiers west of him, to the left of him, had dogs with them and were urging them forward. How motionless the land was. The surrounding air was attacked by the barking and the male voices inducing it. A fierce wind came up and raged through the stalks, the fields, the hollows in the hills, the crowns in the trees, and far off in the distance it made the beach foam.

The teacher remembered that when they passed the barrier guard's house the shutters were open and at the level of the windowsill he had caught a glimpse of two female figures lit by a petroleum lamp sitting at a bed and bending over a child or a dwarf; he remembered the candles on the bedside table throwing light on the stained and crumpled sheets; and he thought, All the sacrilegious howling of dogs and men currently tearing the world asunder will not bring the dead back to life. The dogs drew nearer in a well-controlled formation, covering a precisely defined territory that grew smaller and smaller. The teacher felt a wave of heat flow through his body, and he took off his jacket, undid his watch and tucked it into a fold in the jacket, unbuckled his belt and pulled off his trousers, and, keeping his damp shoes on, tore his shirt in two, kicked his underpants off, then stood and walked through the undulating grain to where he thought the boy was. There he met one of the advance guard, a calm man wearing a thick brown tweed jacket and standing and waiting, hands on hips. The teacher went up to him shivering, sweating, ice-cold, in total wonder. The man bent over and gathered the teacher into two extremely long and hard arms, which then closed around him the way the arms of a boarding school pupil will clench his pillow when dreaming.

(NOVEMBER)

Who is busy talking now with that nasty creature who's supposed to be bringing me my supper and has been getting under my skin lately and won't even give me today's newspaper? Who? My first thought was: it's Korneel reading her the riot act, but now I know better: it is none other than Bogger, that yellowbelly of a porter who worked at the hotel where I lived while I was teaching. Which was nothing to wonder at, because it was so close to the school. You go left past eight houses, turn the corner, and you're on the esplanade; you follow the esplanade till you get to the curve that runs to the north side of town; it's exactly eight blocks plus one square after this street, on the left if you start out from here, opposite the monument to the sailors who died in the war; you can't miss it; there it is, that big, toothy building, a limestone tart with green balconies, the Hotel Titanic, where the porter was pretending to sweep behind the glass partition separating the restaurant from the entrance as I was leaving. That unspeakable Bogger! Who is now jabbering away a mere three-and-a-half meters from my right shoulder! And who comes from the north of France or near the French border and had to flee when a certain smuggling operation – liqueurs or perfume – came to light, and, thanks to the Fish Princess, ended up at the Titantic.

Not that he didn't do a good job. During high season he would wait at the station sporting a Titanic cap. Anyone with an ascot and a suitcase would be accosted by the creep as soon as he got off the train, and told he'd been sent by the hotel the gentleman had booked to report it was full, but he could follow him to its branch (which he sometimes called reverently "sister establishment"). Or he would imply that the poor naïve tourist had booked a hotel plagued by bedbugs and thieves and would be better served by the cheaper but better known and better situated Titantic. A nonchalant salute, two fingers to the cap. Careful diction. Toothless smile. And that scoundrel is out there in the hall jabbering away. Oh my God.

Late at night Bogger would go out dancing at De Witte Zee or Pierlala, and there he'd put away ten glasses of beer with one or two of the twelve middle-aged women who told everybody they were widows. Sometimes he took the lady or ladies to the hotel after the place closed, and they sat with the chef in the kitchen with their Chambertins and Drambuies. A defensive but soft arm was lifted, a hand swatted from a thigh: "Leave me alone." "What's got into you?" "That's not what we came for, right, Irma?" "You can say that again, Alma." "Oh, come off it, my roly-polies." It ended in indecorous moaning and neighing among the fridges, percolators, ranges, and pots and pans and made the slumbering Englishmen in the hotel dream of cats and horses.

What's he trying to put over on Fredine now, here? I can't follow his line, but I can see and hear him deliver it as surely as if I had an endoscope, one of those strange little tubes you attach to a camera and insert into the intestines, a microscope of sorts with a ninety-degree prism. "How about it, you floozy, you stupid slut?" followed by one of his proverbs: "A man may not be a rifle, but he does like to shoot off now and then." While her, the whore, I can't hear. Or see. That's better. He's gone now, Bogger has. On the prowl for other victims. As for her, well, she's still there, in the hallway, her hand in the apron pocket jangling a key-ring. Also in the pocket: glasses, dentures, and hearing aids she's confiscated from others in the building.

(NOVEMBER)
Since the short circuit that made us sit in the dark she thinks everything is permitted her. Before you know it she'll be tipping the inkpot over my papers. What then?

After Bogger disappeared, she came in with yesterday's paper and today's *Les Sports* under her arm. She sat down without being invited. The lady of the house. Looking furtively at my table. She hadn't slept, she said. Me neither, I said. She said she'd kept thinking about me and I was the only friend she had in the world, the only person who would listen to her and wasn't just after you know what. What do you say to something like that? I: Nothing.

"People treat me like shit," she said.

"I don't."

"No, you don't." She sat cowering on the bed. Would not go. "But everybody else does." She coughed. "And I can't do anything about it."

I look at my ink-pot. Superchrome ink writes dry with wet ink. Available in five super colors. Turquoise Blue, Jade Green, Red, Blue Black, and Jet Black. The four humors plus one. Water, fire, earth, air, plus one. Arrival, decline, expectation, return, plus one. Black gall, blood, yellow gall, and white spittle, plus one. Hearts: eros; spades: spirit; clubs: flesh; diamonds: intellect; plus one: the joker.

"You never stop writing. What you get out of it, I . . ."

She slammed the door shut when she left as if she wanted Korneel and the whole asylum to hear. And now that she's gone, it's hard for me to write. "What you get out of it, I . . ." There are flies in the room. How is that possible? I can't get the window open and the door opens and closes so quickly. They must be mating behind the curtain. Now that she's gone, I've got to get back to my writing.

"There's no point in crying." ("Bawling," she said.) I didn't dare tell her it had nothing, absolutely nothing to do with her, with her story, for Christ's sake. I wanted to tell her that I'd lost my glasses and since then I couldn't stand the slightest draft or sunbeam, I couldn't even stand a loud or high-pitched woman's voice or cats caterwauling. But I could in fact stand her and her story. I didn't want to tell her, though. What she told me was:

That she remembered very clearly being at vespers that Sunday, wearing her long, black, woolen stockings and pink ribbon and carrying home her missal with its gilded pages and prayer cards in one hand and the spiral candle for her upcoming First Communion in the other. She gave the candle to Mother for safe keeping, in cotton wool. Father was sitting in the corner near the little vaulted room with his clogs next to him and his feet in a basin of warm water, and nothing was said when I went in. There was a stranger sitting by the fireplace with his feet – he was wearing black shoes – up on the brick border near the flames, which were very high and came from fir logs that smoked but smelled nice. She didn't know the man, but he was from around here: he wore the same kind of corduroy trousers as Father, the kind you buy in Tourhout, and a black jacket like the one in Father's Sunday suit, and his face was brownish like Father's and square and his hands – she'd thought about those hands a lot both afterwards and much later – had the same calluses and tufts of hair on the back and short, rounded nails.

Her father said, "She's the one, Wanten," and the man's bright, light-blue eyes remained glued to her for a terribly long time. Mother left the room to put away the candle.

The man said, "She's a little too old for it, actually."

"I know," Father said.

"And it may not take, Verhagen," said the man.

She thought, Should I run away? and she felt she was going to cry (bawl) because she thought at first the stranger was going to kidnap her, but then she thought Mother would never let that happen.

The man went outside, and Father – Mother, who'd put away the candle in the room next to the kitchen, was taking care of my three little brothers and whiny sister – talked a while with him at the gate, and he nodded slowly the way he did when he called the summer people into the living room and paid them for helping to bring in the harvest. She'd seen him only one more time, for two minutes, just before the operation, when he gave her a dark-green syrup to drink that put her to sleep. Around the time she turned twenty, when she began to see she was going to be taking care of her three brothers and sister all by herself because Mother was dead by then, she realized what the operation was and she thought a lot about the man they called Tall Wanten, though they talked as little as they could about him in the village. He and his sons too were good at slaughtering pigs, taming dogs, and poaching, and he was called in by some of the farms in the area when a girl had to have the operation, most of the time the eldest in a family that kept having babies or seemed likely to. The man had pulled something out of her down there, that much she understood, and when around the time she turned twenty she looked at herself in the mirror in Father's bedroom and saw those heavy hips and broad shoulders and brownish skin, saw the down, no, no, the hair on her chin and above her lips, stared longer and longer at herself, she would curse the man and his hands, and while the muscles in her arms stood out more and more and her chin and cheeks turned blue from the razor, she handled her brother and sister like a man, manhandled them (like somebody no man would ever want to "take," no man or woman for that matter) and sent them into the world and buried her father, who had masterminded the thing.

And while he listened, the teacher thought, "This can't happen in Flanders, where people make pilgrimages to Yser to honor the fallen soldiers and teachers like me receive an extra month of salary" and

"It must be an exception, as when it comes out that a concern set up to provide low-cost housing for workers is making a three hundred percent profit," and turned away from the thing that was talking, was as hairy as an ape, and had the voice of the innkeeper and that was saying, "I've never complained; I'll rest easy when I go to my grave. I'll be able to say I did my duty. Our Lisa's kids are always happy to see me: I give them caramels when she isn't looking. And it's my doing Lisa made such a good marriage and Jan got a job with the customs. Because if it hadn't been for me they'd have had to work in the fields and would barely have seen the inside of a school. The only thing is, I can't get used to life here in town. If I had my druthers, I'd rent a room or a little house in our village. Or be a maid to a priest somewhere in the country. Because people are always in such a rush here. They don't even look at you. They treat you like shit. It's not my fault I . . ."

The teacher stood up from his table and, scarcely able to see the contours of the room for the blinding light, put a hand behind her neck and pressed his forehead to the wiry hair on her temple. She rubbed his back, and her neck became salty and clammy, and she pushed him away and said, "No reason to cry" (bawl) and "Now don't start shouting again; there's no sense in shouting."

He could not see her well: his eyes would not let him and he had on poor-quality glasses that stretched the image into parallel swerves (just as the children in the camp in Poland saw a merry-go-round with horses in an amusement park for the first time in their lives through the distorting windows of the barracks they were locked up in), and he said, "I won't, don't worry."

He was besieged by flies, and the sweat ran down his eyebrows into his wide-open eyes – no one could get so close to him – and when he sat back down at the table, he said, picking at one of the dried fish scales with his pen, "Keep writing, feel like . . ." and thought, "She is a construction whose wood is cracking, the crossbeams of a castle with children playing."

He blew his nose and chased away the flies dancing round him, attracted by his cold sweat.

To the attention of Dr. Korneel van den Broecke

1. I am going to escape.

2. My name is on the back of the door to my room. On whose authority was my name written there? What name preceded it?

3. *The first time* I was beaten by a policeman. Proper steps must be taken. The others called him Zara. He was armed. A black belt. A gypsy. Had been sent to a camp in Poland as a child. District, I believe. Is this policeman hiding in the room next door, number eighty-two, under the identity of the patient Max?

4. I can no longer recall when I was beaten. It is your job to find out. In any case, after the first round, which lasted approxi-

mately twenty minutes, I was taken to Haakebeen's Lumber and Furniture Center. I can show you where it is from the smell of the chemicals used on the wood. As it was daytime and the old man, Edmond Haakebeen, was present – it was he who presided over the second round – it must have been before five o'clock in the afternoon, because at five Mr. Haakebeen goes to the Main Square for his bridge game. From five to eight at La Taverne Brueghel.

5. During the second round the men beating me used *regulation* truncheons and imitated barking, yelping dogs.

6. While having tea at Almout with Miss A.H. and Mr. Sprange (given name unknown), I was slipped a soporiphic. I fell asleep on the spot. The same preparation is being put into my food here. You can be brought to trial for such practices.

7. Crabbe at the hose.

8. This is no *regulation* hospital.

9. The vehicle that brought me here was a van belonging to Pier the Rope Man. Don't think I didn't notice. Again I could tell – like the blind – by the odor: pigs and metal.

10. A possible reservation vis-à-vis 6 above. At Almout we drank tea. Tea keeps you awake. Where does tea come from? According to legend it comes from Bodidharma, who, incensed with himself for having fallen asleep during meditation, cut off his eyelids so that he would *have to keep his eyes open*. The eyelids

fell into the earth and took root as tea-leaves. N.B.: Crabbe was known to have said to one of his men, "If you fall asleep (sleep = lack of consciousness), I'll cut your eyelids off."

11. If Crabbe was a Scharführer, how could Sprange (a born subordinate) be one too? No, Sprange was lying. And is lying now, Doctor, when he comes with you on your rounds and whispers things in your ear about me. What gives Sprange the right to make the rounds?

12. The first two beatings were made by policemen, see 3 above, so he is in any case responsible for some of the injuries inflicted upon me. The first round resulted in a dent in my temple. Proof: I can still feel it. My kidneys are swollen as well, etc. Sensation after the second round: layered glass separating into its layers and cracking. Image: a house collapsing in slow motion as if plucked apart sponge-like by an invisible, careless hand.

13. Your attempt at giving my internment a logical explanation (as if it mattered to me in the slightest) by getting your subordinate, Fredine, to state that I collapsed in school because my ex-wife E. turned up on the playground (*Tu parles!*) failed miserably. I refuse to accept such an explanation, Mr. van den Broecke, because it serves you too well and me too poorly.

14. I am willing to state publicly and at any time that, unlike the violence of the Association membership, the *necessarily* brutal

treatment I received at the hands of your attendants *never* did me any harm.

Your humble servant,

Number 84

P.S. It goes without saying that I am leaving you no forwarding address. Any attempt at finding me is doomed to failure. Me or Crabbe.

Like of an evening a swarm of insects, the veterans of the Eastern Front crossed the garden, despondent and remorseful over the insufficient quantity of men and weapons alotted them and proud of their mutilated limbs and their faith, and I stood at the gigantic statue of a man raising a torch while the lights of Almout beamed across the grounds and the frightened maidservants could be heard blaming one another for the fire as they cleaned up the parquet floor. Although Isaac Luria de Leeuw teaches that a dead man's soul can enter a wretched man's soul to support and instruct him, Crabbe's soul did not come to me. I had nothing to do with the men he wanted to unite with himself and the Leader, men of a high caliber, the elite. His discourse, now dispersed among the voices of his hoplites, was no common property; it was a raging cackle of pitiful, preposterous plots. The icy crust surrounding his soul, an ear-splitting village brass band, a gale!

The gentlemen were gnawing away at their memories.

"It was completely different at Pilau, let me tell you. And when we got to Danzig, Jan and me, it was no joke! Flämen oder nicht, they put us against the wall, can you believe it? with our hands up, and didn't let us budge until the boats were full and on their way. 'Wait here,' Jan says to me, and he comes back white as a ghost. 'Come and look,' he says. It was darker than hell, but we could see well enough. There was one boat still waiting to go and some men had dressed up as women to get on board, and there they were, hanging from a crane on the wharf with their skirts still on and their boots showing and signs on their stomachs. You know Jan, he can take anything; well, he was green. And the bombs raining down on us. So believe it or not, we took all the money we'd saved, about ten thousand marks, and bought a kid each from the women, and Jan and me said in our best Plattdeutsch that we were their fathers and we'd lost everything – which was true: we didn't have a rusty nail to scratch ourselves with – and screamed like a pair of idiots, 'Our wives are on board! Please!' And with bombs exploding like rotten eggs all around us we got away on the boat. Some others after us tried the same stunt using a bundle of baby clothes or just a pillow they kept saying 'There, there, little one' to, and man, they got it in the head from a pistol at close range. There were six of them lying in a heap with their pillows by the time we raised anchor . . ."

". . . so there we were near Koldisy on Lake Vreva. The news was catastrophic, but the way we looked at it was if *we* let go then all of Europe was doomed. We had to shore up the dam, stop the Ivans, no matter what the cost. You remember what that winter was like.

We couldn't get anywhere. I was the youngest, so they dispatched me to deliver a message to Jef Landsman's flank. I couldn't find him. They'd sent him packing long before but kept it a secret. I was riding my motorbike through an ice field when I came to a little village. I thought I might get some food there. I went into a hut and the three old men stood up when they saw me. Remember how close the Ivans were at the time. They didn't say anything, but they gave me some bread and goat cheese and when I left they raised their arms and said, 'Heil!' And they were pure Russians and their fellow countrymen, their liberators, ha, ha, were practically at the other end of the street. I'll never forget it. It will stay with me as . . ."

"We spent our Urlaub in Hamburg!"

"The frightful shortage of young blood has somewhat abated at present. A good thing too. When one has to do without young blood, fresh forces . . ."

"And it seems to me we should be pointing out that eight hundred and seventy of our friends lost their lives thanks to the independence front."

"Yellow and black – those are the colors of our folk, my friend, tiger colors. But if circumstances force us to chose clandestine over open warfare, they become wasp colors . . ."

Thus spake the late Crabbe's courtiers. In their voices the war turned into just another catastrophe, a shift in political alignment, a test of economic prowess, all in the name of their faith.

A courtier picked me up as if I were a sack of salt. He said something soothing or he didn't say a word or he gave me a karate chop in the neck – I don't remember, nobody told me. He handed me his jacket or helped me into it, and once the punishment was over he or she had me admitted here, to be with Korneel, who is paid by somebody – Sandra or the state – to keep an eye on me. It's all a misunderstanding. Against my will. It was a misunderstanding that led me to Sandra. At the time I thought that the more determined and vigorous and dynamic I was in seeking my prey the more readily I would summon it. Prick de Rijckel. But on the way you lost the pang of the hunt, and when the prey did come forth, the first obstacle – that is, Alessandra Harmedam's summoning of Crabbe – set my weapon, my thing, to drooping!

You disappear, Sandra, because you're no good at words. Blinded by passion. Carrion in the trap of clichés, feelings, and memories. The bestial finger exercises you so deftly practice are a part of you – of the keen, dazzling young woman down at the breakwater that night – a part that is fading, melting away and I keep my distance from. Now you're living at Almout with the seed of a man you believe to be Jewish in you. That'll teach you, Sandra of the dyed hair, even under the arms and between the legs. Wash it and it'll turn snow white. You've got the purple eyes of your mother (who sang at Almout) as well. The color comes from injections. The iris of the albino turns purple.

Sandra in a wheelchair. I ride over the lacy esplanade among roller-skaters, I ride over the playground. Sandra with the men, lioness, marionette, crushed by a tank, minced-meat hardtack. Sandra, a dwarf in bed. Your grandmother and your mother pray and knit by your side, and a stranger rushes past at the level of the windowsill, the light from the petroleum lamp just reaching his dripping wet features. Sandra in May 1940, already in high heels (though not nearly so high as the all-steel ones her mother Alice puts on when she poses in the living room in her ball gown for her husband, who is her own brother) and seamed stockings. Sandra with the dyed auburn hair – the softest in the world, displayed at times in a glass case in Louis XV salons, blown from below by an invisible engine that puffs it like a cloud devoid of substance in comparison with which the daintiest pubic tuft of a leukemic Japanese virgin is as mattress filling, seaweed – adorning your dove-egg of a head, Sandra. Sandra in the bleary world of statues and statue-worshippers, amidst balustrades, railings, wrought-iron wicker-work, banners, dwarf palms, church pennants, lowering lashes that cast a shadow on your cheeks, in May 1940, and picking up a furrowed tennis ball like an unfamiliar fruit (a pomegranate) near the Almout tennis court fence and bringing it, the hairy ball, an infant's head, to your swollen lips and biting into it. Another girl comes walking along the hawthorn hedge, a village child with no socks on, a snotnose of a child with a First Communion candle in her right hand and a prayer book in her left. "Hello, Sandra from the castle," she says and you cry, "Mama, Mama, look at her!" and when the child hurries on, embarrassed, you think, "I've got the softest hair in the world, not her."

Sandra from the castle, I won't write to you or phone. If I meet you on the street, I won't acknowledge you. This is the only message from me to you. XXX. Three little kisses.

The teacher thinks: "Even when I'm being kissed (I never kiss), I don't forget I'm a teacher. The word *kiss* comes from the Latin *gustus* and the Gothic *kustus* and *kinsan*, 'to choose.' Elizabeth used to say, 'I can't get out of bed, I can't get up till you give me my morning kiss.' And when her mother came to see us she would say, 'I never see your husband kiss you, Lizzie.' No, Madame, I'm not the kissing kind. Nor am I any better or worse than the assembled tribes of the Balinese, Charmorros, Lepchas, and Thongas."

A courtier by the name of Normand, a former principal of our school, fifty-four, unmarried, bibliography: "The Saerens Clan" (1942), "Our Congolese Brothers" (1961), once said, "It's perfectly clear, old chap, that Crabbe, in a certain sense, if I may put it thus, deceived us. You will find this a bit hard-hearted of me, but is it not so that rather than uniting a Great State with a Great People which, as I'm sure you agree, old chap, had in the past given ample proof of its capability for greatness, our friend, though linked to it by spirit and blood, was perhaps more concerned with solving a personal problem by *using* events he obviously had control over that he, so to speak, in his all-powerful position at Almout, and then as leader of the Association once the Leader was no more, then in the Langemarck stage, and finally in Cherkasy, that is, in a position in which time and time again he was allowed to do entirely as he pleased both in terms of constructive and destructive acts, that he concentrated on the problem of how a man behaves when in an all-powerful position, where, let us call a spade a spade, there is no longer any gap between what is and is not possible, or, rather, how I behave, me, Crabbe, in that void. And don't you think, old chap, that Crabbe may have succumbed to that problem, to wit, a situation that for better or for worse we have never had to face? Or am I going too far? Don't hesitate to tell me if you feel I have overstepped the bounds."

Someone, out of breath: "Well, if you ask me, it does sound a bit, to use the expression one can still hear in the Anhalt region, far-fetched."

"I feared as much."

"He overcame obstacles of a considerable magnitude, after all. I am thinking of the void that reigned in the Central Council of the Movement after 20 May, of the appearance he put in after breaching the Cherkasy encirclement, and so on – tours de force that may well, as you have just intimated, reflect certain personal motivations, a characteristic *Aufklärung,* if you will permit me to express it in German."

"Of course, old boy . . ."

"Thank you. Now where was I? That . . . that this intellectual showdown, inextricably intertwined with the metamorphoses of his physical being, gave him entrée into what Mabille called the 'chamber of light.'"

"Quite."

Someone, keyed up, his mouth full of chocolate: "But when they found that gal – or was it a guy – with the burns down near where you zip up the skirt, some people said he was dark as hell and others that you couldn't hardly see and I know some people who thought – can you believe it? – he was Crabbe dressed up as a nun! No, that's stretching the point; that's barking up the wrong tree."

"The fact that he never knew his mother or his father must have taken its toll. Not that I believe the Madman of Vienna and his claim that everything is over before the age of one, but when you grow up like that, in the wild . . ."

"Wouldn't it make sense to posit that he had reached the point, the decisive point, where you know, you simply know. The point where you can't put anything into words, old chap, so you say nothing at all. You disappear."

"Crabbe was never one for ideas, conscious ideas of the kind we're always coming up with. Remember the totally intuitive way he led us home through Poland and Germany. It was all feeling. I'm afraid we must assume that when Crabbe saw the Leader murdered, saw it with his own eyes, he took upon himself the evil of the situation – the weakness first, then the sin, then the folly of it all – and raising it to a higher power he saw original sin gearing up again, so he concocted a religion of his own – most rituals having struck him as little more than palliative folklore – and practiced it on our men both here and at the front . . ."

"Right. His politics, the practical if fragmentary form of his religious vision, were . . ."

An official: "We were living in Haregem at the time – the local school-master was hiding us – and our oldest daughter said, 'Father,' she said, 'I don't like it here. It smells like dead people.' But we couldn't leave, as you know, because the Whites had smashed our place to bits. Well, I thought she was just being her usual silly self, but she wouldn't stop whining, and one night, bless my soul, they brought in a corpse and put him in the playground shed. The thing is, there was an unguarded railway crossing not far off. It had had a guard once upon a time, but the local council decided it didn't want to pay a man or a woman just to pop their pimples there all day, so of course people got run over by the train now and then, and when they did they were usually taken to the shed, which was also used as a jail for drunkards. Kind of a hospital it was. And our oldest daughter she said, 'Tomorrow or the day after they'll bring Crabbe too.' Well, I'll be darned if in the next six months they didn't bring in four bodies, all four unrecognizable – face gone, head gone, ribs sticking out of the shoulders – and each time she went out with my wife to look. They had a hard time of it for the next week or two, couldn't sleep, but they just had to go and see if it was Crabbe or not. And I swear by all I hold dearest it was never him!"

Leaning against the fireplace, his elbow next to a portrait of a man in uniform (a young man with the corners of the mouth turned down, one continuous eyebrow separating the forehead from the nose and eyes, a jutting, overly long chin, and a malicious look combining spite with pleasure), the teacher spoke for a while but then, seeking a place to rest his twisted ankle, got stuck. He saw Crabbe's courtiers sitting in a circle that straggled at the outer limits and left little space between the rows, and he thought not only of the gas fumes generated by enemies of the Association, who wanted to bring the entire Central Council plus the sleep-drunk teacher under their sway, but also of the fact that no matter what he said the courtiers would interpret it as his homage to Crabbe and that he had stopped speaking in the midst of a terrifying leaden silence and that the circle of courtiers was like a reproduction made by a manufacturer of statuettes (elves and herons for the garden, falling foot soldiers for the marketplace) of Da Vinci's *Last Supper*. It was indisputable. Judas was Sprange, the pouch with the pieces of silver lying before him, the salt cellar overturned; Peter ostentatiously holding out his tortured, disfigured fisherman's hands; and Sandra, as John, with the requisite auburn hair, young and beardless, gazing fearfully up at him, him-the-teacher or him-the-picture-next-to-him. And did not someone say then to the inanimate torsos concealing their frozen or amputated members beneath their togas, "Someone hath betrayed me"?

The teacher (as was his wont when, the wood smoldering, a silence fell after his final words) thought he himself had made the statement, he who had slept in Crabbe's bed, who had been sucked dry and tossed out by Crabbe next to Richard in the garden, and who had recovered by willingly, consciously breaking the law which states that one must take the pain and evil of others upon oneself and expiate their sins. And just as the body changes when shifting from sleep to wakefulness –

blood pressure and nervous energy change – so the Almout meeting room did not grow brighter but changed. The walls in Korneel's room spread, and the teacher (as when on a tennis court a player who has lost his glasses makes too abrupt a downswing with his racket while serving and feels a sudden dizziness and inability to focus, which causes a heaving nausea and the impression of a vast expanse of red gravel stretching out before him – and what populace inhabits that agora, what figures dance in the field of vision of the man with the marketplace phobia?) thought, "What's the matter with me anyway? Gravity ceases to exist once a certain acceleration has been reached. The astronaut floats for several seconds in a blissful, frenzied state of insecurity, doesn't he? What's going on now?"

It was the month when cats stand face to face – in the shade, mostly – and the male laments, three centimeters from the female's seemingly unscathed head; and as her eyes grow glassier – such that the pupil becomes a perpendicular stroke of black in the lemon-yellow iris and she grows more immobile after arching her back and stretching out her paws – the male cries more softly and even breaks off for one indivisible minute; it was the month when oxen bellow to one another, when sailors don their white summer uniforms, the month of May, when two trucks of gendarmes and suspects left Bruges (the Venice of the north) for the south while the Hun was advancing and the Allies taking shelter on the beach before their burning ships. The two trucks drove fast. The driver of the first blew his horn like a madman, winding through roads clogged with refugees; the second truck followed on his tail and often had to swerve out of the way of pedestrians, primarily women, who, when the first truck sped past in a cloud of dust, thought the road was clear and jumped in front of its bumpers without warning.

Once the two trucks had gone, the crowd flocked back into the road to the consternation of the driver of a yellow DKW three hundred or so meters behind the convoy. Owing to congestion at the border town of Menen the DKW had come within nearly fifty meters of the second truck. A number of youths, most of them escapees from the reformatory at Lendelede to which a group of mental patients from the Malderijck sanatorium had attached itself, were trying to stop and storm the first truck. They did not give ground until the gendarmes (whose numbers in their closed vehicles surprised the attackers nearly as much as the gendarmes were surprised to find themselves under sudden attack by numerous raving youths in civvies) started brandishing their pistols and shooting into the air. The gendarmes also threatened to round up all the fugitives upon their return. The hungry, screaming, railing mob, convinced there was no question of their returning, yielded a bit nonetheless and even let the yellow DKW through, assuming it belonged to the armed convoy. The driver, a thin, pale, pimpled youth, tossed a packet of twenty-franc notes to the yammering child victims as he rode past. They scrambled after the fluttering banknotes, cheering and waving the DKW good-bye, then fought among themselves for the money on the sandy road.

On 18 May the convoy arrived in Romazin, a French town of forty thousand known for its procession on the second day of Easter and the industrious nature of its population. A town hall graced the Parc Maréchal Joffre; several battlements of a medieval castle could be seen in their original state; a number of hills raised their rosemary-rich backs around the town. The convoy was poorly received by the inhabitants of Romazin, who had gathered in the marketplace and, at the sight of the Belgian license plates, accused the King of the Belgians of treason for having let the Teutons pass.

Nonetheless, the mayor of Romazin and the colonel of the local gendarmerie greeted the convoy and showed it to the barracks of the Thirty-First Regiment Infantry. Airplanes were crisscrossing the sky, anti-aircraft guns taking pot shots. At about this time the German vanguard arrived in Ruiselede, having executed a number of spies and set fire to the church at Vinkt, whose women and children had been locked inside. Just as the convoy reached the barracks courtyard, the yellow DKW, which had driven down the main street for a few meters, turned into the first side street on the right and parked on a gravel path alongside the barracks wall. The driver then went for a little walk past the main entrance, stopping to ask the gatekeeper what the Belgian vehicles were doing there. The sentry and an orderly with the rank of sergeant explained that they had come because a group of parachutists, spies, and traitors were to be put before the firing squad that very evening after being interrogated by the Sûreté. The young man thanked them and handed the sentry a banknote of fifty French francs, the sergeant a banknote of a hundred, and pronounced his name, which had an aristocratic ring to it, and his Intelligence Service number. They asked for more money, and the young man said, "This evening" and walked off quickly, reproaching himself for having been so gauche. Then he checked into the Hôtel Richelieu, which stood diagonally opposite the bust of a former mayor of the town. The young man spent the entire afternoon and night at the window facing the parade ground and shooting range of the Thirty-First Regiment Infantry. On 19 May the Belgian prisoners, this time escorted by French gendarmes and two lieutenants from the French Army, were transferred to the cellars beneath the stone staircase of the Folklore Museum. They were nineteen in number and included Maurice de Keukeleire and his bodyguard Jan Lampernisse. The young DKW driver spent the afternoon of the nineteenth on the terrace of a café opposite the museum in the company of several drivers who could no longer procure gasoline, playing pelota with them and drinking Pernod while casting an occasional agitated glance at the restless crowd that stood waiting in front of the museum, giving the gendarmes guarding it hell. He spent part of the night in another, adjacent café, and towards morning he sat on a bench in the small tree-lined square likewise facing the museum. At ten o'clock on 20 May the gendarmes and the soldiers of the French Army gave in to the anxiety of the crowd and their own anxiety over the approaching triumphant enemy. Before regaining their houses or fleeing south, the crowd demanded the death of the Belgian spies. Thus it was that at approximately half past ten a platoon of soldiers marched into the square and formed ranks. After the first group of four prisoners were shot in front of the brick wall forming one side of the museum, the young man got up from his bench under the plane trees and joined the crowd. Blinded by the light, Maurice de Keukeleire emerged from the cellar, his arm in the firm grip of Jan Lampernisse. He stiffly, slowly crossed the short distance to the wall, stopping abruptly, an arm's length from it, while the soldiers dragged away the four corpses. He caught sight of the young man. Jan Lampernisse, who had been kicked in the rear by a man from the crowd, said something to Maurice de Keukeleire, and the latter responded without taking his eyes off the young man. The young man was peeling an orange. A nervous tic made him blink. Maurice de Keukeleire smiled at Crabbe, and eight bullets pierced his trunk and thighs. He died on the spot. Jan Lampernisse, who was shot in the nose, lay over the knees of the dead man and was still moving even after the French lieutenant emptied the contents of his revolver into him. Crabbe turned, walked over to his DKW, and rode off in the direction of the Belgian border. Two days later he reached the first German troops and, addressing them in broken German, was let through.

Then in the turmoil of the times Crabbe sought his part in the fantastic banquet laid before a man in pursuit of other men. Defying God or not, he fashioned his personal strategies from the material of the pursued and the pursuing. Apart from the chase and its adrenaline rushes he was caught up by a sort of faith in what he could achieve in wartime, when the case of Europe vs. Asia would be won, to wit, a faith that needed to be cultivated in the people, the nationalism of a bounteous Flanders in das Ewige Reich, and a total faith, faith in oneself, service to the elite, ideological insight, a sense of responsibility, what have you, heavyweight catchwords he was ready, if need be, to pound into the populace, which, inert and unschooled, brooded over its day-to-day sensations with neither outcome nor focus. But the dawn of the technocrats and knights-errant failed to break, the mist thickened and hung motionless in his brain, and then one day he happened upon a camp in Poland and a wooden pavilion that had been put up in two days by a special contingent of carpenters from the Organisation Todt when a visit by a Red Cross inspection team had been announced. They had given it a lot of thought, the O.T. men – an Oriental Pavilion, a fun fair, a merry-go-round with horses for Jewish children – and made a good job of it with an occasional perfectly logical aberration, such as windows that did not open (it was not worth making them open, because the children would spend only one day there, the day the Red Cross passed through for the inspection) and were made of the cheapest glass, glass consisting almost entirely of blemishes, the blemishes of Crabbe and Sprange and the delegates of the Red Cross, whose eyes were more on their shoes in the muck than on the row of children who had come for their sweetmeat rations;

such as horses that did not go up and down because no motor was available, all motors having necessarily gone elsewhere. Crabbe came upon the pavilion two or three days later, when the children were all piled up in rows. Wearing nothing but underclothes, naked blue thighs protruding, pushed into one another in a hook-like pattern. Not one of them had the de Keukeleire smile, the noble, sardonic smirk the leader wore as he was led to his suicide.

After Fredine slammed the door shut, the teacher wiped his dripping face. He had clasped her to him almost as a lover might. He tidied his desk, shoveling all his papers into an envelope and placing a slip of paper on top with instructions to the attention of the doctor treating him.

I had numbered the papers the night before. Korneel could now read everything, the professor's entire story, in one go. I had even left a broad margin for him to make notes in. I could have entered a few of my own: an agoraph here, a claustroph there. Or: third stage. (After flight and defense – attack.) Or schiz. I was thinking of phoning the principal from the telephone booth by the Hazegras Bridge as soon as I went out. I would have told him I was alive and hoped he had cancer and polio. And I might have gone to school afterwards as if nothing had happened. Nothing. No boy. Who was now picking his nose safe and sound at home with his parents. No Sandra. Whom I had chased because of a single gesture – the way she nibbled the knuckle of her index finger when she called the car salesman a Jew – à gesture

I had hoped to see again when she learned in the linen closet next to the kitchen at Almout that I had told the truth when I told her I was circumcised and for the first time she felt defiled in her white albino body. But I did not get that far up the esplanade and so could telephone no one.

Not even Teddy Maertens, the car salesman, who still has Sandra's fur coat. Nor did I get to see the principal's lookout tower at school: they caught me first and brought me back here. Again. For the second time.

Just as sleep brings repose to the body, so boredom soothed the teacher in his nook. He blew the dust off his desk. What is permissible as long as one is under passion's sway is of no consequence once the passion has ebbed. The teacher no longer felt the necessity to cleave to his nook or his story. He thought, "By fleeing this story, this justification, I justify myself." He shoved back his wobbly chair. He spat in the direction of the bottles he had not yet counted or put in order. He opened the door Fredine had slammed. He thought, "This is the house. I am going to explore it. The house I was taken to in the truck with the pig smell."

He stood in the drafty hallway, which still reeked of urine, and failed to recognize the hallway he had been led down. He forgot to read the name written on the door of his room. He walked with his tongue between his teeth, with his eyebrows raised, walked down the hallway on the tips of his squeaky shoes, past white smocks and white trash cans to a frosted glass door, which he opened with ease. Stepped onto the threshold of the servants' entrance. Outside, the sun was shining brightly and a breeze had set the sloops along the cement rim of the esplanade to dancing. He was amazed at the rage he felt within. At first he thought it was the overpowering sea air, but then he felt himself yawning with rage. He walked to the end of the alley and out onto the broad, endless embankment.

We in our country of two hundred and ten airplanes and two submarines, we work hard and have a good reputation abroad – ask anyone – because we are flexible in our transactions and give our all. On Saturdays we'll go for a spin in our big American cars (ninety percent of which, my good man, are bought on credit) to the coast, our coast. We study the rim of West Flanders that lies on the sea. Have a look at the map and you will note that the North Sea presses into our province like a turban into the profile of a weather-beaten fisherman. We complain no more than is necessary. Circumstances, if we are to be believed, are in the hands of others – Providence, foreigners, the government. We do what we can, we do, but circumstances, if you know what I mean . . .

It occasionally happens that while taking a delightful stroll along the embankment at Ostende, that queen of spas, we spy a man coming our way with a frightful, tormented, branded face. We often ascribe it to an excess of wine or women. Sometimes not. Sometimes he is neither filthy nor shock-headed nor in rags, yet we cannot take him for one of our own. We think of him more as someone in trouble. Trouble never happens to us. We never get into trouble. We detest the unwashed, the irresponsible, the antisocial. When we see such a man coming our way, we go back to our bag of frites or fresh shrimp and our thoughts about the elections, which will rightly bring the strongest, the sharpest of us to power. And then, permettez, well, then it is shocking when a man of this sort, right there on the embankment, hands on hips, gazing at the shifting sea, lets out a sudden loud scream, a senseless, violent scream. The teacher thought, I'm going to scream. I mustn't. They'll drag me under the shower if I do. He gazed over the quivering surface and with all the strength his lungs could muster let out a scream. It went on and on. The strolling figures came to a standstill. A gray-haired mother sitting on a terrace opposite the esplanade said to her son, "Did you hear that, darling?"

Her son, though fully grown, was wearing shorts. He was in a wheelchair, and saliva dripped from his lips onto his pink, hairy thighs. "No, no, no!" he said, swinging his heavy head. She carefully dabbed his lips.